WHAT IF HITLER WON THE WAR?

Philip N. Moore

RAMSHEAD PRESS INTERNATIONAL
CORPORATION
Atlanta, GA
1998

What If Hitler Won The War?
Copyright © 1998 by Philip N. Moore
Cover Design/Copyright © 1998 by Philip N. Moore

Published by RamsHead Press International
P.O. Box 12-227, Atlanta, GA, USA 30355-2227
Toll Free: 1-800-RAMS HEAD (1-800-726-7432)
E-Mail: theconinc@aol.com (for questions or
   comments to our authors directly)
Fax: 404-816-9994
Web Page: http.//members.aol.com/theconinc/publish.htm

First Printing
Printed in the United States of America

Scripture taken from the NEW AMERICAN STANDARD BIBLE: HARPER STUDY EDITION (R), © Copyright The Lockman Foundation 1960, 1962, 1963, 1968, 1971, 1972, 1973, 1975, 1977. Used by permission. Quotations of the Hebrew Bible taken from the BIBLIA HEBRAICA STUTTGARTENSIA, © Copyright 1966, 1977, 1983, German Bible Society. Used by permission. Verses marked (The Living Bible) are taken from The Living Bible, © Copyright 1971. Used by permission of Tyndale House Publishers, Inc., Wheaton, IL, USA 60189. All rights reserved. All references designated Yah. Ms. are from the "Yahuda Manuscript," courtesy of the Jewish National & University Library, who own the copyright to this unpublished collection. Reproductions of Jerusalem Post articles courtesy of The Jerusalem Post. The Hebraica and SymbolGreekPMono fonts used to print this work are available from Linguist's Software, Inc., PO Box 580, Edmonds, WA, USA 98020-0580. Tel. (206) 775-1130. Many of the non-credited images printed in this work are digitally produced fiction.

Library of Congress Cataloging-in-Publication Data
Moore, Philip N., 1957-
      What If Hitler Won The War? / by Philip N. Moore.
      p. cm.
      Bibliography: p.
      ISBN 1-57915-996-6 (pbk.)
      1. Fiction—History
      2. Alternative History—World War II
      3. Christianity/Judaism—Political Persecutions of

Library of Congress Catalog Card Number: 98-92925

1933
−1886
47

Special thanks to Teri Hatch for typing this manuscript; to Karen Walters for proofreading; to Mike Bentley and my Uncle Howard Todd, an officer in World War II who helped liberate many Jews from concentration camps, for encouragement.

TABLE OF CONTENTS

"For you [the Jews] are a holy people to the Lord your God; the Lord your God has chosen you to be a people for His own possession out of all the peoples who are on the face of the earth. Lord did not set His love on you nor chose you because you were more in number than any of the peoples, for you were the fewest of all peoples, but because the Lord loved you and kept the oath which He swore to your forefathers, the Lord brought you out by a mighty hand, and redeemed you from the house of slavery, from the hand of Pharaoh king of Egypt. Know therefore that the Lord your God, He is God, the faithful God, who keeps His covenant and His lovingkindness to a thousandth generation with those who love Him and keep His commandments; but repays those who hate Him to their faces, to destroy them; He will not delay with him who hates Him, He will repay him to his face."   MOSES,

The Law Giver - Deutoronomy 7:6-10

"...Unto them [the Jews] were committed the oracles [writings] of God....God has not rejected His people...For I too am an Israelite, a descendant of Abraham,....for the gifts and the calling of God are irrevocable."

The APOSTLE PAUL - Romans 3:2; 11:1-29

DEDICATION

Dedicated to the Jews - a great people who gave the world the word of God, thereby making worldwide totalitarianism impossible, to this very day.

A rabbi recopies a Torah. This is reminiscent of the method in which the Dead Sea Scrolls of the Bible were copied—very meticulously.

"For if it had not been for the Christians, our remnant would surely have been destroyed, and Israel's hope would have been extinguished amidst the Gentiles, who hate us because of our faith....But God, our Lord, has caused the Christian wise men to arise, who protect us in every generation" [1]   RABBI EMDEN, 1757

"..[true] Christianity...distinguished itself, in the particular of rescuing Jewish children, by the highest degree of self-sacrifice. It may be stated without exaggeration that almost the entire remnant of Israel which was found in the liberated countries—no matter how small its number—has the Christians to thank for its preservation, Christians who, by performing this action, placed their own lives in danger." [2]

SHOLEM ASCH, Jewish scholar and author, 1945

"The evangelical community is the largest and fastest growing block of pro-Israeli, pro-Jewish sentiment in this country." [3]   RABBI MARC TANNENBAUM, 1981

INTRODUCTION

This book is in **no way** intended to glorify Hitler. This work is created to illustrate how close the 2nd World War really was! This writing will reveal the horror a Hitler victory would have brought to earth, in a new light, never before imagined. Thus, we will realize anew how thankful we should all be that Hitler was indeed defeated by the hand of God through the victorious allies.

---

[1] Pinchas Lapide, *Israelis, Jews, and Jesus,* New York: Doubleday & Company, Inc., 1979, p. 105. Lapide's source was *Lechem Shamayim* (Hamburg, 1757), p. 30 ff.
[2] Sholem Asch, *One Destiny,* New York: Putnam's © 1945, p. 77, [ ] mine.
[3] The *Washington Post,* Mar. 23, 1981. The late Rabbi Marc Tannenbaum was the American-Jewish Committee's former national interreligious affairs director.

> **"Look in my face; my name is Might-have-been."**
> DANTE GARIEL ROSSETTI, 1881

A few years ago Robert Harris wrote a novel he called, *Fatherland*, which he felt depicted what "might have been" had Hitler won. His novel dealt with Hitler's survival into 1964. He told of Hitler's restricted victory over Europe and his problem of gorilla warfare with the Russians as he attempted to reach a state of detánt with the United States to bring the cold war to an end.

In Harris' novel both the United States and Hitler had the A-bomb.

Many have speculated on "what would have happened if Hitler won" though Harris went to the extreme of writing a novel on this possibility.

It is my belief that if Hitler obtained the A-bomb 'before' the United States, which almost occurred (I document this in Appendix 3), the world would be quite differently organized, beyond Harris' wildest imagination.

Hitler would never have allowed any nation to obtain the bomb, once he had it and Hitler believed in totalitarianism, where he alone would rule—as a **world Führer**.

The very absoluteness of the bomb, upon it's advent, in the hands of such a total totalitarian leader as Hitler would guarantee it's exclusivity to it's new possessor.[4] Anyone attempting to duplicate the bomb would be destroyed by the bomb from a vastly superior stockpile and world military recognizance would detect any attempted research and development attempts.

Few realized Hitler titled himself Führer i.e. leader, after the Roman Ceasars, who ruled most of the known world of their time.

Therefore to answer the speculative question of what would have occurred on our beleaguered planet had Hitler obtained the bomb first and won the war, we will let him win, so to speak, with the aid of science fiction, then we will view the alternative history which there after ensues, but based on *his* beliefs and opinions of who would and who would not be allowed to live.

---

[4] Because the U.S. obtained the bomb first and is not a totalitarian state it did not interfere with Russia's development of the bomb, or any other nation thereafter. The nuclear genie is out of the bottle. It can not be forced back in and nuclear annihilation is an any moment possibility with so many nations presently stockpiling the bomb. However, no one nation can now control the entire world through the exclusivity of the bomb. Had the U.S. been a totalitarian state this would have become the most probable scenario. Perhaps the best case theoretical scenario would have been for us to prevent its development elsewhere through a United States security force while obeying a prime directive, not to interfere otherwise in any way with other external nations goals "which do not threaten our security." In the interest of preventing a future international nuclear holocaust or accident. However, this is no longer possible. Albert Einstein once said, "The bomb should be committed to a world government." *Atlantic Monthly*, November 1945 p 43. He said he feared world government but, the bomb more. I believe once a few bombs are exchanged, probably within 30 years or so, we may be forced into the position of "world government" which will curb human freedom to the limit, no doubt. (See chapter 23 of my work, *The End of History- Messiah Conspiracy* for details).

Truly if Hitler had obtained a global domination over the world it would today be an Aryan world–devoid of democracy, Judaism, Christianity and race, (with acception to the Aryan race). The Jewish scholar, Max I. Dimont, has well noted, "...Because none but German Aryans were qualified to live in the Nazi view, it stood to reason that everyone else would be exterminated. The chilling reality is that when the Russians overran the concentration camps in Poland they found enough Zyklon B crystals to kill 20 million people. Yet there were no more than 3 million Jews left in Europe...Nazi future plans called for the killing of 10 million non-Germanic people every year."[5]

The Bible predicts a future world which **includes Jews** and the return of their Messiah. This alone, predicted in the ancient books of Isaiah and Revelation, could show anyone during the Nazi's Zenith of Power, in 1940, that Hitler had to lose. Even though at that time he seemed absolutely and unequivocally invincible.

If we lay the Bible aside and fantasize a Hitler victory the world becomes an infinitely scary uncertainty. Therefore to truly illuminate "what might have been" we begin our work—showing what Hitler most probably would have done in victory—but based on his documented *assertions* and proclaimed *intentions* using the convicting evidence of his writings and discovered stock piles of German weapons.

---

[5] Max I. Dimont, *Jews, God and History*, New York, New York, Signet Books, © 1962, p. 389, used by permission.

We also shed new light on Hitler's "real reasons" for his cruel and inhumane anti-Semitism[6] and condemn him and all others who would so foolishly dedicate their lives to the destruction of the Jews, who the Bible says are the chosen people of God!

Had the Jew not given the world the Bible the world would not be worth living in. Quite possibly, in that case, there might have been a Hitler or like totalitarian victory at some point in our history. Hitler once said, "Had Charles Martel not been victorious at Poitiers—already, you see, the world had fallen into the hands of the Jews, so gutless a thing was Christianity![7]—then we should in all probability have been converted to Mohammedanism, that cult which glorifies heroism and which opens the seventh Heaven to the bold warrior alone. **Then the Germanic races would**

---

[6] In our factual Appendix 2.

[7] Hitler, well read in much ancient literature, including The Talmud and both Old and New Testaments, which he categorically rejected, realized Christianity [Jewish Messianism] claimed that Jesus was the Messiah i.e. Christ. He knew that New Testament Christianity was the fulfillment (through Messianic prophecy) of at least the first coming portion of Jewish redemptive hopes and aspirations. This is why he speaks of Judaism and Christianity, as one. While cheering on Mohammedanism, which lies totally out of the Judeo Christian biblical realm. Hitler realized Jesus was Jewish and whole heatedly hated him and all that he stood for. For example, Hitler once stated, "These men betrayed their pure Aryan blood to the dirty superstitions of the Jew Jesus—superstitions as loathsome and ludicrous as the Yiddish rites of circumcision....Christianity only added the seeds of decadence such as forgiveness, self-abnegation,...and the very denial of the evolutionary laws of survival of the fittest." Trevor Ravenscroft, *The Spear of Destiny:* York Beach, Maine: Samuel Weiser, Inc. © 1973, pp.49, 70, used by permission.

have conquered the world. Christianity alone **prevented them** from doing so."[8]

Truly the world is in the hands of God, who is the God of Abraham, Isaac and Jacob and God's greatest interlude into human history is on the brink of becoming reality. One day soon the clouds will burst forth and the son of man, who is the ancient of days, will sit on the earth and *true paradise will finally begin,* (Daniel 7:13-14). This is reviewed briefly in Appendix 1, "Israel—Is Real" and my earlier works*, The End of History- Messiah Conspiracy, Volume I,* and *Nightmare of the Apocalypse.* So read, learn, discover, enjoy and be happy - and I will be too! Shalom—שלום

A memorial for the victims of the Holocaust, at Yad VaShem, in Jerusalem, Israel.

---

[8] *Hitler's Secret Conversations 1941-1944,* New York: Farrar, Straus and Young, © 1953, p. 542, translated by Norman Cameron and R.H. Stevens, used by permission, bold mine.

An illustration of the elders before the throne in the
book of Revelation by William Blake (1757-1827).

A War memorial for German soldiers lost in
the Führer's conquest of the United States.

> "The spirit that I have seen may be a devil; and the devil hath power to assume a pleasing shape." HAMLET

1

HITLER IS ALIVE AND WELL ON PLANET EARTH

I, Joseph Jones, woke up from what I thought was a nightmare. As I slept I felt what could best be described as a "sonic boom." I experienced the sensation of a rushing, mighty wind. It was as if time itself had warped and that a new reality had somehow replaced what I had always known to be true. In my sleep I thought I had heard SS troops marching and speaking German but as I awoke I knew that had to be impossible. It was 1950 and the Nazis had been defeated in 1945. As I went over to the window I heard someone speaking German and the words, "Heil Hitler world ruler, in Germany" (*Heil Hitler, Welt Herrscher, in Deutschland*).

I said to myself, "I must still be asleep—still having a nightmare." As I approached the window I peered out and saw SS troops marching–why–how? German Nazis in California? "This could not be," I thought. I picked up a newspaper. It's headlines read, 'Hitler to finalize African Negro extermination this month.' I said, "Oh my God, this can't be true. The Nazis were defeated in '45.' Just then my door was burst down. An SS officer picked up the Bible I had on my night stand and said, "You, you are one too!"

"What?"

"You are a Christian and your best friend is a Jew. We have him and we are arresting you–you and he will report to the same gas chamber."

"This is America and 1950. What are you Nazis doing here?"

He answered, "Plenty," as he handcuffed me and led me away to be incarcerated.

I was thrown into the back of a huge truck which had about 150 Christians and Jews so crammed together we could hardly breathe. I asked, "What is going on?" One gentleman replied, "What's the matter with you, did you just wake up yesterday?" I said, "No, today." He looked disgusted and I was confused.

After a two hour drive the truck we were being hauled in came to screeching halt. Two Nazi soldiers opened the cargo doors and we were pushed out at gun point. Those who didn't move fast enough to suit them were pushed, kicked and rifle whipped. As it seemed, we were to be processed, positively identified, tried, imprisoned, sentenced—all in the same day. Rumors were, tomorrow, we would be gassed and then cremated. Sure enough everyone was identified through their driver's license and social security numbers.

Then we were led into a court room, of sorts, and all at once pronounced guilty of being the wrong race and religion. A single Nazi soldier acted as judge and sentenced all of us to die by gas. We were then loaded into a bus to be transported to a nearby prison.

On the way to prison I saw Nazis and swastikas, statues of Hitler, convoys and a *Time* magazine cover which pictured teams of German soldiers dismantling the Statue of Liberty and I didn't understand any of this.

2

MENGELE'S MOTIVE FOR SAVING HITLER - FUTURE TENSE

In answering Joe's dilemma in how he was awaken by Nazis and the sound of SS troops in 1950 a secret diary was discovered in an underground library which summarized: In the year 2010 a young anti-Semitic (Jew hating) scientist, Adolf Mengele, an illegitimate child of the escaped Nazi war criminal, Joseph Mengele, is hard at work in time travel experimentation. He was always fascinated with time and learned much from Einstein's works on the subject.

Young Adolf was conceived in the late 1970's. His father, Joseph, never saw him, but left a map in his safety deposit box under an assumed name, which would guide his son to one of the biggest stashes of Nazi gold ever to be found.

The cave, which held over fifty billion dollars in gold bouillon, was in western Europe and had remained hidden for almost 70 years.

When Adolf was a young boy he always asked his German, although American born, mother about his father. He wanted to know where he was and why everyone was so hushed on the subject. He would ask about 'Dad' and his mother and all of her friends and family would become silent, looking at each other, as if a bomb had dropped, only to quickly, but subtlety, change the subject.

One day Adolf's mother, when she felt the child was old enough to know the truth, sat him down and told him the entire story of who his father was. She explained that his father was in hiding during the later half of the twentieth century, enduring, she thought, until the late 1980's through the mid 1990's and now was most probably dead of old age. This took a toll on Adolf during his teenage years and he became a very bitter, yet ambitious individual.

He was bitter and upset about his father's having to hide and look over his shoulder for fear of being apprehended and tried for his crimes against the Jews since Hitler was defeated in 1945.

He was ambitious and very excited about his technical research in time travel and now it seemed he had put together a machine which might be able to propel him backwards in time to where he had always wanted to go—back to 1939—to meet the most hated man who had lived to date, Adolf Hitler, his namesake.

His plan was malicious. He intended to give classified military secrets, old videotapes and newspaper clippings regarding the Atomic bomb to Adolf Hitler, six years before the end of the war. He intended to do this so as to convince Hitler to maintain atomic research as a first priority and to insure he obtained the bomb first, before the United States! He intended for Hitler to win the war and change history—forever!

This young devil of a man, now in his thirties, had a grudge to grind with Israel and the Jews. He was very angry with Israel and her secret service for capturing Adolf Eichman in 1960 and bringing him to trial in Jerusalem and thereafter executing him.

He had nightmares where he saw Hitler shoot himself through the mouth only to be delivered to the burning flame.

He was most angry about the Israeli's relentless pursuit of his father, Dr. Joseph Mengele, who had performed experiments of torture on so many helpless Jews. His wicked father had evaded capture until 1998.

At the time of his apprehension Joseph Mengele was in his late nineties. Pursuing tips, the Israeli Intelligence Organization called MOSAD, followed leads that took them to his hide away in Greece.

Thirty-eight years before, he had narrowly escaped the MOSAD from his previous hideout in Venezuela. He had left his home only five days before the MOSAD Agents located his residence, as he was warned by the Nazi underground, the

Brudenschaft, of Eichman's capture, which had just taken place.

However, since that time he had had cosmetic surgery and used the identity of an old jewelry merchant, George Constintine Papadious. But it would seem that his time had run out! Israel's top agent, Isaac Baraak, had closed in on him.

The MOSAD had bugged his cell phone and followed him 24 hours a day. When they had his schedule down pat, they planned his abduction. An agent visited his home one evening impersonating a vacuum cleaner salesman. Mengele, being suspicious of this man, declined his demonstration, insisting that he did not want to buy a vacuum cleaner.

Another man emerged from the car in the drive and came to the door. Mengele, realizing what was about to happen, scrambled to get out the back door. The two agents followed him through the house. Mengele ran out the back only to face two additional agents who were waiting for him there. Three agents tackled him. As he was held on the ground by the three men, the fourth handcuffed, gagged, and threw him in the back of the car. They transported him to a nearby hotel room where they would question him to be sure they had the right man. Once in the room his handcuffs and gag were removed. Two agents stood guard outside the room while two remained with Mengele. As he was being questioned one of the agents took his fingerprints.

His fingerprints matched Israel's file copies and he broke down under interrogation even before his dental records were compared.

Now the truth would be known to all the world at another trial in Jerusalem. This evil man, who tortured untold numbers of Jews and murdered so many, he couldn't remember how many, would now pay the price! It was time for him to be brought to justice. He was to be taken back to Israel in the baggage compartment of a Greek freighter to the Port of Hifa where he would be transported to Jerusalem for trial and execution—just like his fellow Nazi, Adolf Eichman, was in 1960.

However, this time around something would go wrong—drastically wrong. During the night of August 11, 1998, the day before he was to be sedated, gagged, tied up and placed in a padded, wooden crate for transport to Israel, he escaped.

A Greek milk truck driver lost control of his vehicle carrying over 10,000 gallons of milk and crashed into the wooden house where Mengele was being readied for transport. The needle containing the injection of the drug, that would put him out for at least 48 hours, now was only an inch away from his arm. Suddenly the Israeli agent holding the needle was knocked from his feet by the impact of the milk truck's headlights into his chest.

The front end of the truck ended up between the cellar and first floor of that old wooden, abandoned house that was to be the last private hiding place of

Joseph Mengele. Upon impact Mengele was freed. His Israeli captors were dazed and he was on the loose. He ran deep into the nearby woods and almost escaped for a second and possibly the last time. Baraak, the only agent able to run after the crash had taken place, got within shooting range of Mengele and fearing he would escape again, this time forever, through the Nazi underground, fired a shot in an attempt to wound and immobilize him. Mengele fell. As Baraak approached, he saw he had accidently shot him right between the eyes—he was gone!

Later, when the other agents had recovered, a decision regarding the disposal of Mengele was made. His body would be taken to a Greek crematoria where he would be cremated.

Joseph Steinberg, one of the other Israeli agents had paid off John Papageorge, the owner of the crematoria which was built for the few Greeks who for one reason or another passed on burial, the most predominant Greek tradition.

The body was given to Papageorge. One of the other Israeli agents accompanied it as Papageorge rolled Mengele into the chamber where his body was to be transformed into a mere three pounds of ashes. This agent, code named Samuel Simon, watched as the chamber was closed and the fires were turned up. The security team planned to deliver the ashes to the Israeli Prime Minister, Benjamin Netanyahu, upon their return to Israel, in secret.

The plan would precede in this way because of the accident. The entire Mengele fiasco would never be revealed to the public. "Israel would not be perceived as a vigilant," cried the chief agent. And no one would believe the true story of Mengele's attempted escape and the accidental death shot which was meant only to wound in order that Mengele might be recaptured!

It was Friday the thirteenth. Everything was going wrong. Mengele had escaped on the eleventh and died just after midnight on the twelfth and now was being cremated on the day after. Once the cremator began to turn up the fire in his cremation chamber the agent in charge of this final attempt to cover up Mengele's accidental death slipped on the freshly mopped floor & fell. He hit his head on the corner of the adjacent cremation chamber. He was out cold. Papageorge, now in a state of panic, quickly turned off the flames that were to dispose of Mengele and poured cool water over Simon's face.

After a while he came too—but he wasn't himself and didn't even remember that he was an agent working for Israel but he remembered the entire Mengele episode, which remained vivid in his short term memory. He then told Papageorge enough to scare him.

Papageorge called Greek police. Upon their arrival they retrieved the partially charred remains from the cremation chamber and took "Simon," who was still in a dazed state, into custody.

After a few weeks verifiable copies of Mengele's dental records were faxed to Greek Police headquarters. In the end, when Mengele's teeth were compared to his dental records, Greek authorities finally realized what they had stumbled into. "Agent Simon" was in such a state of bewilderment after his accident that he told the police the story of the Mengele capture. They thought he was crazy, that is until they confiscated the dental records and coded material he possessed.

The other agents wondered where "Simon" was and what else had gone wrong. When they discovered what had happened, fearing they might almost be apprehended, they fled to Israel.

This scene was a grim one, the other agents had escaped, "Simon" was in Greek custody and Mengele's body had not been totally destroyed.

The captain of the Greek police unit, which had uncovered all of this, along with eight other police men, were the only ones who knew all the details except the Pathologists who had compared Mengele's teeth to the dental records that the Israeli agent had in his possession, which still bore Mengele's name in code—a code the Greek's broke!

When all was realized, high level talks began between the Israeli and Greek intelligence services. Finally, they decided that all was to be covered up so as not to enrage world opinion against Israel and Greece.

Members of the Greek police were killed—their deaths made to look like an ambush in a phony raid on a band of mob criminals. The only surviving people who knew the story were Papageorge and the members of Israeli and Greek intelligence, who alone trusted each other because they who were sworn to secrecy.

John Papageorge fled in fear of his life once he learned what Greek intelligence had done to the Greek homicide authorities to cover up the Mengele affair. Greek agents were hot on his trail in Germany. He had reasoned that Germany, the scene of the original Nazi crime against humanity, would be the last place he'd be looked for and found.

There he went underground and told the story as to why he was hiding to Gunta Himmler. Himmler was a Neo Nazi, a fact not known to Papageorge. Himmler, a distant kin to Hitler's cohort, Hydric Himmler, couldn't believe his ears, but verified all that he'd been told. Eventually Papageorge was found and killed by Greek intelligence, who never gained knowledge of the Himmler connection with Papageorge.

Himmler had a friend, Fegelein Krebs, grandson of Hitler's last Chief of Staff, General Hans Krebs. Once this story was told to him, Fegelein told his friend, Adolf Mengele, the American born researcher and child of Joseph Mengele's old age, who Fegelein had come to know well through last vestiges of the Brudenschaft, the Nazi underground, formed just after the war to help the German war criminals hide and gain new identities.

Years before, Adolf Mengele had made inquiries to the Brudenschaft, attempting to locate his father, per chance that he may still be alive. Now the mystery of what had happened to Adolf's father was revealed!

Once Mengele had learned of the Papageorge story from young Krebs, he became infuriated. He made up his mind to get even - at any cost!

Albert Einstein

"If money go before, all ways do lie open."

WILLIAM SHAKESPEARE, 16th century

"The distinction between past, present, and future is only an illusion, however persistent."

ALBERT EINSTEIN, 1955

3

A TIME MACHINE BUILT TO FULFILL A MAD MAN'S WICKED DREAMS

Adolf Mengele was a scientist. Though he hated the Jewish people he had, never the less, studied the works of one of the most famous Jews ever to live, Albert Einstein.

He realized from Einstein's equation that if you could travel at the speed of light (186,000 miles per second) time would stand still. Upon learning this he realized if he could go faster than the speed of light then he might be able to travel back in time. He also knew that at the speed of light he would be transformed into pure energy making the trip impossible. But years of research into his time machine innovations had paid off in success. That is, for what would become his dastardly scheme.

He had developed an anti-matter compression chamber that would hold a smaller ship within a larger one with him inside which he believed would shield him from the transfer into pure energy. It would accelerate him fast enough to surpass both the time and zero length barrier which occur at the speed of light. And thereby transport him backwards into time, to a desired, predetermined era.

All was ready!

The Nazi underground gold reserves had been used to purchase the most sophisticated instruments needed to secure the state of the art in nuclear propelled rocket systems and fusion fuel which had been developed by NASA in the year 2008.

The deranged son of Joseph Mengele began loading the ship with enough non-perishable food for a 6-month journey which he had calculated would be needed to successfully travel back to the year 1939. Via making a trip out past the Van Allen belt to the Milky Way through a sling shot projection back around the sun on his return to earth.

He loaded his ship with freeze dried items, personal belongings, sterile drinking water and a 1939 Nazi uniform of his fathers which fit him, to his amazement. He also took many newspaper articles containing stories of the 1945 Nazi defeat, Hitler's suicide and secret burial of his charred remains at Magdeburg by Russian Smirsh (CMEPШ)[*] agents.

---

[*] CMEPШ was a elite police force which reported directly to Stalin and means "Death to spies."

These stories were included on the videotaped television specials, "What Really Happened to Adolf Hitler," (ABC, 1994) And "Russia's War," (PBS, 1997), which told the story of his exhumation (for the fourth time) in 1970 by order of the KGB when his and Eva Brown's bones were ordered crushed by Russian officials and scattered over East German marshlands[*].

However, most importantly, Mengele had detailed articles of the A-bombs dropping on Japan. He also had detailed plans of the H-bomb and portions of weapons grade plutonium which had been smuggled out of Russia when the cold war was seemingly at an end in the late 1990's. He loaded lithium 6 and uranium 235—enough to make six bombs—a few pounds each, which he had carefully encased in lead shielding for safety.

All of this extraordinarily astronomically expensive material was bought from the gold stash his father's map had led him to in France, in an underground cave, which had been long covered over with trash near a forest in the city of Salon, where the house of Nostradamus still stands. There about in those quiet, yet unsuspecting, surroundings lie the entrance to the cave which held the largest gold reserve known to date.

Mengele had dug a hole using a small bobcat style bulldozer he had rented, exactly where the spot marked 'X' was on the map. Once he had broken through, after digging only ten feet, he could see stairs. Mengele proceeded. Carrying a flash light he carefully followed the stone cut stairs to their end.

---

[*] See Author's Notes.

One hundred feet below ground level he saw walls of gold bricks higher than his head. On the bricks were carved swastikas and in the middle of the cave, lined on both sides of these bricks, were sacks of gold bouillon—four feet high.

Mengele and his newly discovered gold stash.

Mengele walked deeper and deeper into the cave, which resembled a tunnel that appeared to be approximately twelve feet high and thirty feet wide. The tunnel—cave, seemed as if it would go on forever. It was over a mile in length and when Mengele finally reached it's end he was in a state of shock and totally dumb founded. There he discovered an eight by ninety foot pile of diamonds, emeralds, rubies and other precious stones.

These gems had been taken out of the safety deposit boxes of the banks of Europe when Hitler took the continent in 1940-41. Many of the other stones had been removed from the gold before it was melted down and composed into the bricks he had found.

Most of the other bricks which did not bear swastika insignias had been taken from the national treasuries of the European states. There was more gold in this cave than in all of Fort Knox in the United States.

Mengele knew that he could never allow anyone to find out about this monumental gold stash if he wanted to cash in on it. He realized the French authorities would move in and confiscate his find. Back in the US the IRS would take most of what he would manage to obtain after the antiquity authorities of France would make their claim of the limited swastika engraved editions of gold bricks from the third Reich no one had known existed.

News like this might arouse as much interest as the fake Hitler diaries did in the 1980's but, of course, this wasn't fake. It would arouse more—and Mengele wasn't going to be on 'Night Line,' after becoming a poor man.

He circumspectly thought out his plan, took a hand full of jewels and left the cave, carefully covering the entrance and booby trapped it lest someone stumble upon the stash, unaware. He covered the dozer with branches he cut from trees, completely camouflaging it and went back to the hotel he had rented.

Later he sold the diamonds, emeralds and rubies to local jewelers and accumulated enough cash to buy the equipment to melt gold. Mengele's imagination wouldn't quit. He bought a krugerand coin, one of the popular gold commodities on the market, only to take several hundred impressions of the coin and produce molds from them.

Once he had acquired and moved a crucible (gold furnace) into the cave along with a portable gasoline generator he had purchased, which he needed to power his entire operation—he began his work. He melted down large portions of Nazi gold swastika bricks and poured off this molten treasure into the krugerand molds, producing hundreds of thousands of counterfeit krugerands made of real gold, which he could now trade on the open market without arousing any suspicion.

He sold them in limited amounts to many buyers to avoid any records that might send tax collectors to his door. He always took cash and gave no receipts and in the end amassed millions of dollars which he kept in thirty different deposit boxes in different banks under thirty different assumed identities. Nothing was left to chance. He would use the money and no one else would get any of it.

Once he had enough money to complete his time machine he covered up the cave. It looked as if he had never been there and he tore up the map. Only he knew where it was and it would always be there—still half full—if he would ever need the money in the future.

Mengele would use the cash he secured from the sale of this gold to purchase millions in sophisticated equipment which only he knew how to put together and use for time travel.

For years he worked and used his secret connections (having formerly worked for NASA and an American Research Military Installation) to buy fuses, circuits and simultaneous precision detonation devices used in plutonium implosion bombs.

These bombs contained a plutonium core and are surrounded with an outer casing of plutonium when all at once, in a billionth of a second the outer casing is smashed into the core, critical mass is achieved and a nuclear explosion occurs.

It was August of 2010 and all was nearly ready.

* * *

Mengele's fusion-fueled timewarp space rocket
being readied for launch.

"...Vengeance belongeth unto me, I will recommence, saith the Lord."   HEBREWS 10:30

"The God of my mercy shall prevent me: God shall let me see my desire upon mine enemies."   PSALM 59:10

"Rejoice, O ye nations, with his people: for He will avenge the blood of his servants, and will render vengeance to His adversaries, and will be merciful unto his land, and unto his people."   DEUTERONOMY 32:43

4

COUNT DOWN, LIFT OFF, POW, BACK IN TIME — 1939

The day had arrived, September 1, 2010, all was loaded. Mengele's equipment included, among other things, an authentic phaser type of hand gun, as seen on sci-fi series in the 1960's-90's. This weapon had been stolen from a US classified[*] weapons lab the year before.

---

[*] See Author's Notes.

The ship was ready and the countdown had begun. Mengele was firmly strapped into his rocket. Everything was automated. He controlled everything from a modified lap top computer including rocket speed acceleration, fuel consumption, rate of time dilation, interior and exterior temperature and even his own vital signs.

He wanted no complications—no one to discover how he would change history. He did not want any traces left behind in 2010 or later, lest someone duplicate his time travel plan and undo what he was about to do.

He wanted revenge on Israel for what had happened to his father. He wanted to glorify the Führer his father worshipped.

He thought to himself, "All that I have ever worked for has meaning today."

His lap top was his command station. He had programmed it prior to entering the ship. It would remind him of all necessary checks that had to take place prior to lift off.

From the speakers of his laptop came the computer generated voice instructing him, "T minus 10 minutes and counting. All lights are green. We have full external power. Begin final status check. T minus 1 minute. Pressure is good. Weather is good. All systems are go."

His eyes gleamed with evil as the countdown ended and ignition began.

LIFT OFF

The rocket, with the anti-matter light speed protection capsule containing the oval shaped spaceship, which he was at rest in, lifted off. He glimpsed at the TV monitor, which was fed by camera lines from outside the craft, to see the clouds of earth disappear out of his sight within seconds.

As the curvature of the earth became visible he shuddered, saying, "I will get revenge on all those Jews who captured my father. Indeed they will never be born."

The entire earth was now visible and the rocket quickly gained speeds many times faster than the moon shots of the late 1970's. In a second it became a tiny blue marble figure. In another instant it became a speck of light as if it were a star—only then to disappear from sight into the blackness of space.

The rocket climbed ever higher as it accelerated away from earth. Weeks seemed like years, months seemed like decades, with no one to talk to, except a TV screen.

Mengele got up each day at 6:00 sharp and did a systems check before breakfast. During the morning hours he would do some exercises and a routine physical exam. After lunch, at 12:00, he would review and edit tapes and clip articles from papers and books. He watched films of Nazi victories from 1939 to 1941. He brought along a video tape recorder and a small TV set with films of Germany's defeat during the years of 1943-45, but only to show the Führer he aspired to have a personal audience with.

The rocket was almost at light speed, 186,000 miles per second. It's length was at 10 feet. It had shrunk from it's original 2,000 foot length, as Einstein predicted all objects do as they near the speed of light. Adolf felt dizzy. Tingles ran rampidly through his body as he glanced at the controls to check his velocity.

At the instant the speed of light was reached, the complete outer ship became pure energy. It's length became zero. But the protective casing inside, which housed his saucer shaped ship, held up. It's anti-matter tritium shell survived the transition and continued to accelerate far past the speed of light. The stars seemed to move in a reverse motion. They appeared to move away from him instead of towards him as he traveled forward.

All was still as he carefully aimed antennas, which were able to capture TV signals from earth, in the direction of the destination from which he'd left in the year 2010. His TV screen was now receiving live TV signals revealing images of 2005. He watched reports of events he'd forgotten about and they were reversing rapidly as he traveled, in fast motion, backwards. He was in awe as he accelerated even faster. The years went backward at a rate of 1 every 10 days. In 1952 his TV screen became black

& white and for a minute he suspected a malfunction and then he remembered he was now in the pre-color TV era. No color TV signals were broadcast until 1953.

Suddenly Adolf realized he had traveled past the Van Allen belt and out and around the Milky Way. He was now approaching Earth's Sun and had traveled back in time almost 70 years, from 2010 to 1940. In a few short minutes he'd arrive on Earth in the time of 1939.

ALMOST DESTROYED BY THE SUN

As Adolf began slowing down to near light speed he approached Earth's sun. He had reduced his speed before nearing Earth, long enough to allow a quick slowing down to sub-light speed in order to re-enter the Earth's atmosphere and avoid being crushed by the tremendous G-forces caused by inertia.

As Adolf neared the speed of light he rapidly slowed down from what were speeds many thousands of times those of light. The sun's gravitational pull bends light rays and if Adolf traveled much slower he would be pulled into the sun as he passed. He well knew this and realized that he had to decelerate to a sub-light speed at the exact distance of the sun from Earth in order to land on the planet intact.

The sun approached rapidly. It's blinding light on the closed-circuit TV monitor hurt his eyes. Suddenly he felt the pull of the sun—still decelerating and about to pass out of range of the sun's gravitational pull the ship was pulled in so close it nearly broke up. Sweat poured off of Adolf's face as the temperature rose to 110 degrees Fahrenheit within the ship and thousands without. He quickly added some liquid nitrogen between the hulls of the ship as he attempted to gain enough speed to steer clear of the sun.

Barely making it past the sun, now the ship's red-hot exterior began to cool. The more the ship slowed, the rougher the ride. All of a sudden the Earth was visible. It's size increased on the TV monitor until it filled the entire screen. Finally all Adolf Mengele could see were clouds and blue sky. His radio was on and a broadcaster had just announced that Germany had split the atom. He had arrived at just the precise time he had planned.

* * *

5

TIME TRAVELER LANDS HIS SAUCER AND MEETS HITLER

Adolf Mengele, the son of the late Joseph Mengele, landed in Berlin. One hundred and twenty-three tanks and over two-thousand troops had surrounded him. Hitler was immediately told that a "flying saucer" had landed. He was on his way in his Chauffeur driven Mercedes Benz to view a "man from another world."

The ship was cooling—still too hot to touch. Liquid nitrogen had cooled the inside enough for it's passenger to survive. Mengele and all his uranium, news reel video taped footage and newspaper articles from 1945 to 2010 were now safe in a 1939 Berlin.

After two hours Mengele had begun to open the door of the space ship. As the door opened a barrage of gunfire hit the door. He was wounded and the ship was burst into by SS officers.

"fliegende Untertasse"
unidentifiziertes fliegendes Objekt

Mengele was unconscious. German emergency military personnel flew him to a nearby hospital and all of his belongings were confiscated and taken to Nazi labs to be disassembled and studied.

German Army intelligence had notified Hitler of the ship almost from the moment it showed up on German radar screens. He had been summoned and was enroute to visit this special captive patient.

Within a short period of time the Führer had arrived at the health care facility as Mengele lay near death in Berlin's top hospital of that day. Every effort was being made to save this "space man."

Hitler approaches the entrance to the hospital where the space man is being cared for.

Hitler now entered the lobby of the hospital and every nurse and every doctor stopped what they were doing, momentarily, to salute him, spewing, "Heil Hitler," as he passed. Once on the elevator with his bodyguards he exclaimed, "This I have to see for myself, a man from another planet?" As he entered Mengele's room Hitler asked the doctors if he was going to be all right and if he could be questioned soon. The doctor, assigned to his personal care, Burgdorf, said it was too early to tell but that it would be at least two weeks before he might be well enough to be questioned.

Hitler stared at this half dead man, who lay in a comma and worriedly picked up the phone and called in the top surgeons of Berlin. He told them that this was a high priority and that anything and everything that could be done to save this man was of the utmost importance.

Hitler calls the top surgeons.

Once his condition worsened Mengele was taken to the Critical Care Unit down the hall from his room. His vital signs were read and recorded. A complete set of x-rays were taken before medication was administered for pain. His eyes were dilated and his skin was pale and clammy. A nurse was assigned to watch him round the clock and guards were posted outside his room.

After following this special patient into ICU, Hitler stood over his bed with a worried look on his face and then patted Mengele on the cheek saying, "You get well, get well soon, for me—I've got questions for you."

As the doctors and nurses looked on—Hitler placed his officer's cap back on his head and left the room commanding the doctor, "Notify me of any changes immediately."

As Hitler exited the hospital a Nazi armored personnel carrier pulled up beside his Limo and an agent from the laboratory, where all of Mengele's things had been taken, jumped out and hurriedly gave the Führer a brief case which contained old newspaper articles and video tapes. The articles appeared to be old, tattered and yellowed, yet dated past that present year of 1939. The man exclaimed, "Here, my Führer, these were in his ship." Hitler took the material and tapes and looked at them with interest as he got into his car.

Hitler began to examine some of the newspapers that Mengele had brought. He had no idea what a TV set was or what these black plastic boxes were that had rolls of tape inside with the English words "video cassette" inscribed thereon. No one would succeed in playing such videos without Mengele's help because the player itself was damaged. However, once Hitler had reviewed the old newspapers from 1939 to 1955 on his way to the man's ship, he wondered if this was some sort of hoax planned by the allies to discourage his war effort. Was it all fake or was this a man from the future as the evidence seemed to indicate.

Hitler was taken to the ship and was amazed as he said, "Even I could not design a plane like this one, what makes it fly! Where are the propellers?" He was at a loss of words and did not sleep that night and was agitated for days afterward. He constantly questioned Germany's top aviation engineers who told him the ship was far above the jet aircraft they were now secretly developing.

Within a few days Mengele's swelling had subsided and additional medication was administered to alleviate his pain. Mengele still did not respond when spoken to or acknowledge when he was touched. The nurses kept him clean and comfortable and exercised his limbs to keep them from stiffening.

At the end of the first week Mengele responded to the nurse by lightly squeezing her hand. Within a few days he would communicate by squeezing the nurse's hand once for 'yes' and twice for 'no'. He was asked a series of basic questions.

"Do you know your name?"

Mengele squeezed her hand once.

"Do you know where you are?"

Mengele squeezed twice.

The nurse told him that he was in a German Hospital and that he had landed here in a space craft and was taken into custody by the German authorities. Mengele squeezed her hand once acknowledging that he knew what she was saying. The nurse continued with questions regarding his health. She asked him if he had any pain and he squeezed once for yes. She began to name body parts in order to isolate where the pain was.

After a few moments of questioning it was determined that the pain was in his chest and shoulders. She asked him to rate the pain in severity by squeezing once for unbearable and twice for tolerable. He squeezed her hand twice. On orders from the Führer his doctor decreased Mengele's medications in hope that he would come out of his dazed state more quickly.

By the end of week two Mengele opened his eyes but was still unable to speak. At this time Hitler, again, was briefed on Mengele's condition. Hitler asked to be informed on a daily basis and would visit him personally the moment he could speak.

At the beginning of the third week he lay on the hospital bed, weak but awake, coherent in speech.

The Führer was immediately summoned and upon his arrival at the hospital a translator was secured and Hitler began to ask questions. Mengele was slow to awake at first, he was unable to answer right off. Hitler became aggravated and asked the nurse by his bed what was wrong. She explained that he was given medication a few hours earlier after becoming overly excited but that he'd be all right in a few minutes.

Hitler started speaking softly and when Mengele was still slow to answer, Hitler lost his patience and began shouting at the man, "Who are you, why don't you speak German? If you are a man from another planet you should know all of our languages, and what is all of this garbage you have brought about my losing the war, committing suicide—crap!"

The man finally awakened saying, "I am not a space man, I am an Earth man."

"What?"

"I am an Earth man from the year 2010. I have come to help the Führer win the war."

"You are mad—you were sent here by the British or the Americans or both to break our spirit of victory with all this pile of lying newspaper articles and propaganda. I am going to have you executed."

As the guards approached, the man said, "Wait - wait, I can prove it." He fell as the guards pulled him from the bed. Hitler smiling said, "Prove it - how? With these printed forgeries." The guards drug him out of the room and down the hall as Hitler laughed saying, "What will they try next—fake space ships—Roosevelt must be desperate."

As the "man from the future" was tied up and readied for execution, on the tenth day after his incarceration, a Nazi physicist who had called Hitler earlier, was now before him saying, "Don't dare shoot that man, there is sophisticated equipment, the likes of which no nation has yet to produce, in his ship. We've taken some of it apart and examined it but we don't know how to operate it."

The physicist showed Hitler a few of the advanced instruments and convinced him that these were not from the world of 1939. His digital, liquid crystal watch fascinated Hitler. He was disturbed and convinced at the same time and feared that Mengele had already been executed. Realizing he must indeed be from the future or an advanced planet, Hitler immediately sent a message to the firing squad. Only seconds before the execution, with all of the rifles cocked and aimed, it was stopped.

Mengele was untied and brought before Hitler. He was brought before Hitler and Hitler yelled at him, "What is this?" Hitler handed him a phazer light weapon which was produced by the United States military in the year 2005. As he handed it to him, Mengele said, "Be careful, you will disintegrate all of us and blow up this whole room." Playing dumb in order to extrapolate all, Hitler said, "What? You are telling me this is that powerful, ha, you must be drunk or as crazed as Roosevelt was for sending you here to attempt to dash our hopes of world conquest and a world without Jews."

Mengele said, "No, I am for you, I want to help you." Hitler sarcastically replied, "Is that so?" as he pressed the photon laser beam weapon into Mengele's hand. The weapon resembled a stun gun of the 1990's and Hitler wanted to know how it worked. He inquired of Mengele, "Show me how this child's 'water pistol' that doesn't even look like a gun can destroy a whole room." Mengele went over to a window as Hitler said, "Go ahead, because when you can't prove it, you're a dead man."

Mengele looked out the window at a large house and said, "I can destroy that structure, may I, for a demonstration." Hitler answered, "O.K. big boy, shoot, I don't know why I am here wasting my time, go ahead, shoot, O.K." Mengele held the light weapon up and aimed it at the house, taking off the combination safety, which only he knew, so it would fire, he pressed the trigger. Instantly a light beam came out of the object and the house glowed, first yellow, then red and finally blue as it vanished from sight, literally into thin air.

HITLER BECOMES A BELIEVER

Hitler's face dropped—he became ashy white as he murmured, "Who - what are you?" Quickly a Nazi body guard grabbed the weapon from Mengele's hand and other guards attempted to put him under arrest.

Hitler yelled, "Stop—let him go—all of you get out, leave him here." One of Hitler's guards warned him, "My Führer, this man could kill you, he is dangerous." Hitler replied, "On my personal authority, leave him here with all of his things—you all get out—that is an order!"

Immediately all the Führer's body guards left and Hitler was alone in the room with this 'man from the future' as he called himself. Hitler asked, "Who are you and why would you want to help me? If you are an American, why would you want to give me this powerful weapon?"

Mengele told Hitler, "I am the future son of Joseph Mengele, who was killed, (after hiding for many years once Germany lost the war), by a future security force of a nation of Jews, called Israel. Hitler shouted, " What? I lose the war and the Jews have a nation of their own in the future? I am starting to think about having you shot again, dear boy."

Hitler began to leave the room and Mengele yelled, "No, no, wait, I can prove all of this. In the future, there is something called television and you lost the power to dominate the world as a result of the United States obtaining the Atom bomb before you. Your 'heavy water,' a key ingredient needed to

produce this powerful bomb, was destroyed by the
underground in Norway in 1944! All of this is on
video tape that can be played on "television," which
cannot be faked. I have brought a TV screen, a video
tape recorder and player to show you."

Hitler looked back over his shoulder with a very
startled look on his face as he asks the man, "You
mean you have some *films* from the future to show
me?"

Hitler challenges Mengele, "Now it is 1939. Can
you show me what will happen between 1942 and
1945?" "O.K., O.K.," shouts Mengele. Hitler
mumbles under his breath, "This I've got to see. I've
got to see this for myself." As a dumbfounded look
appeared on his troubled face, he said to himself,
"How could all this happen to me? Someone from
the future has returned to help me! Can this really be
true? No. Maybe. I must see—see for myself" and
for himself he would.

* * *

"In 1939 news came to Einstein that German physicists had succeeded in producing nuclear fission. The uranium atom could now be split. Germany might be able to develop a bomb."

WILLIAM HURT, Narrator of a PBS special,
"A. Einstein, How I See The World"

"...The key discovery that led to the atomic bomb was made in Germany." COLLIERS ENCYCLOPEDIA. Volume 17, 1997

"For even Satan disguises himself as an angel of light. Therefore it is not surprising that his servants also disguise themselves as servants of righteousness." 2 CORINTHIANS 11:13-15

6

HITLER SEES BEYOND HIS GRAVE

The next day Hitler and Mengele make their way to the Hamburg Military Research Laboratory where all of Mengele's video tapes were stored. German electronics analysts were unable to view these tapes because certain circuits and wires were cut between the TV's components while the Nazi soldiers were breaking in to the ship. Gunfire had stripped two critical wires and Nazi scientists were not sure where to resolder the leads in order to correctly repair a unit which was so strange to them.

Mengele quickly spliced the correct wires together and also repaired the video player. He then loaded a tape of Hitler's 1940 victories which contained a segment announcing Germany's surrender in 1945. Also recorded on the tape were some telecast news reels of Hitler in a near death state greeting the Hitler youth from the outside of the bunker, shortly before his suicide.

As the tape rolled, Hitler smiled as he saw one Nazi victory after another. He laughed and said, "Hey, that's me. I look a little older but look, next year I'll have France. Look that's me in front of the Eiffel Tower." He added, "Good work my boy, maybe you are for real. What a nice box—'a movie in a box—of the future.' What do you call this again, tele?"

"Television," Mengele replied.

Then as the 1945 defeat appeared on the screen and a half-dead Führer was seen patting boys of the Hitler Youth on the cheek, Adolf flinched! Shortly thereafter a blood filled bunker which contained the hanging body of Hans Krebs, Hitler's last Chief of Staff, and the charred remains of Joseph Goebbels was now shown, as the tape continued to play.

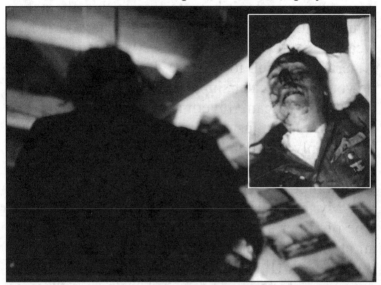

Hans Krebs hanging from the bunker ceiling.

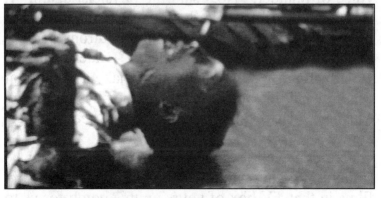

Joseph Goebbels burned to a crisp.

Hitler became white, again. "What's this—are you trying to tell me we lose? What sort of joke is this? I am losing my patience," Hitler fumed.

Mengele replied, "Yes and no."

"What—what do you mean, that doesn't make any sense!" Hitler shouted.

"*Yes*, you did lose in the past, but now, with me here, '*no*', you don't have to lose in this alternative future that I will help you create. There is a new weapon your scientists were working on that America beat you to because the underground blew up your heavy water shipment in 1944 in Norway.

The American Government used this *big bomb* to destroy Japan just weeks after you killed yourself, it took only two bombs and Japan surrendered. One bomb kills over 100,000 in Hiroshima and you could see it's fireball for 200 miles."

"My boy," Hitler shouts, "That's impossible." One of Hitler's physicist, who had split the atom in an atomic experiment only weeks before, was now present with Hitler and Mengele. He quickly spoke up and said, "No!" Hitler said, "No, what?" in a voice of thunder. "No," said the physicist again, "It is not impossible. We have just bombarded the uranium atoms nucleus with slow neutrons and we know that once enough heavy water can be manufactured we may be able to make a bomb that can do what this boy says." Then the physicist asked Mengele, "How do you know about 'heavy water' anyway?"

Hitler's eyebrows raised almost off his face as he stuttered, saying calmly, "Do—do you have any films in that TV box of yours on this bomb for us to see?" Mengele replied, "Yes," and turned on the TV while placing the tape of the bomb in the video player. As old film reels of the dropping of bombs over Hiroshima and Nagasaki were viewed, Hitler's mouth fell open. Hitler appeared dumb founded and asked, "What, how can we get this—where did we make our mistake?"

Hiroshima blast in progress.

The physicist commented, "We knew it would make for a very powerful bomb, but we didn't know it would be that powerful—100,000 in one blast?" Mengele spoke up and said, "And that's the smallest of these bombs. There's also the Hydrogen bomb that came later in the 1950's." Hitler groped and said, "What, what—you are trying to tell me there is something more powerful than the Atomic bomb which you showed me on the television screen."

Young Mengele said, "Yes, I have more films. All you have to do is make sure your heavy water shipment is not sabotaged in 1944. And what's more, I've got some uranium on board the ship already separated and enriched from U238 into U235—a fissionable grade of uranium."

One of Hitler's scientist stood forth and shouted, "How do you know all of this? How do you know what nuclear fission is?" "How?" Hitler, who was now totally convinced, answered, with a glaring look in his eyes, "He's from the future and he's going to help us win the war this time around. Aren't you?" while patting the boy on the back. "Yes," acknowledged Mengele.

Hitler mumbled to himself, "We can win— possibly without the bomb, because we know where all of our mistakes for the next 6 years are going to be made, in advance. We know, we know! Good grief, we now know. However, we are going to build the bomb to make sure we will win, no matter what. All of this must be kept a secret."

Albert Einstein
Old Grove Rd.
Nassau Point
Peconic, Long Island

August 2nd, 1939

F.D. Roosevelt,
President of the United States,
White House
Washington, D.C.

Sir:

Some recent work by E.Fermi and L. Szilard, which has been communicated to me in manuscript, leads me to expect that the element uranium may be turned into a new and important source of energy in the immediate future. Certain aspects of the situation which has arisen seem to call for watchfulness and, if necessary, quick action on the part of the Administration. I believe therefore that it is my duty to bring to your attention the following facts and recommendations:

After reviewing all of the news reels and realizing that Einstein's 1939 letter to Roosevelt was what really got the US Atom bomb program off the ground, Hitler ordered Einstein's capture.

A special highly trained German team of elite soldiers disguised as American scientists would be flown in at low altitude over Einstein's residence. He would be disguised, heavily sedated and smuggled out of the US into German held territory. No time could be wasted. It was July 1st and the letter would soon be written on August 2, 1939.

The team was assembled and sent out that week. Hitler said, "This is one Jew who we Germans will listen to and Roosevelt will not."

Hitler, very weary, called an end to the gathering and told Mengele's son to take the room next to his and retired for the night. Although he tried his best to sleep he got very little that evening. He tossed and turned as he contemplated a sure outcome to the war. A victory which would result in his conquering the entire planet.

* * *

This reality of the Russian conquest of Berlin and a
Hitler near-death with the "Hitler youth" would
never be, because of Mengele's time travel.

7

ENGLAND, RUSSIA AND THE UNITED STATES SURRENDER TO HITLER

Bright and early the next morning Hitler was reviewing news reels on Mengele's video tapes which had been brought back from the future. Hitler was shocked at his sickly, ashy, white gray complexion in 1945 and discovered his physician, Dr. Morel had been giving him pain pills that contained small doses of arsenic which destroyed his body slowly after 1941. Hitler realized this after reading Mengele's 1971 copy of, *"The Last Days of Hitler,"* written by Hugh Trevor-Roper and seeing the movie based on this work. Once Hitler put two and two together he ordered his beloved private physician, Dr. Morel, executed.

DOCTOR MOREL MURDERED

Morel couldn't believe it when a week later he was awakened by SS officers in the middle of the night.

"What's the matter—what are you doing?"

"Orders from the Führer, you are to die by firing squad."

"You don't know what you're doing. Aside from Martin Borman and Himmler I'm the Führer's best friend."

"Just following orders."

Morel was strapped to a post and seconds later shots rang out. Morel, who was to all but poison Hitler in the years to come, through medical quackery, breathed his last.

SPECIAL STEPS TAKEN TO CRACK THE ENEMY'S CODE

Hitler fired Admiral Canaris, his head of intelligence, who he learned would, in the future, fail to inform him that the United States Intelligence Agents broke his military, top secret code. Once he'd done this he established a bureau which was to learn Navajo. Having captured 25 U.S. Navajo Indians he intended for his intelligence to learn that language so well that he would be able to crack U.S. codes which included the segment of Navajo 'code talkers.' The code talkers he learned, from news reels, had translated American codes into Navajo, sent them, and then used Navajo to decipher the codes on the receiving side.

HITLER IN AWE OVER MOON SHOTS

All was now in his favor. He had nothing to lose and he spent many weeks and months reviewing articles and video tapes with Adolf Mengele, the illegitimate son of the captured Joseph Mengele, who was born in the late 1970's.

Hitler said, "You may speak English, look and sound like an American, but you are a pure breed German Aryan at heart. We will win!"

When Hitler saw tapes of the United States moon shot and landing in 1969, he was shocked. "The moon," he exclaimed, "The Americans went to the moon and they used my scientist, Wernher Von Braun, to build their rocket. They stole my technology and went to the moon. What, I can't believe it. If Germany will be destroyed there will be a space race between the United States and that inferior race of Russians, both using scientists they pilfered from me. And those charlatans took my small jet fighter aircraft and expanded it into freighter size airliners and used it for civilians to produce capital. Capitalistic democratic idiots."

HITLER AND HOGAN CAN NOT AGREE

After viewing episodes of Hogan's Heroes from the 1960's, which Mengele had taped from *Nick at Night*, a cable television station specializing in old TV shows. Hitler screamed, "What's this, are the Americans making fun of us after we lose the war—no more, no more!" as he pulled the electrical cord out of the wall.

HITLER AND SPIELBERG

Later Hitler viewed Mengele's videotaped movies: *Raiders of the Lost Ark* and *Indiana Jones & The Last Crusade for the Holy Grail*, produced by Steven Spielberg. He went into a frenzy exclaiming, "The Jews of the future are making movies about me. Fictitious movies with impersonations of me by actors that do not even look like me. Why would I sign the diary of this fool cowboy Indiana Jones and be racing him for a fictious grail?" He passed out.

HITLER SABOTAGES THE AMERICAN ATOMIC BOMB PROGRAM

Back in the U.S., Roosevelt never got the letter which history recorded Albert Einstein had sent. The Italian atomic scientist, Enrico Fermi, who had bombarded uranium with the chargeless neutron and achieved atomic fission, was captured. Dr. Leo Szilard, who was performing atomic experiments was killed and Einstein lay on a cot underground in a German dungeon. He was cold and fed only once a day. He wondered what in the world had happened and why had the Germans captured him.

HOW HITLER CAPTURED ALBERT EINSTEIN

The German intelligence operation of Einstein's capture had gone off like clock work. On July 28, only five days before Einstein would mail the critical letter, a group of men (German soldiers who had parachuted down a half block from Einstein's home) appeared at his door claiming to be physicist. When he discovered they were not, he was accosted, sedated and cleverly disguised. A forged passport with a fraudulent identity was placed in his pocket.

Einstein was injected with a drug which simulated drunkenness. He was unable to speak clearly. He was whisked off with eight soldiers, also possessing falsified pass ports. At the airport they easily cleared through pass port control and boarded a flight to a neutral country where it would be easy to transport him to Berlin.

HITLER PRODUCES
MATERIAL FOR THE BOMB

The next year, 1940, Hitler fortified the Vemork electrical plant in Rjukan, Norway and stepped up production of heavy water to massive proportions. He ordered the production of a gaseous defusing plant as a back up to produce the isotope of uranium 235, which was needed for the bomb.

The next year in 1941, he strategically withdrew from areas where he knew heavy losses were to occur and in 1942 he proclaimed he wanted peace and if the allies would only allow him to cease fire, he would withdraw his troops and return control of certain countries of Europe as good will gestures - and he did. First Greece, then Warsaw—yet he continued to fortify Norway in 1943 as she produced more and more heavy water. In 1944 the ferry sailed and reached it's aspired destination.

A timewarp-Nazi retreat from Greece.

After reading Anthony Cave Brown's 1975 book, "*Bodyguard of Lies*[1]," he had had the explosive plastique meant to sabatogue the delivery of important war material, removed from the ferry which would carry his critical shipment of heavy water moments before it sailed, thereby thwarting it's previous historic destruction, which had been achieved by the underground, in the time before.

HITLER ASSEMBLES THE BOMB AND CALLS FOR A CEASE FIRE

In late 1944 having assembled all the uranium brought to him from the space ship into 6 bombs and having produced enough heavy water in Norway to assemble another 20, Hitler retreated from several countries provided the allies ceased fire on those areas where withdrawal would be executed.

---

[1] P. 370-77, See Appendix 3.

In December of 1945 with all looking well to the world, Hitler ordered three planes be sent out with unknown cargo. He assured the Americans, the Russians and the British that these planes where carrying envoys of peace with new peace agreements which would help to facilitate a quick and more efficient withdrawal from key potential hot spots. The allies agreed to receive the aircraft because Hitler had kept his word to the letter thus far. They wanted peace!

HITLER DROPS THE A-BOMB
ON THE UNITED STATES

As the first plane roared over Washington DC it's port doors opened, it's cargo, a giant cylinder shaped object was released. As it fell ever so gracefully, head long towards a football stadium, the players and crowds looked up. Suddenly a blinding light over took all and after the loud explosion which accompanied the extraordinary brilliance approximating that of the sun—silence was everywhere.

Ground zero and a mile out was deadly silent. Three to five miles out some murmuring could be heard. Farther out screams and blood curdling hysterical cries were heard.

The aircraft traveled on to New York, this time flying low enough to avoid radar. Right before dropping the bomb, the plane gained enough altitude to avoid being taken out with the blast. It's second bomb was released. The Empire State Building, standing 102 stories high, the tallest building in the world, located on 5th Avenue between 33rd and

44th Street, only completed in 1931, was flattened. The city was in ruins. People's shadows were burnt into the concrete where they stood before they fell to the ground, as toasted skeletons.

Actual A-bomb victim of 1945.

An outdoor spiral staircase of 1945 in Japan is shadowed in uncharred paint, during and after the atomic blast. The "white shadow" still exists.

MOSCOW IS DESTROYED - AMERICAN GENERAL'S SURRENDER TO HITLER

The bombs that hit Moscow fell at the same time as the New York bomb detonated. Moscow was raging with fire. No more Kremlin or Red Square. Half an hour later, London got the same. A major air field and half the city burned all night. People were dead and dyeing by the thousands each minute. Farther out people died slower deaths as highly lethal radiation extinguished their lives.

Generals MacArthur, Eisenhower and Patton took careful notice and when they learned Truman and two thirds of Washington and all of New York were no more they decided, before counter attacking, to notify Hitler that a no-fire/retaliation was planned until damage assessments could be taken and terms could be agreed upon provided his attacks be broken off.

Patton and Eisenhower decide to surrender.

As they learned what had simultaneously happened to Moscow and England they would turn themselves in to the German military authorities provided no further bombings were made on the American people.

NO D-DAY—GERMAN VICTORY DAY

On December 10, 1945, Berlin having not been hit with even one bomb as a result of Hitler's well planned false-peace retreat program, received the news that America, Russia and England had surrendered.

German radio Newscasters reported: Washington DC was no more. President Truman was dead. New York was a cinder of fire. Radiation was killing more. Moscow was in shambles. Stalin was dead. Marshal Zhukov, the Russian Army's top General, had surrendered. London was gone, a sight of horrible flame, in ruble. Churchill could not be found and the head of England's army had delivered the letter to Hitler which said, "We surrender, please, we will do whatever you want us to. We will even let you have our Jews, fundamentalist Christians, Gypsies and all of our gold and anything else you desire. We will be your slaves, but please in Satan's hell don't drop another bomb like that on us."

Mengele was at Hitler's side as news came of complete allied surrender. Hitler patted him on the back and told him how indebted he was to him and that he would give him anything he wanted. Hitler introduced him to the most beautiful woman he had ever laid eyes upon. In the coming months Mengele would be married to Fräulein Helga and three years later she would bare him twin sons.

As German victory was announced to all German citizenry, Hitler and his "space man" friend, Mengele, could be seen walking and conversing, both had evil gleams which spelled tyranny, in their eyes. Both walked around as though they owned the world and in reality, they did. Mengele's origin and his time travel were not announced to the public. These facts were kept secret on orders of military intelligence. The soldiers and civilians who witnessed the ship's landing were killed to protect what would become Germany's most guarded secret. This secret along with the knowledge of the bomb would belong to no one—no one but the Führer.

Mengele was appointed foreign minister to help unite the world's nations into a "planetary state," Hitler would found as the Führer's "Global Germania."

The Führer's Global Germania.

Hitler congratulates the pilot who dropped
the A-bomb on the United States.

Hitler is congratulated for his conquest of the U.S.A.

"Colonel Hogan...you didn't fool me for one minute with that story about the water. I deliberately went along with your little joke so you would think it was spring water from Norway...It was <u>heavy water</u> to be used for a <u>new</u> type of <u>bomb</u> that will bring the <u>allies</u> to their <u>knees</u>."

"COLONEL CLINK"...to Hogan in an episode
of "Hogan's Heros" regarding a secret allied mission
to sabotage a German heavy water delivery.

"If these Germans do win they will turn the whole world into one big execution yard, not just for Jews."

The "American Minister" TUTTLE in 1942 from
War and Remembrance. A made for TV serial, 1989.

8

THE FÜHRER VICTOR
BECOMES WORLD DICTATOR

With America, England and Russia at Hitler's knees—he ordered his top Generals and most elite troops to occupy the continental United States, Canada, Russia, England and the Orient. The Feeble nuclear experiments which had barely begun in the U.S. were smashed. All nuclear scientists who were not German or loyal to Hitler were ordered shot. This action was repeated in every country which had begun the slightest work in atomic research.

HITLER ORDERS JEWS AND CHRISTIANS EXTERMINATED

The entire earth was entering a dark age. Hitler ordered all Evangelical Christians[*] and Jews to be shot on sight and buried on the spot. Large numbers of either group, if found together, were to be transported, gassed and cremated! His genealogical record society began tracing everyone's lineage, in an attempt to uncover the slightest amount of Jewish blood in any person's family. Anyone who had any Jewish ancestry was to be executed. Hitler ordered the construction of a museum in Berlin called, *The Relics of an Extinct People,* where he put Jewish prayer shawls, yamacas, Torah scrolls and Bibles.

All other Bibles[†], both Christian and Jewish versions, were deemed propaganda, which were to be burned! It became a death sentence for anyone to hold a Bible or assemble in a Jewish or Evangelical house of worship.

SYNAGOGUES BECOME MUSEUMS

Synagogues were kept only to show where a forgotten people once gathered. They were turned into local museums with their own Nazi tour guides permanently in place. After every tour was a warning not to read the sacred writings of the Jews or the New Testament of their offspring, the Christians, on penalty of death.

---

[*] See Author's Notes.
[†] Ibid

THE PEOPLE OF THE MIDDLE EAST, CHINA, INDIA AND AFRICA ARE GASSED

In the Middle East, China, India and Africa, gas chambers and crematoria were constructed on a mass scale. Hitler following his belief in Houston Stewart Chamberlain's book, *Foundations of The 19th Century*, was beginning his plan to exterminate the world's "inferior races." Within a short period of time China[§] was completely depopulated—the Chinese people were no more. In their place Hitler established German colonies who continued the trades of silk clothing, producing, growing and exporting rice and the mining of tungsten[*]. Germans took over the mining of coal in the world's largest open pit coal mine close to Fu-shun Liaoning province using British slave labor. The coal was dug and exported world wide for use in industrial plants and homes.

In the Middle East Arab populations were seen lined up for blocks waiting to "take a shower and be deloused" in gas chambers—cleverly disguised as showers. Early on, before the end of the war, Hitler had considered the Arabs his allies in his common cause with them against the Jews.[†]   But now he

---

[§] See authors note on Hitler's view of China.
[*] A metal used in light bulb filaments.
[†] This was documented in the book, *The Mufti and the Führer*, by Joseph B. Schechtman. The book quoted, a letter by Freiherr von Weizsaeeker, "The Germans and the Arabs have common enemies in the Jews and are united to fight against them." The book notes that the Arab's construction of gas chambers in the Middle East was for the Jews in anticipation of Hitler's break through to that area.

would deal with the Semites, who were not Jewish, the half brothers of the Jews, who were far from Aryan.

Mengele reminder Hitler of the Arab's cooperation and help in his attack against the Jews, reminding him of Schechtman's book he brought back from the future. Hitler replied, "I know, but they ARE NOT ARYAN and we don't need them anymore." Hitler told Mengele, "The only pure human creatures on earth are the Aryans and they include Germans, English, Irish and Scandinavians. All others must go—no exceptions—none!"

THE GERMANS OCCUPY THE MIDDLE EAST, INDIA AND AFRICA TAKING OVER THEIR WORLD TRADE

Once the Arabs were exterminated German troops manned the oil wells in this area of the world and supplied Hitler's incoming freighters with an infinite supply of petroleum to fuel the world's third Reich which grew stronger and more efficient with every coming day.

In Africa, natives, through interpreters, were told to line up to be bathed in the newly constructed showers or face depravation of food rations. Millions were murdered and turned to ashes in the short space of six months with over 2,000 gas chambers and crematoria covering the entire continent of Africa—within five years the black race was no more.[*]

Hitler dispatched German mining crews to Africa to continue the mining of precious minerals

---

[*] See author's note on the black race.

including diamonds which were exported mostly to German royalty i.e. the upper echelon of German society, who would be able to afford such gems.

India's 1,263,068 square miles, about half the area of the continental United States, became a waste land used as a giant pollution dump after Hitler affected the countries complete depopulation. However, before the gassing of all Indians, selected Indians were forced to teach their art of carpet manufacture and embroidery of gold and silver threads to German craftsmen so these arts wouldn't be lost to Hitler's world.

Hitler made use of the iron ore which is on the Bihar-Rissa state borders for steel production. The mica* mines that were taken over became a precious commodity for the Führer's military, along with the radio active metals of thorium and uranium which Germans mined and stored for future production of the new atom bombs.

The Kolar Gold Mines in Mysore, which are the world's deepest, were continually mined to retrieve even more gold to back Hitler's new world Reich Mark. Of all the ancient architecture of India only the Taj Mahal was salvaged and in it's interior was placed a golden statue of Adolf Hitler.

HITLER BUILDS HIS CITIES AND TAKES OVER THE EARTH AS LORD SOVEREIGN

Hitler began construction of his planned cities— night and day. Construction crews assembled these cities chiefly designed by Hitler's architect, Albert Sphere, before 1945. Sphere and Hitler had laid the

---

* A mineral needed for the manufacture of electrical devices.

cities out in miniature models but now with his victory, the cities of the Führer would finally become reality.

Marble or gold pagan statues of Hitler's image were placed everywhere. He proclaimed, "Germany was he and he was Germany." And Germany was now the world and he was "Führer - Lord" of the world. An invincible pagan god-like figure who ruled the earth with the all powerful A-bomb at his disposal proclaimed, "If any province should get out of line or fail to honor the Führer, even for a short space of time, the bomb will be used."

The Führer's study at his chancellery in Berlin (above) would never see destruction. Instead his great cities were built from the models[*] of architects, Giesler, Kreis, Malwitz, Klage and Speer.

---

[*] The following photos of models and architecture differ somewhat from those traditionally known because Hitler changed his mind regarding many of his previous designs, after his victory.

NSDAP Military Academy.

Hitler's Hall of Soldiers.

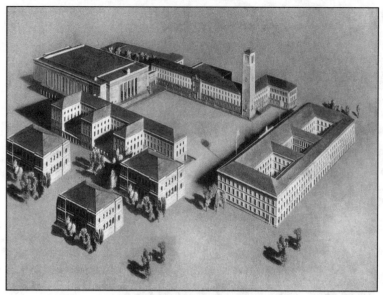

Adolf Hitler Square.

Nuremberg Stadium.

Stamp design commemorating
Hitler's World Victory.

The Führer's replacement of
the Empire State Building.

Statues cast from the above prototype made everyone in the world aware of who the Führer was after
the war.

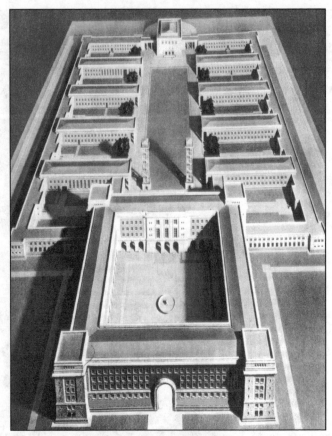

Hitler's Institute of War Technology.

Hitler's Circular Plaza in Berlin, 1950.

Entrance to NSDAP Academy, Bavaria, 1952.

The Führer's Great Hall to be would seat fifty thousand people. The dome would be 1,050 feet high and the eagle atop the dome with it's claws sunk into a model of the globe represents Hitler's rule over Earth.

Mengele, acting as both world foreign minister and co-advisor of atomic weaponry, was unofficially second to Hitler in power. He dispatched troops to newly formed German provinces and negotiated surrender in small pockets of resistance. At times Hitler would smile at Mengele and call him co-Führer, jokingly. When anyone would ask where he came from, Hitler would claim that he was a long lost nephew who he adored and changed the subject rather abruptly. Mengele felt that he was "set for life." Only within another 35 years would he begin to grasp the real hell he had created for the world and especially for himself! Meanwhile he acted as State Consultant for the construction of new atomic plants while Hitler alone maintained sovereignty over the bomb itself!

HITLER TAKES OVER FORT KNOX
AND PLACES HIS OWN STATUE
IN THE LINCOLN MEMORIAL

In January 1946 Fort Knox was handed over to Hitler's SS elite guard without incident. The SS disarmed and loaded the Fort Knox security personnel up and sent these poor souls off to the gas chambers. Hitler replaced them with his own security and renamed the National Gold Reserve, Fort Hitler. He placed a giant stature of himself, made out of gold, at the entrance to the newly claimed "Fort Hitler."

Shortly thereafter, Hitler ordered the giant statue of Abraham Lincoln, which was housed by the marble building of the Lincoln Memorial, destroyed. For weeks Nazi engineers and construction crews carefully sawed it up, so as not to damage the beautiful Lincoln Memorial Building around it. First the head was removed, then the arms and chest, with the help of a small crane and steel cables. Finally, the legs were sawed into several pieces with the help of several hundred cement saw blades.

After Lincoln's statue was removed, piecemeal, a new statue of the same size was placed in Lincoln's giant chair but this statue was of Adolf Hitler. The Lincoln Memorial in Washington DC was renamed, "Führer Memorial."

The Führer Memorial.

Lincoln Memorial after Hitler's conquest of the U.S.

HITLER SETS UP GERMAN
LANGUAGE SCHOOLS WORLD WIDE

In February 1947, special schools were set up in every city of every country (now German provinces of the greater "Global Germania") for the teaching of the German language for two and a half hours each day. German linguistics specialists were sent to existing schools. Attendance was compulsory.

HITLER ORDERS JEWISH
ARCHEOLOGICAL DISCOVERIES
DESTROYED—TO REWRITE HISTORY

In 1949 in Palestine, where the Jewish nation of Israel would never be reborn[*], German occupational troops demolished all archeological evidence which authenticated the Bible. The wailing wall, the tomb of Abraham and the Garden Tomb of Jesus were demolished with the use of explosives. Within a few weeks, after the ruble was cleared, not a trace of antiquity was left to prove that they had ever existed.

---

[*] See the conclusion in Appenix 1, *Israel- Is Real* to understand why this fictional scenario, which was Hitler's goal, could have never become reality.

In their places Hitler seeded the area with ancient German relics and claimed that the Germanic peoples of ages past were the first to inhabit this land.

HITLER TRIES TO EXPLAIN AWAY THE BURNING OF THE JEWS

As the 1950's dawned, no Christians or Jews were to be found. Day and night the world over crematoria bellowed smoke and the stench of burning flesh. Hitler claimed the smell was that of animals cooking which was food for the poor to eat. No one really believed this dastardly lie, but were all afraid to speak up for fear of their families safety.

Nazi soldiers arrive at the Washington Monument as they occupy the United States.

Some questioned how Hitler could accomplish all that he was doing. How he could simply march in a few troops and just "take over" the world—just like that? The A-bomb was a very powerful tool. There was no defense against this destructive weapon. Hitler only had to disperse a small number of troops to each nation and they built small armies of soldiers when they arrived. There was very little opposition to their rule.

A SMALL RESISTANCE IS FORMED—TO NO AVAIL

A few knew that death was inevitable and decided, for the sake of future generations, to retaliate so that their children and grandchildren might experience the freedom they once knew. However, these rivals were few and easily dealt with. The fear of the bomb was great enough to gain almost total and universal cooperation.

THE WORLD LEARNS OF THE EXTERMINATION OF THE JEWS—BUT CAN DO NOTHING

The news had also circled the globe through underground networks about the mass murders of the Jews and other "inferior races[*]" however, no one dared to cross this extraordinarily evil and nefarious man and his small army of soldiers for fear of precipitating a nuclear holocaust.

In reality Christians and Jews burned all day—every day. The Führer's deputy, Martin Borman, instituted pagan worship rights to all nations where Hitler was worshipped as Führer and God.

---

[*] In Hitler's warped opinion and view.

EVA BROWN ENCOURAGES
HER SON ABOUT HIS FUTURE

Eva Brown's son, born five years earlier, was to take his father's place as Führer in 20 years or so. Eva told him constantly, "You are the new Führer and when your father is eighty years old, you will take the throne as the new, all powerful prince of Earth. You and your son after you will rule in a world of complete submission because you have what no one else has or will ever have—the Atomic bomb."

A WORLD FÜHRER CURRENCY
AND COINAGE ARE ISSUED

In the late 1950's all currency and coinage world wide were shredded and melted down with exception of small amounts, hoarded by collectors, who risked their lives by doing so. The newly issued money was a world currency and coinage inscribed with the German words, *"Dem Führer vertrauen wir"* (In The Führer We Trust). It bore likenesses and images of Adolf Hitler. These likenesses resembled the faces carved in the statues that were placed around the world with the words, "Führer, Adolf Hitler reigns supreme and is Lord—Solver of the universal miseries of humanity."

In reality Hitler had caused most of humanity's miseries by exterminating the black race, the Christians and Jews worldwide, polluting the oceans and large areas of land with nuclear fall out which caused untold varieties of cancers, etc., yet he felt he was the glory of the human race and was just what the world needed in a supreme leader.

Many of the statues throughout the world were in color. They included his black hair, blue-gray eyes and pale complexion. Perhaps this compensated for television which remained black and white, even in the 1980's and 90's.

If there was anything every city had in common in Hitler's new world it was three things: every city had a school that taught the German language, a security force dedicated to preventing nuclear secrets from being revealed and it's own gas chamber/ crematoria combination.

In Africa alone 2,000 gas chambers and twin crematoria had been constructed. For five years smoke rose in their chimneys from—1945 through 1950. The black race had been removed from the face of the earth.

In the 1050's the Earth only sustained one race of humanity, the Aryan, the sole survivors of Hitler's "racial purification program." These included the German, English, Irish and Scandinavian peoples.

The new American Germanian White House built over the rubble of the original.

"Veni, Vidi, Vici [*I came, I saw, I conquered*]"

CAESAR, 47 BC

9

HITLER'S WORLD REIGN
1960-1986

As the years passed and the 1960's dawned, Earth only had 1/4 billion citizens. Germans in China Germania produced silk cloth for Germany. America produced TV sets, stereos, steel, electrical appliances of all sorts and a variety of agricultural products. England mostly produced cars. Almost all were VW Bugs for common world citizenry and a few Mercedes Benz for the Government elite.

Hitler decided to produce replicas of portions of his German city in several areas of the world where he would stay during visits involving governmental affairs. These meetings were held to discuss Government advances and newly instituted rules which would further the world state of the Germanian Reich.

HITLER REWRITES HISTORY

Hitler took extraordinary steps to rewrite history. One of his main goals was to erase the achievements of the Jewish people from public record. He also intended to blot out anything positive written or spoken about the Jews by any respected or famous person or author. One case in point which he relentlessly pursued were the religious writings of Sir Isaac Newton. These writings were part of a private collection owned by Professor A. S. Yehuda[*]. They spoke very highly of the Jews, their Bible, their Messiah and their place in history.

Hitler ordered the collection burned and in fact ordered all other books authored by Newton destroyed. This striking of the name of Sir Isaac also included any books which had been penned about Newton by others. In the end Newton would be written out of history for his pro-Semitic stance.

AMERICA GERMANIA NEVER LANDS ON THE MOON

The space age never dawned. Rocketry was restricted to the military. "Who cared about the moon when there was much work on Earth to be

---

[*] See Author's Notes.

done!" Hitler exclaimed. Besides, the critical technology needed was not available in Mengele's alternative history. Perhaps a moon shot would have been a great challenge had Germany competed for it with another country, but there could be no space race with Germany as the sole runner. 1969 came and went and America, now a province of Germania, (The United States of Germania), never landed a man on the moon.

Computers were never allowed for civilian use. Only the Government and Hitler's top officials had clearance for the use of computers. As the 1980's approached, no computers appeared in businesses, homes or schools. The Internet was restricted for military use only among the newly formed provinces of Hitler's world wide state of Germany he called "Global Germania."

The world continued on in the dark ages as technology never passed the lead of the mid 50's in most areas.

Because Global Germania now ruled Earth with a universally supreme weapon, there were no super powers to compete with each other for defense weaponry and the race to the moon, which in the world before, had brought "the age of advanced computers and miracle medical technologies" to the civil populations of the Earth, therefore the world of advancement as Mengele had known it had never dawned.

MEDICINE IMPAIRED BY
MENGELE'S TIME TRAVEL

Mengele, upon having chest pains, visited the doctors who told him he had an incurable heart condition. Mengele knew that his problem was curable in the previous future from which he had come and a valve replacement was all that was needed. The doctors told him, "Such technology was not available at this time."

Mengele had accidentally taped an educational special on a heart valve replacement procedure on the end of one of his Hitler specials he had recorded for the Führer, which aired in the 1980's. He frantically took the movie to the doctors to show them what he was talking about, in the hope they would understand and somehow get on with this simple, yet routine, operation.

The doctors were amazed and inquired, "What sort of fictional movie have you brought us?" They exclaimed, "This type of operation, in reality, won't be perfected for at least 20 years." Mengele shuddered and realized that tampering with time, as he did, had created an alternative history in which many medical technological advances had never taken place and the few that did had come about at a much slower rate.

Realizing that this could cost him his very life, he became frantic. He went to the U.S. hoping things would be different there. However, the U.S. was a province of the Reich and the doctors there gave him the same story.

In the years to come, as Mengele's heart deteriorated as he slowly headed towards a death he would have never had to experience in the time before, he began to regret what he had done in giving Hitler victory.

THE END OF FREEDOM
BRINGS UNIFORMITY

Freedom and democracy, as it had existed in the world before, ended in Hitler's 1945 victory. Eighty percent of the Earth's population were driving VW Beetles, a car jointly designed by Adolf Hitler and Ferdinand[*] . One thing was for sure, everyone knew the word *Volks Wagon meant people's wagon* because the people of the world, that was left after the war, all spoke German. Hitler wanted the world's masses to own a vehicle, which would be affordable to most of the common people. This was an inexpensive and efficient automobile that all common people could afford. However, the elite Government officials all drove Mercedes Benz luxury cars.

The 1970's brought massive witch hunts for a few Jews and Evangelical Christians, who had somehow managed to evade capture and murder early on.

---

[*] See Author's Note.

HITLER'S SON—PROMOTED

Hans Hitler, Adolf's son, had studied at the University of Berlin and once he had graduated he became more or less a lazy, yuppie type bum working at a stock brokerage firm part-time.

In 1975, when Hitler was 86 years old, and strangely enough, still in a fair state of health he brought his son, at only 30 years of age, into a prominent position in his government.

Hans spent an unusual amount of time playing tennis and skiing in Austria's most elite resort. Finally Hans was appointed Vice Führer. His father coached him in the old ways of the Reich as modern Nazism continued to develop into an even more brutal form of totalitarianism.

RECOLLECTION OF AN ASSASSINATION ATTEMPT

This development resulted from the paranoid fear Hitler continually harbored—a fear of governmental over-throw and assassination. These were well founded fears because in 1974 Hitler was nearly killed in an assassination attempt by one of his top Generals, formerly known as Major Brug, who had planted a huge bomb in Hitler's palace.

Hitler, in the middle of a sleepless night had ventured into the bunker, which was underneath his palace, in search of some additional information regarding his family tree he had stored there three years before. He hoped the material would once and for all disprove any possibility of partial Jewish[*] ancestry. While he was in the palace bunker, the bomb went off. The entire palace collapsed but Hitler was safe and used the military bunker hot-line to call crews to excavate the wreckage and rescue him.

Shortly after the explosion Brug was seen near the premises and arrested for questioning. During his interrogation he was given truth serum. Thereafter he admitted the entire plot to assassinate the Führer.

Hitler ran the Reich from his "bunker prison" underground. By phone he gave orders to his most trusted soldiers and elite government officials. He was informed of the General's assassination attempt on his life. Hitler advised his contacts to wait until his rescue before sentencing the General. He wanted to speak to and question Brug personally.

It took two weeks of digging to finally free the Führer. The bunker was well stocked with non-perishable items, water and a TV. Hitler daily watched world wide news reports of how the 85 year old Führer of Earth was being rescued by Germany's experts in the field of excavation.

Finally, when he was dug out of his "palace prison," so to speak, General Brug, who had made

---

[*] See the last two pages of Appendix 5.

the assassination attempt on the Führer was released from jail and questioned by Hitler himself.

Once Hitler was satisfied that Brug acted alone, he was executed on world wide television for all to see. Military sirens on every corner of the globe sounded. Everyone was either awakened or took a break from whatever they were doing to watch the execution of the man who had attempted to slay the Führer. He was hung with piano wire and films were made of his hanging. The films were re-aired world wide every year on the day of the attempted assassination. This went on for 12 years until Hitler was 97 years old in 1986. *born in '86*

The year before in 1985 Hitler had suffered a heart attack and there after was bed ridden for 3 months. He became gravely ill and decided to hand the work of governing over to his son, Hans. Towards the end of that year he suffered a stroke and complained of continual pain.

He constantly awoke screaming & sweating from terrible nightmares that haunted him. He repeatedly stumbled over the priceless heirlooms and works of art that had been stolen from museums and other royal palaces the world over after Germany secured world dominion in 1945. One day he became so disgusted during a bout with pain that he even threw eggs at the original Mona Lisa, which hung in his living room.

Hitler acquired the world's finest pieces of art including: the <u>Danae</u> by Rembrant, 16(3)6; The

Mother and Child by Pablo Picasso, 1921-22; The marble statue The Kiss, 1886-98 and the bronze sculpture, The Thinker, 1879-89 by Augustine Rodin; The engraving of Adam and Eve by Albrecht Dürer; The lime composition Head of Buddha 3rd-4th centuries A.D.; The Moses by Michelangelo and The Last Supper mural by Leonardo da Vinci, 1495-98, which was removed from the Stanta Maria delle Grazie, a Dominican cloister in Milan, Italy and then reassembled in Hitler's palace, in a large showroom, especially built for this work, which measured 15 feet high and 28 feet across.

Hitler stocked many thousand of additional works of art, which there was no room for in his palace in the "Führer's Berlin Museum of Art" which he founded for a showcase to display the world's finest art.

The Last Supper

Mona Lisa

The Thinker by Augustine Rodin

THE SACRED ARK HAUNTS HITLER

The golden Hebrew Ark of the Covenant, (the most sacred artifact of the ancient Hebrews) which his archeologists had discovered under the Mosque of Omar in Palestine where the 2nd temple stood, sits in the entry hall of Hitler's palace.

Fine art from all over the world lined his walls, ancient artifacts and fine furnishings adorned every room and famous statues stood in the courtyards surrounding the palace.

Although he adored all of these furnishing his pain never left. It would seem, from the time he obtained the Ark, as if the pain accompanied him constantly as some sort of divine judgment. Plaques of mice and boils overwhelmed him. These rodents ravaged his private gardens and the boils mutilated his appearance. It seemed a replay of ancient history, when the Philistines had taken this priceless, mystical article.[*] Neither exterminators or dermatologists were able to help rid the Führer of these things.

THE DEATH OF THE FÜHRER

He continuously took pain pills of all sorts. In the end he begged family members to give him stronger & stronger medication and finally morphine. Having over dosed on pain pills, he went into a comma and became a living vegetable only to expire at the end of that year where upon his son, Hans, took the throne and the title of Führer then he began to rule the world with an iron hand at the age of 41.

---

[*] I Samuel 5-7

1889-1986

The Führer's Funeral in 1986.

Mengele contacted Hans and expressed sympathy over the death of his father. Although Mengele had already begun regretting some of the things he had caused by his time travel, he offered Hans his support if needed. This was primarily until Mengele could get a feel for Hans. He did not want to become an enemy at this time because of the power he knew Hans had.

Hans was not at all ready to welcome Mengele or his help. This was his world and he would rule it his way. He told Mengele that his support and advise was not needed nor was it wanted. One day in the Führer palace Hans Hitler told Mengele "If you do not like the world of the new Führer you can go back to the world from which you came."

Mengele thought quietly to himself, "This would be a good idea, go back in time before I went back before—go back to 1938, a year before '39 and undo what I have done, then the world would be a better place for me, for I am now trapped in a time in which I do not belong. I could even get my heart fixed and see the moon landings."

Suddenly he was jolted back into reality—out of his daydream—realizing that would be impossible, forever, in his lifetime. Because to go back in time again, he would need to surpass the speed of light and for that he would need an advanced space ship. He was now experiencing, first hand, the consequences of his actions. Remembering what he'd done, in altering time, had destroyed the 1970's technology for simple moon rockets. He now knew there would never be a 2010 fusion fuel rocket or the parts needed to build a ship capable of reaching and surpassing light speed. He wept.

> "...Radioactive poisoning of the atmosphere, and hence, annihilation of any life on earth, has been brought within the range of technical possibility."
>
> ALBERT EINSTEIN on the H-bomb

10

1987-HANS HITLER TAKES GLOBAL RULE

Upon Hitler's death his body was flown around the world and viewed by every major dignitary in every major German province on the globe. His was the most elaborate funeral in history costing $100 million and lasting two weeks.

After Adolf Hitler was buried, in a casket of solid 24 karate gold set with rubbies and diamonds, with full military honors in Linz[*], his son, Hans, wasted no time in taking the reins of power. Many, the world over, felt Hans was negligent and irresponsible and not suited to rule the Earth. Hans

---

[*] See Author's Note.

Hitler was especially spurned by the Canadian province of Germania. As time passed this province began to assemble weapons underground to form a resistance.

HANS RULE IS NOT WELCOME BY CANADA GERMANIA

The people of Canada did not welcome or respect the new ruler, Hans. The people began to unite and start a revolt, having theorized that this young new ruler would not resort to using the bomb, which was at his disposal. The newly founded Canadian Army and government served notice to Hans that they were proclaiming their independence from Germany and would declare war if there was any opposition from Global Germania.

Hans was furious and insulted and cried, "How dare they try to overthrow my rule? If war is what they want, war is what they will get." He yelled as he slammed his fist against his desk and called a state of emergency. The troops were dispersed and told to shoot first and ask questions later with regards to any Canadian who openly defied the world rule of the Führer.

Canada did not back down from the Führer and his threats. War was declared.

The Canadians had an underground network that had been building and stockpiling weapons for sometime. They felt sure that they could stand up to and outlast the German army.

Hans' German Global Army walked the streets of Canada day and night shooting anyone who was openly rejecting the Führer. The Canadians returned the fire and people, young and old, both Canadian and German, lay in the streets. The war had begun.

MENGELE PLEADS WITH HANS NOT TO KILL HIS KIDS

After a week the Führer warned that if Canada did not surrender, that a blast, the likes of which they have never known, would bring them to their knees. The Canadians stood tall ignoring his warning.

Mengele came to Hans and asked him to please allow his relatives out of Canada—to spare the lives of his children and grandchildren. He asked for a special pass to go in and rescue them and bring them to safety. Hans refused saying, "I do not care how much you helped my father or our cause. All those who remain in Canada will be used as an example to reveal the consequences of those who choose to defy me. I can not help that some of those are your kin. None will be spared if this Canadian Army does not surrender. If you want to spare their lives then your sons should talk to those in authority in Canada Germania and convince them to surrender."

HANS MOCKS MENGELE

Mengele pleaded with Hans for several more minutes to no avail. Hans knew full well that Mengele and his sons could not turn the tide of the revolt. Mengele was on his hands and knees begging, "In the name of God," even though he, nor Hans, believed in God, "Please spare my sons and grandsons. You would not be here if it were not for me and my time travel."

Finally when Hans had heard enough, he said, in a reserved, cool tone of voice, "I know," and then called upon his guard and commanded him to remove Mengele from the palace. Once Mengele was taken out of the palace Hans looked out over Berlin from his window, poured a drink and as he lifted it to his lips said, "Poor fool. Who is he to beg of me? Nothing terrible enough could happen to him for that."

MENGELE WARNS HIS KIN TO FLEE UNDERGROUND

Mengele contacted his sons and told them to get their families to safety. He knew of the devastation that the H-bomb could cause and pleaded with them to go underground and take food and water with them. He would be unable to come and rescue them but if they moved immediately, several stories underground, they may be able to escape the worst of the blast that was going to take place.

Hans gave a final warning to the Canadians to cease-fire and surrender within 24 hours or he would use the H-bomb to end this war. The Canadians ignored his warning, once again. They dared him saying, "You can not be so inhumane as to use such a devastating weapon against those wanting freedom. No human being could be so cruel and evil."

A Canadian Germanian spokesman addresses Hans, "You can not take away our hopes of independence and freedom. We took the abuse from your father for years and we will not take it from you any longer. We do not think you will use the bomb. We will not cease fire nor will we surrender. We will be free!"

HANS USES THE H-BOMB

On February 1, 1987, according to schedule, Hans Hitler wiped out the German province of Canada, using the H-bomb, when large numbers of people refused to cease their revolt. This was broadcast around the world via global Germanian television.

Hans, from his office in the Führer palace, turned on his television. TV cameras had been set up to view the bomb. He walked over to this telephone, called the military on his hot line and ordered that the jet fighter aircraft circling Quebec release it's bomb.

The relatively small object was seen falling from the sky. Then as it hit, a blinding light filled the screen. Hans said, "They got what was coming" and laughed pouring his favorite drink, a Schnaus.

The fire ball of the Hydrogen bomb used was 2 miles in diameter. It destroyed 800 times the area as did the smaller A-bombs Hitler had used on the U.S. in 1945 to secure a German victory and speedy end to the war.

The Hydrogen bomb used by Hitler's son incinerated 2 million people instantly. Another million died within a week and another 2.5 million died before the end of the month. Hundreds of thousands died every month thereafter for nearly the rest of the year from the lingering radiation. Hitler had ordered that this bomb be encased with cobalt and other radioactive compounds to maximize its lethality through radiation poisoning.

Entire areas were quarantined. Medical attention was not allowed to be given to anyone under any circumstances. The people of the world, daily, viewed the horror of a slow death for months after— from that one, incredibly destructive, bomb.

Television news crews covered the dyeing and interviewed those in terrific pain. They were asked by Hans Hitler's reporters, "Wouldn't all had been better if you had not attempted to revolt against the Führer Hans?" They always replied, "Yes," as they blindly stared into the television cameras and the Führer's television camera was the world's eye.

The entire world population, fearful of similar consequences, should they be perceived as traitors to the Führer, fell into an about face. Anyone suspected of anti-Führer politics was killed, not necessarily by the army, but by their fellow workers or family, for fear they might invite nuclear retaliation.

MENGELE'S FAMILY DIES— HE REGRETS GIVING HITLER THE BOMB

Adolf Mengele, the time traveler who had traveled back in time from 2010 to 1939, to give Adolf Hitler the bomb witnessed the death of his family, who had settled in Canada years earlier. Though they had indeed gone hundreds of feet underground in a hide away, that coal mine was taken out with the blast leaving a crater two thousand feet deep. Mengele became so bitter and sorry that he had given the knowledge and materials necessary to build the bomb to a totalitarian power which had become absolutely corrupt. He cried night and day and contemplated revenge on Hitler's son, Hans.

The H-bomb dubbed "Mike" the diameter of it's fireball was three miles.

DEADLY AFFECTS OF RADIATION ARE USES AS FÜHRER PROPAGANDA

Day and Night the globe was engulfed in an inhuman, animal like, irrational fear of perpetual agony. The news reels rolled on, every week, year after year, showing old footage of the Canadian holocaust. No one dared to deny the Führer or even to speak against him. Those with radiation sicknesses were taken around the world and were shown to thousands in person so the masses could see the deadly results of revolt. No hair, sores that would not heal and horrible cancers were among the dire side affects of this new bomb demonstration. Truly, many commented, "Death would have been more humane."

HANS HITLER BECOMES AN ALCOHOLIC

In 1992, when Hitler's son Hans was 47, he became an alcoholic, very belligerent and unbelievably vain. Mourning the death of his father daily, he visits the tallest bell tower in Linz which contained Hitler's crypt with an eternal flame that burns constantly which marked where his body lay.

The SS allowed only dignitaries and family to enter the grave sight entrance. Television's national German anthem always closed with pictures of the Führer's grave at 2:00 am every morning before a picture of Hans was shown which millions saluted saying, "Hail to the Führer of antiquity and his son Hans."

HANS MARRIES

In 1993 Hans was married to Fräulein Magda Barnheart. A blond haired, fair complicated daughter of Alfred and Hannah Barnheart, friends of the Goebbels' family from two generation back. Having a moody, but interestingly intellectual personality, she played a part in almost every political decision of Hans after their marriage on January 12, 1993.

As Hans invited old girlfriends to visit him Magda took careful note and thereafter each and every one mysteriously disappeared. She used her clout and agents, which had been assigned her for security detail. They were ordered to kill anyone she suspected of flirting with her husband. Fifty-three women were reported missing within a short period of 6-months.

ADOLF HITLER'S GRANDCHILDREN ARE BORN

In late September she bore Hans a son who she called Hans Adolf Hitler, II. In January 1994, the royal baby was brought onto the terrace of Adolf Hitler's palace which had been restored from the ruble after the bombing of years before. Millions viewed her holding the 4-month old prodigy. The third in the royal line of the Führer.

Magda held the child close as she proclaimed, "The third Führer whom you see in my arms will rule the earth of Global Germania with an iron hand, as did his Grandfather and Father before him, in the coming 2030's." Hans smiled and viewed the multitude of people, with a smile similar to that of Prince Charles on his lips, as he both bowed and saluted "Zig Heil" to the huge crowds and television cameras which carried this event to every city in the world.

In 1995 a second child was born to Hans Hitler. A daughter he named Gertrude. She was blond haired and blue eyed, like her father, and the sunshine of his life. In 1998 when she was three and a half old, he constantly held her before Magda, her mother, and said, "I adore my pure Aryan baby, don't you?" She always replied, "Yes and she's as pure as we are."

WORLD TOTALITARIANISM
GAINS STRENGTH

Hans and Magda had willed global dominion to their two children and their spouses, whoever they would be. As the children reached their teenage years in the 2010's of our calendar they were taught by their parents to be as ruthless as they were and to not flinch or bluff if ever they would have to use the bomb to keep a German province in line.

The world was so different in the 2010's. Completely totalitarian, no privacy, television cameras and microphones lined every store, every telephone pole, every business and residence in every district. Television sets had cameras inside them which transmitted the details of whom ever was near the screen back to Gestapo intelligence, as did all other mounted and hidden cameras. Anyone suspected of anti-Nazi sentiment based on any action viewed was considered an enemy of the global state of Germania and the Führer and thereafter arrested & executed.

Most people were cremated however, some where put in mass graves. Huge holes were dug and the bodies were just thrown on top of each other and covered over with dirt.

The United States flag had stripes but no stars. In the place of the 50 stars there lie an over-sized, embroidered swastika.

The same went with the flags of other nations. Though initially they had replaced flags of conquered countries with their *own national, socialist* flag, the Germans now wanted enough of every flag preserved to illustrate it's national representation before Nazi conqueror—before Hitler dropped the A-bombs world wide in 1945, to show German victory. But those flags always had a Nazi swastika clearly visible on them.

THE HANDICAPPED ARE NO MORE

In hospitals, all over the world, lethal injection rooms were added to exterminate infants born with the slightest deformity and were to be used to execute all who had incurable conditions. Every polio victim of the 1950's was put to death as he or she contracted the disease.

There would never be a wheel chair factory or handicap facility, ramp or parking space because the handicapped were considered, by Hitler's government, to be "inferior people" that placed unnecessary burdens on society.

Hitler ordered the concept of "the survival of the fittest," (first introduced by the Victorian philosopher, Herbert Spencer[1], as a label for Darwinism, which was the natural end of the philosophy of evolution that was taught in schools everywhere) in an attempt to smother the guilt many felt when those who were terminally ill were executed. Most didn't like or buy this but it was the law of the world handed down by Adolf Hitler and it was enforced.

CHAMBERLAIN GETS HIS WAY

Everyone had to read Houston Stewart Chamberlain's, *Foundations of the Nineteenth Century,* before the age of 14. It's reading was compulsory. This crude and sickening work, along with the beliefs of Richard Wagner & Friedrich Nietzche, had earlier convinced Hitler of racial superiority and he and his son after him believed that it would also convince the world.

---

[1] Spencer, 1820-1903, "gained a wide reputation as a philosopher, but scientist later proved many of his theories wrong." *The World Book Encyclopedia.*

"There is a way that seems right to a man but it's end is the way of death." PROVERBS 14:12

11

THE FÜHRER KILLS THE LAST OF HIS ENEMIES—THE BAD DREAM ENDS

In 1999, Adolf Mengele, now in his old age, walked the streets as an ordinary person. No one, except Hans, knew that he was the one responsible for giving Adolf Hitler victory with the bomb in 1945, over fifty years before.

Occasionally Mengele spoke to Hans Hitler who realized he himself, the son of the Führer, would never have been born had it not been for Mengele's time travel, however, Hans shunned Mengele and only pretended to be his advocate. He felt obligated to Mengele and hated the feeling of being obligated to anyone.

Mengele hid his grudge towards Hans. He felt that if he pretended to forget what Hans had done in Canada, which caused the death of his sons, he might one day catch the Führer off guard and be able to take revenge on him—by assassination. His life long dream since Hans had, in essence, murdered his sons and grandsons while making an example of the Canadian's rebellion by dropping the H-bomb on them, was to get even by assassinating Hans. Even though Mengele's sons went underground the H-bomb's blast and deadly radiation had spared no one.

On Monday, December 10, it would be Führer Day. A day Adolf Hitler had instituted to recognize and remember his 1945 victory of world conquest. The day the US, Russia and Britain had surrendered after having the atom bomb dropped on them in unison. Adolf & Helga Mengele were invited to the celebration which would include a banquet with the Führer, Hans, & Magda Hitler.

HAN'S ASSASSINATION IS PLANNED

Mengele had made a gun out of a new composite material he had developed for this event. This ceramic like material would be strong enough to maintain its composure, so as not to shatter as a bullet traveled down its barrel, yet it would not be picked up by the newly developed metal detectors used in the Führer's palace.

He had made an ink pen, of gold, he'd claim would be a gift for Hans on Führer Day, however, the pen was hollowed out and held two bullets that would be used in the ceramic gun. No one would suspect these bullets since the pen was metal and would be placed in the basket for inspection while Mengele passed through the magnetic metal detector with the undetectable ceramic gun in his pocket, along with his wife, Helga, and other honored guests.

As he passed and the golden pen, with an effigy of Adolf Hitler's head carved on it's upper half, was inspected from outside, no one imagined this "gift" was a "Trojan horse," of sorts, for the projectiles meant to end the Führer's life.

MENGELE SLIPS THROUGH THE FÜHRER'S SECURITY WITH HIS LETHAL WEAPON

Mengele and his wife, who was unaware of what was about to take place, passed effortlessly through the Führer's security. The pen was rewrapped and handed back to him.

The guards commented, "What a nice gift," while smiling at Mengele.

Once inside Mengele sat down to dinner, after seating his wife, he began to eat as he anticipated his revenge. When everyone was done the Führer, Hans Hitler, took his place behind the podium. He was to deliver a Führer Day speech on the 54th year of victory for the world wide German Reich.

As Hans began to speak, Mengele carefully unscrewed the pen and removed the shells under the table while all were giving Hans their full, undivided attention. Mengele slipped the ceramic gun out of his pocket, under the table, out of view. He then opened the gun and slipped the bullets into the chambers from which they were to be fired.

Mengele concocted a story of feeling faint and asked his wife if she would go to the car and get him some aspirin that he had in the glove box. After she had excused herself and he felt she was safe, he stood up and pretended to cough, covering his mouth with the hand that held the unusually small gun. Knowing he would only have one chance he slung his hand out and aimed at Hans—quickly firing off two shots. Upon the second shot he was wrestled to the ground.

THE FÜHRER FALLS

Hans had fallen, his face covered in blood. Mengele was arrested and taken into custody. As it turned out Hans was only grazed. His wound, although superficial, was a burst vein on the side of his forehead. The Führer would live on! However, Mengele would be made an example of.

Mengele yelled and screamed at the Führer's security detail, "He killed my kids with his H-bomb and I gave his father power. I am a time traveler from the future and came back to give Adolf Hitler the nuclear bomb. His wicked son used it on my kids when he destroyed Canada."

All thought, "This is absolutely crazy!" These are the insane words of a mad man who needs help in the worst sort of way.

FROM RICHES TO RAGS

As Mengele sat in jail that night he schemed and planned his escape. He offered the security guard a bribe in exchange for his cooperation and silence. He told the man about the large stash of Nazi gold in the cave that he had secretly left behind for future needs. Before the guard agreed to the offer he investigated Mengele's claim. Upon investigation the cave was found to be empty. Mengele's tampering with time had allowed for different circumstances. The Führer had withdrawn from Europe and returned spoils of gold, as he secretly developed the bomb. The gold had been returned before 1945. Mengele was truly poor and appeared to be delusional.

MENGELE IS DECLARED INSANE

The following day the SS called in a psychiatrist. They sat down with Hans and in a world television broadcast the Doctor labeled Mengele a paranoid schizophrenic mad man who had finally cracked. He would be executed to ensure the safety of all. That night Mengele's hanging was broadcast on global television.

MENGELE'S LAST WORDS

His last words were, "I have done the work of Satan and for this I desire to die, but not for my attempted assassination of Hans Hitler, but for saving his father, Adolf, in 1945. And to my dear Helga, mother of my sons, I am forever sorry. My misguided hate and anger ultimately took your sons and grandsons and will leave you a widow. I didn't know! I am sorry."

An SS Officer placed a canvas bag over Mengele's head, pulled the rope down from above and placed the noose around his neck and tightened it. At that moment Mengle could be heard saying, "I've brought misery to this world." Then the SS officer kicked the stool that Mengele was standing on out from underneath him as he fell to his death.

In late 2010, when Hans Hitler was 65 years of age, the Gestapo discovered there were untold numbers of hidden Bibles, and books about the Bible, stashed around the world. An entire new crop of Evangelical Christians, who considered themselves enemies of the Führer, had come to be. They printed Bibles secretly in underground caves with old style offset printing presses they had managed to smuggle into their refuge under ground.

There was something about Jesus which caused Christians to despise the Führer and his totalitarian rule. Jesus had promised love, forgiveness and power to tread over the enemy (Satan who inspires the murder of the innocent). The Führer believed in hate and power to enforce ruthlessness in his rule.

Jesus had said, "And ye shall know the truth, and the truth shall make you free" (John 8:32). The Führer maintained he was the truth and that no one could be free.

NAZIS PLAN ANOTHER DEATH RAID
FOR JEWS AND CHRISTIANS

For this reason the Nazis planned to instigate a 3rd Christian extermination. The Christians considered themselves a kin to those of the second century AD who hid from Rome and Caesar in the underground catacombs.

There were also a few Jews, only about 700, who had managed to Escape the 2nd Jewish extermination a few years earlier. Some of these Jews believed in Jesus as Messiah and attempted to convince others, believing He would return in the 2030's and liberate the Earth from the Hitler line of Führers.

No one was safe. The Gestapo relentlessly hunted the Christians and the Christians protected the Jews, continuously. Once in awhile, when some of them were discovered, they were publicly tortured and executed. Their executions were filmed for the Führer and broadcast world wide with the warning that these were forbidden religions and that it was a death sentence for anyone to hide or protect Jews just as it was in the 1940s[*] of the last century.

Only one hundred and one of the last Jews that survived all round ups, to date, were Israeli (from Palestine—what would have become the land of Israel, in 1948, had the Führer failed in his endeavor of victory) and they could read, write and speak fluent Hebrew. Only 36 of these were experts in the ancient biblical Hebrew and only 12 were Jews of Persian descent and knew the Aramaic of which portions of the ancient book of Daniel were written.

There were prophecies in Daniel that gave the true Christians and Jews hope in the midst of a terrified world. They were hunted day and night by Nazi special agents who were trained to recognize Hebrew and knew the intricacies of the holy rights of the Jews.

JEWS AND CHRISTIANS HIDE OUT UNDERGROUND

These Jews, along with some Christians, lived primarily in Palestine's Bell and Bar Kochba caves situated deep within the Middle East. The Bell caves also provided shelter.

---

[*] See Author's Notes.

In the United States of Germania another group
of Jews and Evangelical Christians hid out in an
abandoned gold mine several hundred feet
underground. An underground stream provided
enough fish for food and the water was pure enough
to drink as they were away from civilization and
hidden in the wilderness.

Wood was gathered from outside the entrance of
the mine to make fires for both light and cooking.
Oil lamps were used for light during the night.

The Palestinian survivors had enough exterior
light which came down into the cave from the small
opening at the giant Bell cave from which the shelter
had been carved nearly 2000 years ago.

The caves were cut from the tops of mountains
which were isolated in the wilderness. No one knew
they existed except a select few Jews and Christians
who's families had lived in Palestine from generation to generation, from the time of the well known
Rabbi Bar Kochba (his name was Hebrew and meant
"son of the star") an ancient messianic title.

Bar Kochba had lived in the second century. The
caves were known to him and a small band of
Rabbis who had attempted to save the culture of the
Jewish people once the Roman dispersion was
complete. The dispersion was precipitated when
Rome attacked Israel in 70 AD and again in 135 AD
exiling every Jew they could find, forbidding them
to re-enter Israel, which had remained Palestine on
pain of death. Only a few dozen hid out and escaped
discovery and only their children and close friends
knew of these well hidden caves and of course they
only told their children and so on, right on down to
the 21st century.

Bell Caves of Palestine.

In the caves the leaders were Maja and Isaac. They wore animal skins and came out only at night to plant wild harvest and later to gather them.

Occasionally recognizance Nazi flights flew over all areas of the world which included the Middle

East in a standardized security which was carried out to assure the German Government that no unauthorized persons were about who might go unnoticed and thus become a threat to world state security.

Scrolls of the Tora were read by all who had taken refuge in the cause—daily. These Holy writings were kept in a small makeshift synagogue. There were a few Christians who cohabited with their Jewish brothers and sisters. These also had their own Tora scrolls, along with a few tattered, but still readable, copies of The New Testament.

NO HOPE ON THE OUTSIDE

Some of the Jews debated and engaged in long visits and discussions with their Christian friends. Both groups studied and ate together because there was nothing for them on the outside—no hope of life or survival. They lived on until 2025 when the Nazis developed a global net of primitive, yet infra red, satellites for global surveillance around the clock. These were equivalent to those used in the pre-Mengele time warp era of the 1980's.

NO HOPE ON THE INSIDE

Every square mile could be seen and because the satellites were so sensitive, even to body heat, these last survivors would be apprehended. The Nazis could see human shaped figures surfacing at night, planting crops. One evening, under cover of darkness, they sent in five hundred troops of whom ten entered the cave as the rest surrounded the caves and stood guard.

At once, all were shocked—an SS officer, who had surprised everyone by his presence in their hide away, picked up a New Testament and a Jewish Tora scroll and read a portion of the 31st chapter of Jeremiah, "Thus saith the LORD, which giveth the sun for a light by day, *and* the ordinances of the moon and of the stars for a light by night, which divideth the sea when the waves thereof roar: The LORD of hosts *is* his name: **If those ordinances depart from before me, saith the LORD,** *then* **the seed of Israel also shall cease from being a nation before me forever.** Thus saith the LORD: If heaven above can be measured, and the foundation of the earth searched out beneath, I will also cast off all the seed of Israel for all that they have done, saith the LORD."

Laying the scroll aside, the SS man said, as he laughed sarcastically, "You're Jewish—you're a Christian. God does not exist because He is supposed to have promised your preservation and now we are going to kill the last of all of you!"

The Christians and Jews said, "I guess you are right!"

A NIGHTMARE ENDS

At that very moment Joseph woke up and realized he had awaken and that he truly had had a nightmare. Before he'd only dreamt he'd awaken—now he was awake for real. He pinched himself to be sure and said, "That last line of my dream, '...you are right.' was wrong, dead wrong and I know why."

Philip Moore, with some of his Israeli friends, near
Megiddo, in Tiberius, Israel, 1986.

CONCLUSION

Why?—the Jews and Christians did not lose to a Nazi victory is because the scriptures predicted the Jew would go on. The Nazi's planned to murder all the Jews. That is why this novel of Hitler's victory is *fiction* and the reality of Jewish/Christian survival and Israel's prophetic rebirth is proof that those sacred words of Jeremiah are *true*.

However, I developed this story of horrifying proportions to illustrate no matter how close things came there could have been no Hitler victory in the providence of God. God himself kept the bomb from Hitler! Though the Jewish divine words in the Bible itself promise the Jewish people will be severely disciplined for unbelief in their God (Deuteronomy 28:63-68), the same Bible tells us that the Jews will never be destroyed!

Hitler's plan was to annihilate the Jew from the earth. God has promised this would never happen (Jeremiah 31:35-37).

There are some within the liberal school of theology who would have doubts and deviate from traditional Jewish hopes, writing, "The events of the Holocaust have shattered for me the historical religious ideas of our Jewish people and have forced me to rethink the entire process of my Jewish identity...I no longer believe as did my Grandfather, killed by the Nazis, believed; I reject the God that my father rejected because that God, too, died in those same camps, along with our family and our historical ideas."[1]

Nothing could be further from the truth! To give in to Hitler and allow him to redefine one's biblical view of God is irresponsible because Hitler and the Nazis failed and are dead! The people of the Bible live on in hope of the fulfillment of the end time prophecies which will soon culminate in the Messiah's coming.

It is my opinion and speculation that this great event may very well occur before the year 2040. Though, as the Messiah Himself revealed in the 24th chapter of the book of Matthew, no one knows the day or the hour of His return, we know we are the generation who will witness His historical arrival.

In the book of Acts in the New Testament chapter 1 verse 6 tells us, "When they [the disciples] therefore were come together, they asked of him, saying, Lord, wilt thou at this time restore again the kingdom of Israel?" (KJV)

---

[1] Rabbi Steven Jacobs, *Rethinking Jewish Faith*, New York: State University Press of New York, © 1994, p.108, used by permission. Interestingly enough this Rabbi is presently reading all of my other books.

Jesus told his disciples it wasn't *the* time for them to know this saying, "It is not for you to know the time or the seasons which the Father hath put in His own power" (Acts 1:7). However, we, as his modern day disciples, are clearly instructed that when we would see the fig tree bud to "know that it [the time of the Messiah's return] is near, even at the doors" (Matthew 24:33 KJV).

The parable of Israel (the budding of the fig tree) started in 1948, when Israel became a nation, and will culminate in Jesus' second coming. One ancient second century Jewish Christian commentary (only recovered since 1910) which illuminates the prophetic implications of the fig tree parable— recorded: "...receive ye the parable of the fig tree thereon: as soon as its shoots have gone forth and its boughs have sprouted, the end of the world will come...Dost though not understand that **the fig tree is the house of Israel**?"[2]

According to the Old Testament passage of Genesis 15:13-16, the length of a biblical generation is not more than 100 years; therefore we may gather (regarding his return) that because Jesus said, *"This generation* [the one witnessing the end time return of Israel] shall not **pass**."[3] His coming to inaugurate world redemption as Messiah might very well occur long before a one hundred-year generation passes, possibly in the late 2020's to mid 2030's.[4]

---

[2] G.Alon, *The Jews in their Land in the Talmudic Age, Vol. I* Jerusalem: EJ Brill, © 1980, pp. 619-620, used by permission. Bold mine.

[3] Matthew 24:34.

[4] Truly Jesus said we could not know the day or hour of His return (Matthew 24:36), but that we would know the *generation* of his coming

An illustration of the Second Coming,
as predicted in the Scriptures.

The Hasidic Rabbi, Y'huda hehasid, who authored
sefer Hasidim, a renowned Jewish work, also wrote,
"...No man knows about the coming of the

in relation to certain end-time events, including Israel's rebirth (Luke
21:28). Illustration by Cathy Taibbi.

Messiah."[5] (A statement almost identical to Jesus on the subject recorded in Matthew 24:36). Never the less Rabbi Y'huda hehasid believed in the Jewish historical certainty of his[6] coming! This is a stark contrast to Rabbi Jacobs statement quoted earlier.

This coming of the Messiah, to resurrect the dead, including those killed in the Holocaust and give new eternal bodies to those of us who believe, who are living at the time is a chief tenant of both Orthodox Judaism and Evangelical Christianity.

ORIGINAL HEBREW TEXT WRITTEN 534 BC

וְרַבִּים מִיְּשֵׁנֵי אַדְמַת־עָפָר יָקִיצוּ אֵלֶּה לְחַיֵּי עוֹלָם וְאֵלֶּה לַחֲרָפוֹת לְדִרְאוֹן עוֹלָם:

וְהַמַּשְׂכִּלִים יַזְהִרוּ כְּזֹהַר הָרָקִיעַ וּמַצְדִּיקֵי הָרַבִּים כַּכּוֹכָבִים לְעוֹלָם וָעֶד:

דניאל יב:ב-ג

OLD TESTAMENT SCRIPTURE TRANSLATION

"And many of those who sleep in the dust of the ground will awake, these to everlasting life, but the others to disgrace *and* everlasting contempt. And those who have insight will shine brightly like the brightness of the expanse of heaven, and those who lead the many to righteousness, like the stars forever and ever."
Daniel 12:2-3 NASB

ANCIENT RABBINICAL COMMENTARY

"R. 'Azaria said: 'The Holy One, blessed be He, opens the graves and opens the storehouses of the souls and puts back each soul into its own body....' "[7]   **Pirqe R. Eliezer, ch. 34**
"Rabbi [Y'huda haNasi] said....the Holy One, blessed be He, too, will bring the soul, cast it into the body, and judge them as one."[8]
B. Sanhedrin 91a-b

NEW TESTAMENT RECORDED 31 AD

"Do not marvel at this; for an hour is coming, in which all who are in the tombs shall hear His voice, and shall come forth; those who did the

---

[5] Raphael Patai, *The Messiah Text*, Detroit: Wayne State University Press, © 1979, p.57, used by permission.

[6] The Jewish Messiah's coming—identity anonymous.

[7] Raphael Patai, *The Messiah Texts*, p. 202.

[8] Ibid, p. 219.

good *deeds* to a resurrection of life, those who committed the evil *deeds* to a resurrection of judgment."
John 5:28-29 NASB

MODERN RABBINIC COMMENT/REFUTATION
"However, the life after which there is no death is the life of the World to Come, in which there is no body. For we believe it, and it is the truth [held] by all those who have a mind, that the World to Come is souls without bodies, like the angels."[9]
***Treatise on Resurrection*, by Maimonides, p. 17**

AUTHOR'S COMMENT—EVANGELICAL CHRISTIAN POSITION
Again, we have Maimonides (Rambam—Rabbi Moshe ben Maimon), who presently has many admirers and followers, advocating an off-the-wall, controversial, contrived position, contrary to the Bible's promise of resurrection. The Scriptures promise that we will receive bodies at the resurrection in which our souls will reside during the eternal world to come.   **Philip Moore**

To view, in greater detail, the immense evidence of why Hitler could never win, from a biblical standpoint, and see God's plans for the future of our planet including the coming of the Messiah, Jesus, יֵשׁוּע to bring peace through the reborn state of Israel, read my inspirational thrillers: *The End of History-Messiah Conspiracy,* 1238 pages and *Nightmare of the Apocalypse,* 370 pages (available through Ramshead Press International, 1-800-RAMSHEAD).

In order to balance and contrast the horror story of "what might have been," had Hitler won, if there were no God, with the truth of ongoing, prophetic revelations I provide the following appendix, "Israel - Is Real." Enjoy!

---

[9]Raphael Pati, *The Messiah Text*, p. 206. While Maimonides lived in the thirteenth century, he originated this modern rabbinical view.

"...And in a word it was the ignorance of the Jews in these Prophesies which caused them to reject their Messiah and by consequence to be...captivated by the Romans...."[1] "The Jews will return to Jerusalem in the 20th century."[2]

SIR ISAAC NEWTON, 1600's

"When the ships of the kingdom of Russia will cross the Dardannels you [Israel] should dress in Sabbath clothes because this means that the arrival of the Messiah is close."[3]

Rabbi ELIJA BEN SOLOMON, the famed Vilna Gaon, 1700's

"Israel's regathering to its land is the trumpet of the Messiah that is blasting out over the earth. Already we hear the footsteps of the Messiah in the corridors."[4]

Israel's first Prime Minister, DAVID BEN-GURION, 1973

"Everywhere you turn in Israel today the Bible is coming to life. I'm not talking only about archeological discoveries, but about the international political scene as it affects us today. If you read the Biblical prophecies about Armageddon and the end days, and you look at the current realities in the world and especially the Middle East, things certainly begin to look familiar. 'The vast number of archaeological discoveries in Israel have all tended to vindicate the pictures that are presented in the Bible. If therefore the Bible has been proven true concerning the past, we cannot look lightly at any prognostication it makes about the future.' "[5]

Israeli Major General, CHAIM HERZOG, 1977

"I have the survivability of a super power."[6]

Israeli General, ARIEL SHARON, 1987

"We [Israel] will have a war with Russia because Ezekiel 38 and 39 predicts it."[7]   Israeli President, YITZHAK NAVON, 1993

APPENDIX 1
ISRAEL—IS REAL

God promised Abraham, nearly 4000 years ago: "...I will make of thee a great nation, and I will bless thee, and make thy name great; and thou shalt be a

---

[1] *Yahuda Manuscript 1* Courtesy of Jewish National & University Library, Jerusalem.

[2] Ruvic Rosenthal, "The Ostracized Newton," *Al Hamishmar*, Tel Aviv. July 26, 1985, p. 10.

[3] ירושלים.קלה p. קלה.חבלי משיח בומנו, רפאל הלוי אייזנברג, © 1970, used by permission.

[4] Birgitta Yavari, *Min Messias*. Jerusalem: Rahm & Stenström Interpublishing, © 1979, p. 10, used by permission.

[5] Hal Lindsey, *The 1980's: Countdown to Armageddon*. New York: Bantam Books, Inc., © 1980 The Aorist Corporation, Inc., p. 35, used by permission.

[6] Morris Cerillo, "Evangelical Newsletter," 1987.

[7] *Perhaps Today*, Troy, MI, Jack Van Impe Ministries, May/June 1993, p. 7. [ ] mine.

blessing: And I will bless them that bless thee, and curse him that curseth thee: and in thee shall all families of the earth be blessed....in thy seed shall all the nations of the earth be blessed; because thou hast obeyed my voice" (Genesis 12:2-3; 22:18 KJV).

Few realize that Sir Isaac Newton, known today as the greatest scientist to ever live, was also a prophetical *Bible commentator*. In our opinion, he is unsurpassed in history. He foresaw Israel's return.[8]

---

[8]Our design consists of a portrait of Sir Isaac Newton and a modern satellite photo of Israel and the ancient Sinai.

The promise meant that one day all the world will return to the God of Israel from the pagan and atheistic culture that had developed in the 2000 years between Adam's creation and Abraham's time. This plan included the very redemption of man from the Fall, described in the Torah book of Genesis, and the creation of the "New World," commonly referred to in Hebrew tradition as the *olam haba*, which will even surpass that of the Garden of Eden before the Fall.

It was the Messiah who would come out of this nation, Israel, and be a blessing to all the world. The Messiah had two clearly predicted roles: one of suffering servant and one of kingly redemption.[9] When He came at the exact time that Daniel said He would, He was rejected, as predicted in Isaiah 53, ushering in this suffering role. Because of the rejection, His earthly kingdom was postponed 2000 years (Hosea 5:15-6:2).

These Messianic events had profound implications for the dispersion and return of Israel. Moses had already outlined the two dispersions, and Jesus pinpointed the time of the second one.

THE FIRST JEWISH DISPERSION (AND RETURN), FORETOLD IN ITS SEVERITY AND LENGTH BY ISAIAH, JEREMIAH AND MOSES HIMSELF

Moses predicted in his fifth book, Deuteronomy: "The LORD shall bring a nation against thee from far, from the end of the earth, *as swift* as the eagle flieth; a nation whose tongue thou

---

[9] For details of the Messiah, son of Joseph and Messiah, son of David teachings which existed within ancient Jewish tradition. See chapter 3 of my book, *The End of History—Messiah Conspiracy*

shalt not understand;   A nation of fierce countenance, which shall not regard the person of the old, nor shew favour to the young...." (Deuteronomy 28:49-50 KJV).

This occurred when the Babylonians overran Jerusalem and carried its inhabitants to Babylon in the year 606 BC. This was predicted by the prophet Isaiah: "Behold, the days come, that all that *is* in thine house, and *that* which thy fathers have laid up in store until this day, shall be carried to Babylon: nothing shall be left, saith the LORD" (Isaiah 39:6 KJV).

Jeremiah the prophet indicated that the captivity would last for seventy years. "And this whole land shall be a desolation, *and* an astonishment; and these nations shall serve the king of Babylon seventy years" (Jereremiah 25:11 KJV).

Of course, every detail occurred precisely as predicted. The Jews were invaded by Babylon and there they remained captive exactly seventy years (II Chronicles 36:15-21). At the end of the Babylonian captivity, the Jews were permitted to return to their land (II Chronicles 36:23) by King Cyrus! If you check Isaiah 44:28-45:4, you may be amazed to see that this king was predicted by his very name two hundred years before his birth: "That saith of **Cyrus**, *He is* my shepherd, and shall perform all my pleasure: even saying to Jerusalem, Thou shalt be built; and to the temple, Thy foundation shall be laid....For Jacob my servant's sake, and Israel mine elect, I have even called thee by thy name: I have surnamed thee, though thou hast not known me" (KJV; bold mine).

MOSES FORETOLD THE SECOND DISPERSION (70 AD), GIVING ISRAEL'S DISOBEDIENCE AS THE REASON FOR GOD'S DISCIPLINE

Moses, nearly four thousand years ago, in his famous discourse in Deuteronomy, went on to warn the Jewish people that a second dispersion would occur. However, unlike Babylon's, which was local, it would be a worldwide event in which the sons and daughters of Israel would be *scattered into all nations* (Deuteronomy 28:64). This of course, would occur because of Israel's disobedience. Moses wrote: "Moreover all these curses shall come upon thee, and shall pursue thee, and overtake thee...because thou hearkenedst not unto the voice of the LORD thy God, to keep his commandments and his statutes which he commanded thee...." (Deuteronomy 28:45 KJV).

Chief among these statutes was the **acceptance** of the Messiah, mentioned in Deuteronomy 15:18; thus when Israel rejected her Messiah (Jesus), this predicted worldwide dispersion became a historical reality! Moses continued: "And the LORD shall scatter thee among all people, from the one end of the earth even unto the other....And among these nations shalt thou find no ease, neither shall the sole of thy foot have rest: but the LORD shall give thee there a trembling heart, and failing of eyes, and sorrow of mind: And thy life shall hang in doubt before thee; and thou shalt fear day and night, and shalt have none assurance of thy life: In the morning thou shalt say, Would God it were even! and at even thou shalt say, Would God it were morning!....And the LORD shall bring thee into

Egypt...and there ye shall be sold unto your enemies for bondmen and bondwomen, and no man shall buy *you*" (Deuteronomy 28:64-68 KJV).

Nazis hold Jews at gunpoint during the Holocaust.

JESUS, THE GREATEST PROPHET, PINPOINTED THE SECOND JEWISH DISPERSION TO HIS VERY OWN GENERATION, THIRTY-SEVEN YEARS BEFORE THE FACT

Jesus pinpointed the time of the second dispersion, of which Moses warned, in His discourse in the Gospel of Luke shortly before He was arrested and crucified.   Jesus, the greatest of the Hebrew prophets (being the Messiah), foretold: " But woe unto them that are with child, and to them that give suck, in those days! for there shall be great distress in the land, and wrath upon this people. And they shall fall by the edge of the sword, and shall be led away captive into all nations: and Jerusalem shall be trodden down of the Gentiles, until the times of the Gentiles be fulfilled" (Luke 21:23-24 KJV).

Jesus also remarked that it would be His generation that would see this dispersion: "Verily I say unto you, All these things shall come upon **this** generation" (Matthew 23:36 KJV).

JESUS WANTED TO SAVE THE FIRST CENTURY JEWISH NATION—WITH TEARS IN HIS EYES HE PREDICTED HER FATE, EXPLAINING WHY

Jesus also implied that, had He been received, He would have remained and saved Israel under His wings. He said these words with tears in His eyes: "...'If thou hadst known, even thou, at least in this thy day, the things *which belong* unto thy peace! but now they are hid from thine eyes. For the days shall come upon thee, that thine enemies shall cast a trench about thee, and compass thee round, and keep thee in on every side, And shall lay thee even with the ground, and thy children within thee; and they shall not leave in thee one stone upon another; because thou knewest not the time of thy visitation....O Jerusalem, Jerusalem, *thou* that killest the prophets, and stonest them which are sent unto thee, how often would I have gathered thy children together, even as a hen gathereth her chickens under *her* wings, and ye would not!' " (Luke 19:42-44; Matthew 23:37 KJV).

JESUS WOULD HAVE SAVED ISRAEL HAD THE RELIGIOUS LEADERS NOT MISLED THE PEOPLE REGARDING HIS IDENTITY AND ABILITY TO BRING PEACE

Because the religious leaders and political factions succeeded in convincing the majority of the people to continue to reject the Jewish Messiah instead of setting up a royal kingdom, Jesus, the *rejected* king, left the scene forty days after the resurrection and ascended into the clouds with the promise to return upon **acceptance**. What righteous king would force His kingdom? Some of Jesus' last words to the religious leaders who rejected Him were: "...how often would I have gathered thy children together, even as a hen gathereth her chickens under *her* wings, and ye would not! Behold, your house is left unto you desolate. For I say unto you, Ye shall not see me henceforth, till ye shall say, Blessed *is* he that cometh in the name of the Lord" (Matthew 23:37-39 KJV).

AFTER JESUS LEFT, HIS AND MOSES' PREDICTIONS OF DEFEAT, DISPERSION, SLAVERY AND WORTHLESSNESS BECAME REALITY

Luke's eyewitness testimony of the departure of Jesus included: "And He led them out as far as Bethany, and He lifted up His hands and blessed them. And it came about that while He was blessing them, He parted from them. And they returned to Jerusalem with great joy, and were continually in the temple, praising God" (Luke 24:50-53 NASB).

As history has recorded, less than forty years after these events, Titus and the Roman armies destroyed Jerusalem and dispersed her inhabitants into "all the earth." The Romans slaughtered hundreds of thousands by "the sword." Some survived, and were shipped to the slave markets in Egypt. When the supply of slaves there exceeded the demand, they "became worthless, even as lowly slaves." Moses' prediction said, as you recall: "And the LORD shall bring thee into Egypt **again** with ships...and there ye shall be sold unto your enemies for bondmen and bondwomen, and no man shall buy *you*" (Deuteronomy 28:68 KJV).

THE PROPHET MOSES PREDICTED THE GREATEST OF ALL PROPHETS (JESUS), BUT BECAUSE HIS PEOPLE REFUSED TO "HEARKEN" AS MOSES FORESAW, MUCH TRAGEDY EXISTS TO THIS DAY!

No prophets have been more precise regarding the dispersion than Moses and Jesus. Remember, the Bible of the Jews predicted through Moses: "The LORD thy God will raise up unto thee a Prophet from the midst of thee, of thy brethren, like unto me; unto him ye shall hearken....And the LORD said....I will raise them up a Prophet from among their brethren, like unto thee, and will put my words in his mouth; and he shall speak unto them all that I shall command him. And it shall come to pass, *that* whosoever will not hearken unto my words which he shall speak in my name, I will require *it* of him" (Deuteronomy 18:15, 17-19 KJV).

This was the Messiah Jesus, for He, like Moses, dealt with the true interpretation of the Jewish law (Matthew 5-7)![10] Because Israel's religious leaders

---

[10]The lives of Jesus and Moses were beautifully paralleled in events and meanings. For example: "Both were preserved in childhood, Ex. 2.2-10; Mt. 2.14,15. — Contended with masters of evil, Ex. 7.11; Mt.

did not hearken to this prophet's words spoken in God's name, remember Jesus said, "I am come in my Father's name, and ye receive me not...." (John 5:43 KJV). It truly was and still is being **required** of Israel, for there was a terrible dispersion, and anti-Semitism[11] continues to the present day!

An illustration of the destruction of Jerusalem and dispersion of Jews by the Romans (70 AD).

4.1. — Fasted forty days, Ex. 34.28; Mt. 4.2. — Controlled the sea, Ex. 14.21; Mt. 8.26. — Fed a multitude, Ex. 16.15; Mt. 14.20, 21. — Had radiant faces, Ex. 34.35; Mt. 17.2. — Endured murmurings, Ex. 15.24; Mk. 7.2. — Discredited in the home, Nu. 12.1; Jn. 7.5. — Made intercessory prayers, Ex. 32.32; Jn. 17.9. — Spoke as oracles, De. 18.18. — Had seventy helpers, Nu. 11.16, 17; Lu. 10.1. — Established memorials, Ex. 12.14; Lu. 22.19. — Re-appeared after death, Mt. 17.3; Ac. 1.3." Frank Charles Thompson, D.D., Ph.D., "Condensed Cyclopedia of Topics and Texts," *Thompson Chain Reference Bible.* Indianapolis, IN: B.B. Kirkbride Bible Co., Inc., © 1964, p. 95.

[11] Our point is that had Jesus been accepted, He would have set up the kingdom, defeated Rome and created a world free of disease, hunger and war. As we will see in our chapters 29 and 30 of my book, *The End of History—Messiah Conspiracy*, He will accomplish of all this soon. Had His nation accepted Him, He would have accomplished this in the first century and there would be no opportunity for anti-Semitism today. Jesus would not have allowed this. His reign, which will be free of anti-Semitism is still in our future, but moving ever closer! I believe we are within approximately forty years of this date.

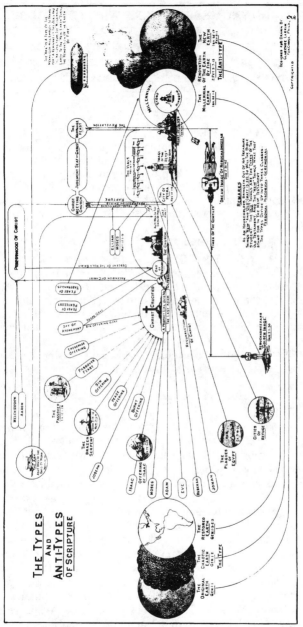

A chart by Reverend Clarence Larkin, entitled,
"The Types and Anti-Types of Scripture."

ORIGINAL HEBREW TEXT WRITTEN 1451 BC

נָבִיא מִקִּרְבְּךָ מֵאַחֶיךָ כָּמֹנִי יָקִים לְךָ יְהוָה אֱלֹהֶיךָ אֵלָיו תִּשְׁמָעוּן: .... וַיֹּאמֶר יְהוָה אֵלַי
הֵיטִיבוּ אֲשֶׁר דִּבֵּרוּ: נָבִיא אָקִים לָהֶם מִקֶּרֶב אֲחֵיהֶם כָּמוֹךָ וְנָתַתִּי דְבָרַי בְּפִיו וְדִבֶּר
אֲלֵיהֶם אֵת כָּל־אֲשֶׁר אֲצַוֶּנּוּ: וְהָיָה הָאִישׁ אֲשֶׁר לֹא־יִשְׁמַע אֶל־דְּבָרַי אֲשֶׁר יְדַבֵּר בִּשְׁמִי
אָנֹכִי אֶדְרֹשׁ מֵעִמּוֹ: אַךְ הַנָּבִיא אֲשֶׁר יָזִיד לְדַבֵּר דָּבָר בִּשְׁמִי אֵת אֲשֶׁר לֹא־צִוִּיתִיו לְדַבֵּר
וַאֲשֶׁר יְדַבֵּר בְּשֵׁם אֱלֹהִים אֲחֵרִים וּמֵת הַנָּבִיא הַהוּא:

דברים יח:טו; יז-יט

OLD TESTAMENT SCRIPTURE TRANSLATION

"The LORD your God will raise up for you a prophet like me from among you, from your countrymen, you shall listen to him....the LORD said to me'....I will raise up a prophet from among their countrymen like you, and I will put My words in his mouth, and he shall speak to them all that I command him. And it shall come about that whoever will not listen to My words which he shall speak in My name, I Myself will **require** *it* of him.' "

Deuteronomy 18:15, 17-19 NASB

ANCIENT RABBINICAL COMMENTARY

"Behold, my servant, the Messiah, shall prosper; he shall be exalted, etc. 'Behold, my servant shall deal prudently.' This is the King Messiah. 'He shall be exalted and extolled, and be very high.' He shall be exalted more than Abraham; for of Him it is written, 'I have exalted my hand to the Lord' (Gen. XIV. 22). He shall be extolled more than Moses...."[12]   **Yalkut in loco**

"Rabbi Berachia said in the name of Rabbi Levi: 'As the first redeemer, so the last....' "[13]   **Ruth Rabba, sec. 5**

---

[12]Rev. B. Pick, Ph.D., *Old Testament Passages Messianically Applied by the Ancient Synagogue*, published in the compilation *Hebraica, A Quarterly Journal in the Interests of Semitic Study*, Vol. I, p. 268. Though this rabbinical commentary says the Messiah will be more extolled than Moses, which is a point in our favor, the learned scholar, Risto Santala, enlightens us with a Hebrew Targum on this very verse in Deuteronomy. He tells us: "The Targum attaches an interpretation to this verse which from the point of view of Christian theology is of great importance: 'The Lord your God will raise up from your midst a prophet by the Holy Spirit who will be like me', and, 'A prophet I will raise up from amongst your brethren, through the Holy Spirit.' " Santala's footnote to Holy Spirit reads: "In Hebrew, respectively, *be-Ruah qudsha* and *de-Ruah qudsha*." Risto Santala, *The Messiah in the Old Testament in the Light of Rabbinical Writings*. Jerusalem: Keren Ahvah Meshihit, © 1992, p. 58, used by permission. Available through Keren Ahvah Meshihit, POB 10382, Jerusalem, Israel.

[13]Rev. B. Pick, Ph.D., *Old Testament Passages Messianically Applied by the Ancient Synagogue*, published in the compilation *Hebraica, A Quarterly Journal in the Interests of Semitic Study*, Vol. II, p. 30. In

NEW TESTAMENT RECORDED 33 AD

"And now, brethren, I know that you acted in ignorance, just as your rulers did also. But the things which God announced beforehand by the mouth of all the prophets, that His Christ should suffer, He has thus fulfilled. Repent therefore and return, that your sins may be wiped away, in order that times of refreshing may come from the presence of the Lord; and that He may send Jesus, the Christ appointed for you, whom heaven must receive until *the* period of restoration of all things about which God spoke by the mouth of His holy prophets from ancient time. Moses said, 'THE LORD GOD SHALL RAISE UP FOR YOU A PROPHET LIKE ME FROM YOUR BRETHREN; TO HIM YOU SHALL GIVE HEED in everything He says to you. And it shall be that every soul that does not heed that prophet shall be utterly destroyed from among the people.' And likewise, all the prophets who have spoken, from Samuel and *his* successors onward, also announced these days. It is you who are the sons of the prophets, and of the covenant which God made with your fathers, saying to Abraham, 'AND IN YOUR SEED ALL THE FAMILIES OF THE EARTH SHALL BE BLESSED.' "

Acts 3:17-25 NASB

"Now the Passover, the feast of the Jews, was at hand. Jesus therefore lifting up His eyes, and seeing that a great multitude was coming to Him, said to Philip, 'Where are we to buy bread, that these may eat?' And this He was saying to test him; for He Himself knew what He was intending to do. Philip answered Him, 'Two hundred denarii worth of bread is not sufficient for them, for everyone to receive a little.' One of His disciples, Andrew, Simon Peter's brother, said to Him, 'There is a lad here who has five barley loaves and two fish, but what are these for so many people?' Jesus said, 'Have the people sit down.' Now there was much grass in the place. So the men sat down, in number about five thousand. Jesus therefore took the loaves; and having given thanks, He distributed to those who were seated; likewise also of the fish as much as they wanted. And when they were filled, He said to His disciples, 'Gather up the leftover fragments that nothing may be lost.' And so they gathered them up, and filled twelve baskets with fragments from the five barley loaves, which were left over by those who had eaten. When therefore the people saw the sign which He had performed, they said, 'This is of a truth the **Prophet** who is to come into the world.' "   **John 6:4-14 NASB**

MODERN RABBINIC COMMENT/REFUTATION

"Furthermore there is no evidence that the original passage (Deuteronomy 18:18) speaks of the Messiah at all. The verse merely

---

this Midrash it is understood that the first redeemer is Moses and the second is the Messiah.

states that the future prophets of Israel in general would share Moses'
saintly qualities."
The Real Messiah, by Rabbi Aryeh Kaplan, *et al*, p. 54; 1976

AUTHOR'S COMMENT—
EVANGELICAL CHRISTIAN POSITION
Rabbi Kaplan should have read his Midrashim and Targumim more
carefully! It is an accepted fact within Judaism, and particularly in the
rabbinic writings produced by the Jewish sages, that the Messiah would
be extolled **more** than Moses!
Philip Moore

The land of the prophets is once again blooming,
as predicted by Ezekiel (chapter 37) nearly 3000
years ago.

"....the Apostles and those who in the first ages propagated the gospel urged chiefly these Prophesies and exhorted their hearers to search and see whether all things concerning our Saviour ought not to have been as they fell out. And in a word it was the ignorance of the Jews in these Prophesies which caused them to reject their Messiah and by consequence to be...captivated by the Romans....Luke 19. 42, 44."[14]

Sir Isaac Newton's comment on Jewish dispersion in 70 AD

For the next 1800 years, until 1948, the Jewish people wandered over the earth. They were people without a country, persecuted in every land through which they passed, just as Moses and Jesus had warned. Genuine Evangelical Christians were virtually the only ones who offered true love and shelter, as we document in Appendix 6 "Christian Zionists (Lovers of Israel) Past and Present[15]". Remember Moses' warning: "...thy life shall hang in doubt...." (Deuteronomy 28:66); and Jesus' words: "...they shall fall by the edge of the sword, and shall be led away captive into all nations...." (Luke 21:24 KJV).

---

[14]Frank E. Manuel, *The Religion of Isaac Newton*, London: Oxford University Press, © 1974, pp. 108-109. Manuels source was the *Yahuda* manuscript 1. Courtesy of the Jewish National & University Library, Jerusalem.

[15] This subject is covered in greater detail in chapters 13-15 of my book, *The End of History—Messiah Conspiracy*.

We see that Israel, her dispersions and judgments, have truly been a sign to all other nations, as Moses predicted. "And thou shalt become an astonishment, a proverb, and a byword, among all nations whither the LORD shall lead thee....And they shall be upon thee for a **sign** and for a wonder, and upon thy seed for ever" (Deuteronomy 28:37, 46).

Israel has indeed become a sign before the entire world because she was warned, did not heed that warning, and suffered the consequences, which fell exactly as foretold by the Bible. This shows all who reverence the scriptures that God is not playing games. He is to be taken seriously and truly loves all of us who return. The same prophets who foretold the dispersion, including Jesus, also foretold the second ingathering of Israel to her land, which occurred in 1948, when Israel became a sovereign Jewish State.

Schoolchildren playing a Hanukkah game in their classroom.

This sign, which reads in Hebrew
"Blessings to Those Coming to Jerusalem"
(ברוכים הבאים לירוּשלים) lies at Jerusalem's entrance
to welcome all who love her—we do!

ORIGINAL HEBREW TEXT WRITTEN 713, 587 BC

וְהָיָה ׀ בַּיּוֹם הַהוּא יוֹסִיף אֲדֹנָי ׀ שֵׁנִית יָדוֹ לִקְנוֹת אֶת־שְׁאָר עַמּוֹ אֲשֶׁר יִשָּׁאֵר מֵאַשּׁוּר
וּמִמִּצְרַיִם וּמִפַּתְרוֹס וּמִכּוּשׁ וּמֵעֵילָם וּמִשִּׁנְעָר וּמֵחֲמָת וּמֵאִיֵּי הַיָּם: וְנָשָׂא נֵס לַגּוֹיִם
וְאָסַף נִדְחֵי יִשְׂרָאֵל וּנְפֻצוֹת יְהוּדָה יְקַבֵּץ מֵאַרְבַּע כַּנְפוֹת הָאָרֶץ:

יַשַׁעְיָה יֹא:יֹא-יֹב

וָאָפִיץ אֹתָם בַּגּוֹיִם וַיִּזָּרוּ בָּאֲרָצוֹת כְּדַרְכָּם וְכַעֲלִילוֹתָם שְׁפַטְתִּים: .... וְלָקַחְתִּי אֶתְכֶם
מִן־הַגּוֹיִם וְקִבַּצְתִּי אֶתְכֶם מִכָּל־הָאֲרָצוֹת וְהֵבֵאתִי אֶתְכֶם אֶל־אַדְמַתְכֶם:

יָחֶזְקֵאל לֹו:יֹט-כֹד

OLD TESTAMENT SCRIPTURE TRANSLATION

"Then it will happen on that day that the Lord Will again recover the second time with His hand The remnant of His people, who will remain, From Assyria, Egypt, Pathros, Cush, Elam, Shinar, Hamath, And from the islands of the sea. And He will lift up a standard for the nations, And will assemble the banished ones of Israel, And will gather the dispersed of Judah From the four corners of the earth."

Isaiah 11:11-12 NASB

"Also I scattered them among the nations, and they were dispersed throughout the lands. According to their ways and their deeds I judged them....For I will take you from the nations, gather you from all the lands, and bring you into your own land."

Ezekiel 36:19, 24 NASB

ANCIENT RABBINICAL COMMENTARY

"When Moses our Master heard these words in the presence of Messiah ben David, he rejoiced with great joy, and turned back his face to the Holy One, blessed be He, and said to Him: 'Master of the World! When will this built-up Jerusalem descend?' The Holy One, blessed be He, said: 'I have not revealed the time to anybody, neither to the first ones nor to the last ones. How could I tell it to you?' Moses said to him: 'Master of the World! Give me a hint of the events!' The Holy One, blessed be He, said to him: 'I shall first scatter Israel with a winnowing fork in the gates of the earth, and they will be dispersed in the four corners of the world among all the nations....Then I shall stretch forth My hand a second time and shall gather....' "[16]

B'reshit Rabbati, pp. 136-37

"He who wrought miracles and portents in those days and at that time, may He work for us miracles and portents in these days and in this time, and gather us from the four winds of the world and lead us to Jerusalem, and make us rejoice in her, and let us say Amen, *Selah*!"[17]

Midrash waYosha', BhM 1:56-57

---

[16]Raphael Patai, *The Messiah Texts*, p. 228.
[17]Ibid, p. 218.

NEW TESTAMENT RECORDED 65, 37 AD

"...when they had come together, they were asking Him, saying, 'Lord, is it at this time You are restoring the kingdom to **Israel**?' He said to them, 'It is not for you to know....' "

Acts 1:6-7 NASB

"Now learn the parable from the fig tree: when its branch has already become tender, and puts forth its leaves, you know that summer is near; even so you too, when you see all these things, recognize that He is near, *right* at the door. Truly I say to you, this generation will not pass away until all these things take place."

Matthew 24:32-34 NASB

MODERN RABBINIC COMMENT/REFUTATION

"In 1862 Zevi Hirsch Kalischer, an Orthodox rabbi, wrote...redemption would come about through human initiative and natural causes rather than through God's intervention and miracles. He urged Jews to colonize Palestine...."

What Christians Should Know About Jews and Judaism, by Yechiel Eckstein, p. 218; © 1984

"We consider ourselves no longer a nation, but a religious community, and therefore expect neither a return to Palestine, nor a sacrificial worship under the sons of Aaron, nor the restoration of any of the laws concerning the Jewish state."

"Pittsburgh Platform," *Encyclopaedia Judaica Jerusalem*, p. 1415; © 1885

ON THE SPOT EYEWITNESS REPORT, MAY 1948

"The first independent Jewish State in 19 centuries was born in Tel Aviv as the British Mandate over Palestine came to an end at midnight on Friday....As 'Medinat Yisrael' (State of Israel) was proclaimed, the battle for Jerusalem raged, with most of the city falling to the Jews."

Palestine Post (now the *Jerusalem Post*), Vol. XXIII, May 16, 1948

MODERN FACTS HISTORICALLY RECORDED IN SECULAR NEWS

"With the war won, Israel soon became a sort of modern miracle....the nation sprang almost overnight from a picturesque wilderness to an enclave of clanging energy. Deepwater ports were dredged, power and irrigation plants built, modern cities and industries created. The desert bloomed, the orange trees blossomed, and Israel was suddenly the land of milk and honey. For 14 wondrous years, its gross national product soared by at least 10% a year, until by 1964 Israel had achieved a standard of living that rivaled Western Europe's."

"Israel: A Nation Under Siege," *Time*, p. 40, June 9, 1967

AUTHOR'S COMMENT—EVANGELICAL CHRISTIAN POSITION

There are many "Bible teachers" today who deny that the New Testament speaks of the rebirth of Israel, which occurred in 1948. The dominion theologists and liberals are a good example. Gary DeMar, in his book, *Last Days Madness*, claims that the New Testament is silent on the subject of Israel's rebirth, and that Ezekiel's prophecy refers to the first restoration from Babylon. Nothing could be further from the truth. This is expressed by Jesus' words when questioned on the subject of Israel by His apostles. Notice that He did not tell them, "You are wrong, Israel will not be restored." In answer to their question, He clearly told His disciples that they were not to know when it would occur. In retrospect, we see that though some rabbis of a hundred years ago denied Israel's miraculous rebirth, the secular news magazine, *Time,* described it as a "miracle." Interesting, isn't it? In addition, the prophetic Christian writer, Lance Lambert, noted in his book, *Israel: A Secret Documentary*: "An Israeli captain, again totally irreligious, said that at the height of the fighting on the Golan, he looked up into the sky and saw a great, gray hand pressing downwards, as if it were holding something back. In my opinion that was exactly what happened. Without the intervention of God, Israel would have been doomed. Shimon Peres, once a key adviser to Golda Meir and the present Minister of Defense, has said, 'The miracle is that we ever win. The Arab nations occupy eight percent of the surface of the world. They possess half the known oil resources and are immensely rich. They have more men in their armies than we have people in our state, and on top of the Arabs come the Russians, who have built for them a great war machine. On our side we have only America....[Lambert detailed of the '73 war] Three days before the war began the Soviet Union launched two orbital Sputniks, which crossed Israel at the best time for aerial photography. Russia then relayed information to Syria and Egypt as to whether Israel was prepared....the war was originally planned for six o'clock in the evening of Yom Kippur, but was moved up to two o'clock. The Russians had passed on the information that preparations had begun on the Israeli side."[18] Hence, even though the enemy used the most modern, sophisticated, scientific technology of the time, Israel won as a result of God's miracles.

Philip Moore

THE BIBLE SAID THE WORLD
WAS ROUND BEFORE SCIENCE
FIGURED IT OUT MATHEMATICALLY

Remember the quote we used to illustrate Israel's rebirth, Isaiah 11:12, mentioned "four corners." Well, many philosophers have tried to use

---

[18]Lance Lambert, *Israel: A Secret Documentary*. Wheaton, IL: Tyndale House Publishers, Inc., © 1975, pp. 15-17, used by permission.

this to claim that the Bible said the world was flat instead of round. Hence, they maintain that the Bible is wrong and that there really is no God. I will never forget my high school English literature teacher, Mrs. Linda Young, who always tried to pound this idea into my head.

The Scripture uses figurative language to describe the future of God's regathering of Jews from all areas of the earth. Thus, Isaiah says "corners." Since the voyage of Christopher Columbus,[19] Bible critics have used this verse of scripture to try to convince the world that the good book is in error (I Timothy 6:20-21)[20] because it states the world is flat. Thus, it is not a reliable document in which to place one's faith.

Let it be known, from now on, that the Bible taught the world was spherical and suspended in space long before Columbus took his first breath or the advent of modern science, which made it possible to photograph the earth from the moon. The oldest book of the Bible, Job, written over 3500 years ago, says: "He stretcheth out the north over the empty place, *and* hangeth the earth upon nothing" (Job 26:7 KJV). Isaiah, writing over 2600 years ago, added: "...have ye not understood from the foundations of the earth? *It is* he that sitteth upon the circle of the earth, and the inhabitants

---

[19]Columbus was a Jewish-Christian. I document this in *The End of History—Messiah Conspiracy,* chapter 16 , "Was Christopher Columbus a Messianic Jew?"

[20]I Timothy 6:20-21 of the New Testament reads: "O Timothy, guard what has been entrusted to you, avoiding worldly *and* empty chatter *and* the opposing arguments of what is falsely called 'knowledge' — which some have professed and thus gone astray from the faith. Grace be with you" (NASB).

thereof *are* as grasshoppers; that stretcheth out the heavens as a curtain, and spreadeth them out as a tent to dwell in...." (Isaiah 40:21-22 KJV).

The ancient rabbinical writing, *Midrash Rabbah Numbers*, intended as a commentary on the Old Testament and written before the time of Columbus, reads: "He brought ONE SILVER BASIN (MIZRAK) as a symbol of the world which is shaped like a ball that can be thrown (*nizrak*) from hand to hand."[21]

AS WE CAREFULLY STUDY THE WORDS OF JESUS, WE SEE THAT HE KNEW THE WORLD WAS ROUND 2000 YEARS AGO

Only recently was it scientifically accepted that winds blow in cyclic currents. Yet the Bible foretold thousands of years ago: "The wind goeth toward the south, and turneth about unto the north; it **whirleth** about continually, and the wind **returneth** again according to his **circuits**" (Ecclesiastes 1:6 KJV bold mine). This is illustrated in this photo of Earth taken on the way back from the moon—notice the white **swirls**.

These are cyclic wind patterns which illustrate that what the Bible says about the nature of wind is

---

[21] *Midrash Rabbah Numbers*, Vol. II, Rabbah 13:14. New York: The Soncino Press Ltd., © 1983, p. 528.

true. Jesus illustrated His knowledge that the world was round and that it rotated on an axis. He said that when He came the second time, two would be working and sleeping at the same time, thus inferring day on one side of the earth and night on the other side.

We believe Columbus, being a believer and ardent Bible student, realized from these verses that the world was not flat. He was not afraid, as many were, of falling off the edge when navigating the globe, because Jesus, in the Gospel of Luke, had predicted: "I tell you, in that night there shall be two *men* in one bed; the one shall be taken, and the other left....Two *men* shall be in the field; the one shall be taken, and the other shall be left" (Luke 17:34, 36 KJV).

"Field" implies day because at that time people did not work at night. Since this statement of Jesus' consists of one instant in time, when we will be Raptured (see my book, *The End of History—Messiah Conspiracy,* chapter 25, "The Rapture Factor" for details), it shows Jesus knew that the world was not flat, but round. In order to have day and night at the same moment, a spherical Earth would have to have one side facing toward the sun while the other would obviously have to be facing away. The Hebrew word translated as "circle" in Isaiah 40, means a three-dimensional sphere.

* * *

JESUS GAVE SPECIAL INSTRUCTIONS FOR JEWISH SAFETY, WHICH APPLIED TO THE ERA AFTER ISRAEL'S BIRTH BUT IMMEDIATELY BEFORE HIS SECOND ADVENT

Jesus foretold warnings to the Jews living in Israel during the general time of His return! Thus, we are able to observe from His words, He was aware that after dispersion, His people would be regathered into their own land. Jesus remarked, "But pray ye that your flight be not in the winter, neither on the sabbath day...." (Matthew 24:20).

From Jesus' special instructions for Jewish safety just prior to the terrible war which He will return to stop, we see that there would have to be a new Israel in existence and that Jesus, as a prophet and the Messiah, clearly saw this nearly 2000 years earlier. As a matter of fact, the Temple (not yet rebuilt), according to Jesus' words, will soon be erected. He said in Matthew 24:15: "When ye therefore shall see the abomination of desolation, spoken of by Daniel the prophet, stand in the holy place, (whoso readeth, let him understand:)...." (KJV).

The "abomination of desolation" refers to the taking of an unholy thing into the Holy of Holies chamber of the Temple. It occurred once before in 165 BC, when a pig was sacrificed in the second Temple.

Paul, in the New Testament book of Thessalonians, described Jesus' warning regarding Daniel's prophecy. The apostle wrote: "Let no one in any way deceive you, for *it will not come* unless the apostasy comes first, and the man of lawlessness is revealed, the son of destruction, who opposes and exalts himself above every so-called god or object of worship, so that he takes his seat in the **temple** of God, displaying himself as being God....that lawless one will be revealed whom the Lord will slay with the breath of His mouth and bring to an end by the appearance of His coming...." (II Thessalonians 2:3-4, 8 NASB).

THE FIG TREE (ISRAELI NATION) HAS PUT OUT LEAVES, INDICATING OUR ERA AS THE GENERATION TO SEE JESUS ARRIVE AT THE PROPHETIC DOOR

Jesus also used the parable of the fig tree. The fig tree is an Old Testament symbol of Israel, along with the olive tree, clearly foretelling Israel's rebirth as a key apocalyptic sign for His return. His presence at the door, ready to return to save His people, is imminent. In His very words: "Now learn a parable of the fig tree; When his branch is yet tender, and putteth forth leaves, ye know that summer *is* nigh: So likewise ye, when ye shall see all these things, know that it is near, *even* at the doors" (Matthew 24:32-33 KJV).

If you are asking, as many have in past times, "Who is the fig tree?", we will make use of a first century document, *The Apocalypse of Peter*, for our answer. This early writing, which only fully came to light in 1910, identifies the fig tree parable Jesus used as a reference to Israel. It also speaks of the future Antichrist's attempt to kill those who reject his (Antichrist's) claim that he is Messiah. Although we realize this is not a canonical part of the New

Testament, and therefore not divinely inspired, it nevertheless sheds light on our understanding of the New Testament in reference to the age of Jesus and Israel today, in relation to the parable of the fig tree. It reads: " 'And ye, receive ye the parable of the fig tree thereon: as soon as its shoots have gone forth and its boughs have sprouted, the end of the world will come.' And I, Peter answered and said unto him 'Explain to me concerning the fig tree...' And he answered and said unto me: 'Dost thou not understand that **the fig tree is** the house of **Israel**?'....Verily I say unto you, when its boughs have sprouted at the end, then shall deceiving saviors come and awaken hope, saying: 'I am the Savior who am now come into the world.' And when they shall see the wickedness of their deeds (even of the false saviors) they shall turn away after them and deny him to whom our fathers gave praise, the first Messiah whom they crucified and thereby sinned exceedingly. And this deceiver is not the messiah. And when they reject him he will kill them with the sword, and there shall be many martyrs..."[22]

Jesus cursed[23] the fig tree for unbelief. This tree was a representation of Israel's unbelief at that time. This disfavor for unbelief peaked in Israel's dispersion in the first century. However, Jesus blessed it in a parable of the future, exclaiming it would one day again bring forth fruit!

---

[22]G. Alon, *The Jews in Their Land in the Talmudic Age*, p. 619. Bold mine.
[23]Matthew 21:19-21 KJV. The literal meaning is "disfavored."

This began in 1948 with the rebirth of Israel. Jesus said that the generation[24] which saw Israel reborn would not pass until all (which includes His Second Coming) would be fulfilled. In reference to the generation of the fig tree, Jesus said: "Verily I say unto you, **This generation** shall not pass, till all these things be fulfilled" (Matthew 24:34 KJV; bold mine).

HOW LONG CAN A BIBLE GENERATION BE? APPROXIMATELY ONE HUNDRED YEARS — ISRAEL IS ALREADY FIFTY YEARS OLD — CLOSE, MAYBE IN YOUR LIFETIME!

Genesis 15:13-16 says a generation can be as long as one hundred years, thus some Bible teachers believe that sometime within the next few decades, before 2048, we may see the Second Coming of Jesus, the resurrection of the dead and world redemption. However, this author refuses to set any exact dates because Jesus said, "But of that day and hour no one knows...." (Matthew 24:34 NASB).

Genesis 15:13-16 is God's prophecy to Abraham, given approximately one hundred and fifty years before the fact, predicting that the Israelis would be captive for four hundred years, which would be four generations before they would return to Canaan (Israel). The Amorite mentioned in verse 16 was given four hundred years to repent, but did not.

---

[24]See my book, *A Liberal Interpretation on the Prophecy of Israel—Disproved* for the opinion of a writer who denies the prophecy of Israel as told by Jesus. This work goes into greater detail with regard to the fig tree and quotes many authorities on the prophetic rebirth of Israel.

While Israel was in Egypt, the Amorites (a name used for the people who occupied Palestine in that day) sacrificed their children to demon gods, yet God gave them every opportunity to turn away from paganism and to Him. They had their last chance four hundred years later, and their iniquity (sin) became full, as the Genesis passage mentions. Only then did Moses lead the Hebrews to their land, Canaan, which today bears the name Israel.

Our main point is that God clearly identifies to Abraham that a generation is one hundred years; four hundred equals four generations! A "generation" is specifically named in Jesus' time clock for His Second Coming in connection with Israel, in Matthew 24 and Luke 21.

According to the prophecy of Genesis 15, a generation (one hundred years) may not pass after the rebirth of Israel *before* redemption will be realized. The fig tree of Israel, as Jesus called it, blossomed forty-eight years ago (as we look back from 1998). We are at the halfway mark. If you are in your twenties, thirties, or even your forties, it may very well occur in **your** lifetime. Keep in mind, a full generation is not required to pass. Jesus said, concerning these events leading up to and during His Second Advent: "...This generation shall not pass, till all these things be fulfilled" (Matt. 24:34 KJV). Thus, perhaps ninety-nine years, or eighty, or seventy may tick off out of this hundred before He returns. It could happen tomorrow, but no later than one hundred years. So, don't think that if you are old you have no hope. You do! It could happen tomorrow!

***

RECENT ISRAELI POLITICAL EVENTS AND WAR RESULTS/PREPARATIONS ARE INDICATIONS THAT THE SIGNS OF THE SECOND ADVENT OF JESUS ARE *ALMOST* AT THE DOOR

Though we realize we can not know exactly when, Jesus did give us indications of the approaching *nearness* of His return! These signs of His Second Coming include: 1. The Rapture of all true believers sometime after Israel's rebirth—obviously yet to occur, if you are a believer[25] still on Earth reading this book (see my work, *The End of History—Messiah Conspiracy,* chapter 25, "The Rapture Factor" for details); 2. The coming of the Antichrist, whose rule will last seven years (see ibid, chapter 23, "The False Messiah Armilus Equals Antichrist"), ending at Armageddon, at a point three and one-half years after he enters the rebuilt Temple in Jerusalem to proclaim himself God (II Thessalonians 2:3-4). This is called the abomination of desolation. Jesus spoke of it in Matthew 24:15 when He warned His future Jewish people to "flee to the mountains for safety" (see my book, *Nightmare of the Apocalypse,* Appendix 9, "They Escaped to Petra").

The construction of this Temple would be impossible unless Israel owned the area of old Jerusalem. In the Six Day War of 1967, Israel's victory over five Arab armies put this strategic piece of real estate, along with their most sacred holy shrine (the Wailing Wall), back into their hands for the first time in two millennia. Thus we are one step closer to the rebuilding of the Temple.

---

[25]That is, if you were born-again before it occurs.

After the victory, the Israeli General Moshe Dayan marched to the Wailing Wall and proclaimed: "We have returned to our holiest of holy places, never to leave her again."[26] "No power on earth will remove us from this spot again."[27]   Later, Israeli General Ariel Sharon said: "I have the survivability of a superpower!"[28]

The full thrust of this statement was later revealed in a *Time* magazine article written during the Yom Kippur War, which quoted Dayan and Prime Minister Golda Meir. " 'The Third Temple (a term for modern Israel) is falling,' Dayan reportedly told his prime minister.   'Arm the doomsday weapon.'   One of the world's worst-kept military secrets is that Israel has strategic nuclear capabilities."[29]

Recently, an Israeli nuclear technician publicly confirmed that as of 1982, Israel had at least two hundred nuclear weapons.[30] During the 1991 Gulf War, Prime Minister Shamier put Israel on full nuclear alert. Had Iraq dropped a chemical bomb on Israel, she would have gotten more than Saddam Hussein bargained for.   Shamier said: *"Our retaliation will be so terrible that it will be impossible to imagine. Iraq will never be able to forget it."*[31]   Thus, even from a practical military point of view, it is clear that Israel is not going to just disappear because her enemies dislike her!

---

[26]Hal Lindsey, *The Late Great Planet Earth*, Grand Rapids, MI.: Zondervan Publishing House © 1970, p. 55.
[27]Grant R. Jeffrey, *Armageddon, Appointment with Destiny.* New York: Bantam Books, © 1988, p. 109, used by permission.
[28]Morris Cerillo, "Evangelical Newsletter," 1987.
[29]Hal Lindsey, *The 1980's: Countdown to Armageddon*, p. 39.
[30]Grant R. Jeffrey, *Armageddon, Appointment with Destiny*, p. 203. This was also confirmed in the May 16, 1982 issue of the *Toronto Star*.
[31]This author heard Shamier's address on Israel TV in Jerusalem.

THE FUTURE JEWISH TEMPLE, PRESENTLY FORESHADOWED BY THE PRODUCTION OF ITS ORNAMENTS

At present, ornaments are being manufactured for use in the new Temple by the Temple Institute. Richard K. Ostling, in a *Time* magazine article entitled, "Time for a New Temple?", commented: "During six years of research, the institute has reconstructed 38 of the ritual implements that will be required when Temple sacrifices are restored; it will complete the other 65 items as funds permit. A museum of the completed pieces has drawn 10,000 visitors...."[32] The same article mentioned: "Temple restoration is also a fixation for literal-minded Protestants, who deem a new Temple the precondition for Christ's Second Coming. Two Talmudic schools located near the Western (Wailing) Wall are teaching nearly 200 students the elaborate details of Temple service."[33]

In a more recent article by the national news magazine, *U.S. News & World Report*, which had the words, "Waiting for the Messiah" blazing across the cover of its December 19, 1994 edition, the latest and most startling information was revealed. The article was entitled, "The Christmas Covenant." A profile of the article regarding the anticipated rebuilding of the Temple pointed out: "The first step, says Chaim Richman of the Temple Institute, is replication down to the precise detail of Temple objects, half of which have now been made. In

---

[32]Richard K. Ostling, "Time For a New Temple?", *Time*, Oct. 25, 1989, p. 63, used by permission.
[33]Ibid, p. 62.

addition, a Mississippi cattle farmer has agreed to provide special unblemished red heifers, the ashes of which are required for a purification ritual.

Others also prepare for the miracle. Rabbi Nahman Kahane of the Old City has created a data base of all Jews descended from Aaron, the priestly brother of Moses. They will be called into service if the Temple is rebuilt."[34]

Gershom Soloman, an Israeli member of the Temple Mount Faithful who is greatly interested in working for the Temple's rebuilding, said recently: "We must start immediately the rebuilding of the third Temple because this is a condition for the coming of the Messiah."[35]

I will not be surprised if Soloman's wish is accomplished within thirty to forty years of our writing!   However, it will be the Antichrist's negotiation of a temporary peace between Israel and the Arabs which will allow this Temple to be rebuilt.

THE *GLORY* OF THE MESSIAH'S RETURN, WHEN WILL IT BE? PSALM 102 GIVES US A CLUE—ZION

Because God is faithful, it will not be our fate that His Messiah will be late. He will be right on time. His scheduled time to arrive is to be found in Psalm 102:16.

When Jesus came 2000 years ago it was a Coming in humiliation, to suffer. However, He made

---

[34]Jeffrey L. Sheler, "The Christmas Covenant," *U.S News & World Report*, Dec. 19, 1994, p. 70, © used by permission. Quoted from the profiles by Gareth G. Cook and David Makovshy, "Jerusalem Temple, Preparing for the Messiah," *U.S. News & World Report*.
[35]*The 700 Club*, Christian Broadcasting Network, Dec. 8, 1994.

reference to His Second Coming "when the Son of Man shall come in all of His **glory**" (Matthew 24:30). The Jewish Bible references this glory as follows: "When the LORD shall build up Zion [Israel], he shall appear in his glory" (Psalm 102:16 KJV; [ ] mine).   Thus according to David's inspired line, He will be right on time.

Jesus could not have returned to Earth until Israel became a nation in 1948, as this Psalm clearly says that when He shall build up Zion (Israel), the Lord (Messiah) shall appear (come) in His glory to save the earth and usher in the royal Messianic Kingdom. This kingdom was promised by hundreds of prophecies, inspired by God, throughout the Old Testament. So, since He promised to come in the generation of Israel's rebirth (Matthew 24:32-34), and a generation cannot be more than one hundred years (Genesis 15:13-16), and since Israel was born in 1948,[36] we do not have long to wait!

---

[36]Risto Santala comments: "The Talmudic scholars picture the Messiah arriving in the middle of a crisis for humanity.   These birth-pangs connected with the last generation relate to individual morals, the history of the nations and the whole of creation.   Just a short example of this: *'If you see kingdoms arming themselves one against another, you can expect the coming of the Messiah.'*   *'The Messiah, the Son of David, will not come until the whole world is filled with apostates* (Heb. *minût,* by which the Rabbis seem to understand the 'Christians'). *'The Son of David will not come until judges and authorities cease to be in Israel.'   'The Messianic footsteps will appear when insolence increases....'*   We could add here the so-called *'Messianic signs'* according to which *in that time there will be dreadful diseases, plagues and epidemics', 'the whole world will be bathed in blood' 'the sun will be darkened and the moon changed to blood'.*   There are descriptions corresponding to these both in the words of Christ and the letters of Paul.   It is worth keeping this symmetry in mind when studying Jewish scholars' expositions of psalm 102, which gives a description of the *'last generation'.*"   Risto Santala, *The Messiah in the Old Testament in the Light of Rabbinical Writings,* Jerusalem: Karen Hahvah Meshihit, ©

The front page of the May 16, 1948 edition of what
is now *The Jerusalem Post* reporting the rebirth of
Israel. Courtesy of *The Jerusalem Post.*

1992, pp. 141-142. Santala's footnote to "blood" reads: "Jellinek, *Beit ha-Midrash,* vol. II pp58-63 'The Messianic signs' and vol. V1117-120 'The wars of the Messiah-King'." Ibid, p. 142. The rabbinic writings maintain that in the time before the return of the Messiah, there will be "dreadful diseases, plagues, and epidemics." Jesus said the same thing. His predictions on this are recorded in the twenty-fourth chapter of Matthew's gospel. I cover the predictions of plagues as they relate to current developments in modern germ warfare and genetic engineering in my book *Nightmare of the Apocalypse,* Appendix 12. "Designer Germ Warfare".

This is the school presently preparing the ornaments for the Temple. It is located in Jerusalem's Old City, next to the Moriah Bookstore.

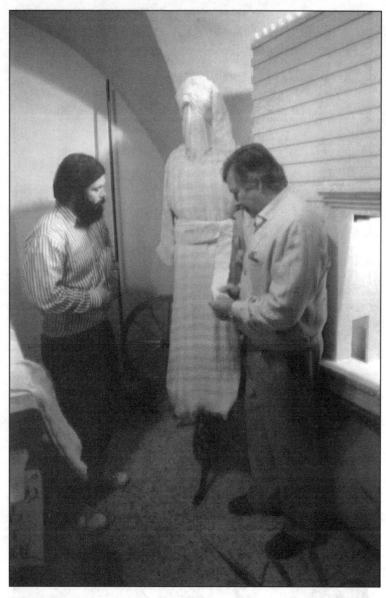

The author and Hal Lindsey examine the garments recently woven for the high priest at the Jerusalem school. These garments may one day be used by a future priest in the Temple.

"Yea, though I walk through the valley of the shadow of death, I will fear no evil: for thou *art* with me; thy rod and thy staff they comfort me."
Psalms 23:4 KJV

HAVE NO FEAR—JESUS AND AMOS ASSURE US THAT ISRAEL WILL BE SAVED, NEVER AGAIN TO BE PLUCKED UP OUT OF HER LAND!

Before the final war is over, it is predicted that Jesus will return to save Israel by wiping out her enemies and thereby inaugurating the millennial kingdom. Jesus said those days would be cut short: "And except those days should be shortened, there should no flesh be saved: but for the elect's sake those days shall be shortened" (Matthew 24:22 KJV).

Amos, the Old Testament prophet, foretells that Israel, once regathered the second time from all the nations, will never be scattered again. "And I will bring again the captivity of **my people of Israel**, and they shall build the waste cities, and inhabit *them*; and they shall plant vineyards, and drink the wine thereof; they shall also make gardens, and eat the fruit of them. And I will plant them upon their land, and they shall **no more** be pulled up out of their land which I have given them, saith the LORD thy God" (Amos 9:14-15 KJV, bold mine).

GOD SPEAKS TO THE JEW, THROUGH EZEKIEL, IN THE FIRST PERSON, "I....WILL BRING YOU INTO YOUR OWN LAND," AND HE IS STILL DOING IT!

The prophet Ezekiel had much to say about Israel's dispersion, regathering and last war, recognizing her Messiah and her permanent re-establishment on the land God gave to Abraham! Ezekiel tells us: "Therefore say unto the house of Israel, Thus saith the Lord GOD; I do not *this* for your sakes, O house of Israel, but for mine holy name's sake, which ye have profaned among the heathen, whither ye went. And I will sanctify my great name, which was profaned among the heathen, which ye have profaned in the midst of them; and the heathen shall know that I *am* the LORD, saith the Lord GOD, when I shall be sanctified in you before their eyes. For I will take you from among the heathen, and gather you out of all countries, and will bring you into your own land. Then will I sprinkle clean water upon you, and ye shall be clean: from all your filthiness, and from all your idols, will I cleanse you. A new heart also will I give you, and a new spirit will I put within you: and I will take away the stony heart out of your flesh, and I will give you an heart of flesh. And I will put my spirit within you, and cause you to walk in my statutes, and ye shall keep my judgments, and do *them*. And ye shall dwell in the land that I gave to your fathers; and ye shall be my people, and I will be your God. I will also save you from all your uncleannesses: and I will call for the corn, and will increase it, and lay no famine upon you. And I will multiply the fruit of the tree, and the increase of the field, that ye shall receive no more reproach of famine among the heathen. Then shall ye remember your own evil ways, and your doings that *were* not good, and shall lothe yourselves in your own sight for your iniquities and for your abominations. Not for your sakes do I *this*, saith the Lord GOD, be it known unto you: be ashamed and confounded for your own ways, O house of Israel. Thus saith the Lord GOD; In the day that I shall have cleansed you from all your iniquities I will also cause *you* to dwell in the cities, and the wastes shall be builded. And the desolate land shall be tilled, whereas it lay desolate in the sight of all that passed by. And they shall say, This land that was desolate is become like the garden of Eden; and the waste and desolate and ruined cities *are become* fenced, *and* are inhabited. Then the heathen that are left round about you shall know that I the LORD build the ruined *places, and* plant that that was desolate: I the LORD have spoken *it*, and I will do *it*" (Ezekiel 36:22-36 KJV).

EZEKIEL'S 2600-YEAR-OLD EXPOSÉ ON ISRAEL IN THE LAST DAYS— FULFILLMENT IS IMMINENT

"After many days thou shalt be visited: in the latter years thou shalt come into the land *that is* brought back from the sword, *and is* gathered out of many people, against the mountains of Israel, which have been always waste: but it is brought forth out of the nations, and they shall dwell safely all of them. Thou shalt ascend and come like a storm, thou shalt be like a cloud to cover the land, thou, and all thy bands, and many people with thee. Thus saith the Lord GOD; It shall also come to pass, *that* at the same time shall things come into thy mind, and thou shalt think an evil thought: And thou shalt say, I will go up to the land of unwalled villages; I will go to them that are at rest, that dwell safely, all of them dwelling without walls, and having neither bars nor gates, To take a spoil, and to take a prey; to turn thine hand upon the desolate places *that are now* inhabited, and upon the people *that are* gathered out of the nations, which have gotten cattle and goods, that dwell in the midst of the land....And the heathen shall know that the house of Israel went into captivity for their iniquity: because they trespassed against me, therefore hid I my face from them, and gave them into the hand of their enemies: so fell they all by the sword. According to their unclean-ness and according to their transgressions have I done unto them, and hid my face from them. Therefore thus saith the Lord GOD;   Now will I bring again the captivity of Jacob, and have mercy upon the whole house of Israel, and will be jealous for my holy name; After that they have borne their shame, and all their trespasses whereby they have trespassed against me, when they dwelt safely in their land, and none made *them* afraid. When I have brought them again from the people, and gathered them out of their enemies' lands, and am sanctified in them in the sight of many nations; Then shall they know that I *am* the LORD their God, which caused them to be led into captivity among the hea-then: but I have gathered them unto their own land, and have left none of them any more there. Neither will I hide my face any more from them: for I have poured out my spirit upon the house of Israel, saith the Lord GOD" (Ezekiel 38:8-12; 39:23-29 KJV).

THE CRISIS OF THE LAST WAR IN ISRAEL, AS DESCRIBED IN ZECHARIAH AND EZEKIEL, BRINGS MANY ISRAELIS TO FAITH IN JESUS!

Hal Lindsey accurately said: "...these prophets forecast that Israel will be brought to the brink of annihilation just before the coming of the Messiah, who will save the Israelis (see Zachariah chapters 12-14 and especially chapter 13, verses eight and nine). According to Ezekiel, Israel's great crisis will cause many Jews to believe in their true Messiah.

Zachariah speaks of this holocaust and the repentence which follows: 'And I will pour out on the House of David and all the inhabitants of Jerusalem the spirit of grace and supplication, so that they will look on Me whom they have pierced; and they will mourn for Him as one mourns for an only son' (Zachariah 12:10)."[37]

WE WILL SOON BE CELEBRATING ISRAEL'S FUTURE VICTORY AND ENJOYING TABERNACLES WITH THE PEOPLE OF ISRAEL AND JESUS— EVERY YEAR!

For those of us who know the Bible's predictions, we have nothing to fear and have only to wait. If we are believers now, we will one day soon enjoy seven years in Heaven, while these terrible end-time events, which unbelieving men will perpetrate on themselves, occur.[38]

After this seven-year period, we will enjoy Israel's victory with Jesus, thereafter dining with all the world's peoples who receive Him, in Israel, as they are granted entrance. Zechariah tells us: "...it shall come to pass, *that* every one that is left of all the nations which came against Jerusalem shall even go up from year to year to worship the King, the

[37]Hal Lindsey, *The 1980's: Countdown to Armageddon*, p. 46.
[38] See chapter 25 of my work, *The End of History—Messiah Conspiracy* for the full story.

LORD of hosts, and to keep the feast of tabernacles" (Zechariah 14:16 KJV).

Jesus will sit with the twelve tribes of Israel. Remember what He promised at the last Passover supper: "That ye may eat and drink at my table in my kingdom, and sit on thrones judging the twelve tribes of Israel" (Luke 22:30 KJV).

We conclude our chapter on Israel with a collection of photographs representing all walks of life within the land of Israel.[39]

The Mount of Olives is one of the highest places in Jerusalem. Many Evangelical Christians and some Jews believe the Messiah will return to the vicinity of the church here, located at the top of this majestic mountain, as He comes to bring peace. This location is Jesus' biblically predicted re-entry point (Acts 1:11, Zechariah 14:4).

---

[39]The following photos, courtesy of the State of Israel Government Press Office, photography department, with the exception of above, below, Ben Gurion's Bible, El Al Office, Pisgat Ziev, The Jerusalem Great Synagogue, McDavid's, Talithakumi, the Danish underground boat, entrance to Yad VaShem and following four which were taken by this author.

This face of the Mount of Olives reveals thousands of Jewish gravesites, placed there by Orthodox Jews in anticipation of the Coming of the Messiah, to resurrect the dead (Daniel 12:2-3, Job 19:25-26).

David Ben-Gurion,
during a 1956 address in Tel Aviv.

David Ben-Gurion's personal Bible, including the New Testament, sits atop his desk at his home in Israel. (For in-depth documentation of Ben Gurion's immense interest in Jesus, see my work *The End of History—Messiah Conspiracy*, chapter 15.)

A closer look reveals the words *Brit Ha Dasha* (ברית הדשה), the "New Testament" in Hebrew.

David Ben-Gurion and George Lauderdale at
Ben-Gurion's home in Kibbutz Sdeh-Boker, Israel.

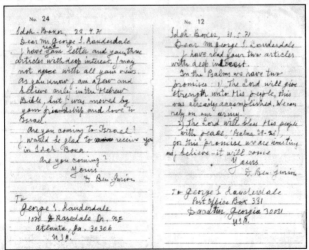

Two letters from David Ben-Gurion to Reverend
George Lauderdale of Atlanta, Georgia.

Dr. Chaim Weizman, the first President of Israel.

David Ben-Gurion, first Prime Minister of Israel,
and 1948 and 1967 Israeli war victories.

Yemenite Jews, who resemble
Arabs in their dress, immigrate to Israel.

Israeli Prime Minister, Golda Meir.

Israeli school children and scenic views of Israel.

Sabras (natives of Israel) and the flag of Israel.

Israeli settlements and an Israeli Army air show. The planes fly in the formation of
the Hebrew initials meaning the "Army of Israel's Defense"
("TSA-HAL" or צהל), and the Star of David.

Israel is built and trees are planted as the desert is pushed back.

Downtown Israel, the suburbs, and a new sabra in his baby carriage.

Pisgat Ziev condominiums,
settlements, and a farm owner.

McDavid's fast food restaurant, and Israel's replica of the U.S. Statue of Liberty, in front of the Kol Bo Shalom department store.

Israel's statue of Abraham Lincoln, and
a replica of the U.S. Liberty Bell.

The Israeli Army, the Temple Mount as viewed from the summit of the Mount of Olives, and the Western Wall on Yom Ha Zicharon ("Day of Rememberance," for those lost in the Holocaust).

Eshcol Lake, and Israel's army and weaponry.

The Jerusalem Theater, a morning service under a prayer shawl prior to a Barmitzva on the top of Masada, and a bonfire during Lag b'Omer (a Jewish festival commemorating an unsuccessful revolt against the Romans in the second century AD).

An Israeli hospital, kibbutzniks at work, a drill team forming the Star of David, an amphitheater, religious holiday, and a field of flowers.

Religious ceremonies and sights in Jerusalem.

An Israeli child builds a menorah in the sand,
and an aerial view of a circular moshav (private farm) called Nahalal .

Landscape and religion in Israel.

Religion and the army in Israel, and a soldiers'
memorial at Kyriat Anayim.

Names of fallen Israeli soldiers memorialized, and a German shepherd equipped with a gas mask in the service of the Israeli Army.

en the Messiah comes, He will arrive through the Golden Gate as the shofar sounds
and the religious realize He is Yeshua—Jesus...

...then all will celebrate and rejoice.

True Christians will stand by Israel until the redemption arrives.

Until the end.

Philip Moore (left) with Israeli military personnel,
Tamar Borria, and Shosh Abraham, at Base
Machena Natan, in Beersheba, Israel.

International Christian Embassy Jerusalem

THE JERUSALEM **POST**

SUPPLEMENT – April 11, 1988

Second International Christian Zionist Congress

Massive support for Israel

AN HISTORIC conference of Christian supporters of Israel from around the world, gathering in Israel for the first time, has opened at Jerusalem's Binyenei Ha'uma. The four-day Second International Christian Zionist Congress, spearheaded by the International Christian Embassy Jerusalem, coincides with Israel's 40th anniversary and gives voice to an international show of Christian support for Israel.

"Delegates to the Congress are involved spiritually, educationally and practically in demonstrating their commitment to Zion," declares Johan Lückhoff, director of the ICEJ. "We are looking to the participants to mobilize all the great Christian support for Israel in all parts of the globe. During the congress they will attend in-depth seminars examining issues ranging from the biblical basis for Christian Zionism to analyses of anti-Semitism and anti-Zionism.

The discussions at the congress embrace a view of history with contemporary reality. The delegates will gather today in Tel Aviv at the museum where independence was declared in 1948 and then proceed to an open-air concert in Malchei Ysrael Square.

A gala banquet in the Knesset on Tuesday will be preceded by a reception with prominent Israelis present.

Wednesday's activities will be devoted to a memorial to Holocaust victims, culminating in a session calling on Christians to aid the causes of Soviet Jewry and aliya. Ida Nudel will deliver a message to the congress.

Melanie Rosenberg

At Mount Herzl the congress delegates will unveil a plaque commemorating Reverend William Hechler, an Anglican Church cleric from England who a century ago used his good offices to convince the Grand Duke of Baden to grant Theodor Herzl an audience. The Duke consequently opened the door for Herzl to be received by the Kaiser.

Director Johann Lückhoff points out the special significance of the Christian Zionist Congress being held on the occasion of Israel's 40th anniversary. "Biblically speaking, the number 40 holds a very great significance. It often marks the entry into a new phase. Just as the Children of Israel ended 40 years in the desert to inherit the land promised to them, so Israel today is on the threshold of entering a new dimension of its existence.

"The Christian world, too, must grasp this moment to understand and the challenge facing us. What happens in Israel is reflected in the Church. The 40th years offers us a unique opportunity to consider our responsibility to the Jewish people in the light of our spiritual inheritance.

"The Christian Congress in Jerusalem is our tribute to the Jewish People and the State of Israel. Israel has many friends. We're convening here to deliver that message to the Israelis and to the nations of the world."

The spirit of Basel

THIS WEEK'S International Christian Zionist Congress in Jerusalem was conceived three years ago at the first congress of world-wide Christian supporters of Israel in Basel, Switzerland.

"In retrospect Basel was a turning point in Christianity's global mobilization to strengthen the State of Israel," attests ICEJ Director Johann Lückhoff. "The interest and excitement generated in that historic meeting - in the same hallowed hallways where Theodor Herzl convened the first Zionist Congress nearly a century before - set the tone for our ongoing work."

At Basel 600 delegates from 27 countries participated in the deliberations and decision-making, in addition to western countries, delegates from Gabon, India, Zaire, Sri Lanka, Ivory Coast and a number of other countries that do not even maintain diplomatic ties with Israel, played active roles.

The Congress adopted several resolutions urging world recognition of Jerusalem as Israel's capital, Jewish sovereignty over all of the Land of Israel, and aliya as a main principle of Diaspora Jewish life. Anti-Semitism and anti-Zionism were forcefully condemned.

"We are especially gratified that resolutions calling for Ethiopian Jewish aliya and Spain's closing the diplomatic vacuum with Israel preceded their actual occurrence," says ICEJ spokesman Jan Willem van der Hoeven. "And more recently our activists in Europe were able to nip the first signs of corporate boycotts of Israeli products in the bud through effective counter-pressures.

Even as all eyes turn towards Jerusalem, the vision expounded at Basel in 1985 will continue to grow today in the Binyenei Ha'uma.

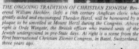

THE ONGOING TRADITION OF CHRISTIAN ZIONISM: Reverend William Hechler, (left) a 19th century Anglican cleric who greatly aided and encouraged Theodor Herzl, will be honoured by a plaque to be unveiled at Mount Herzl during the Congress. Above right is Orde Wingate, the British officer who trained units of the Jewish underground in pre-State days. At right is a scene from the First International Christian Zionist Congress, in Basel, Switzerland, three years ago.

Congress Highlights

SUNDAY	7:30 p.m. Opening night at the Binyenei Ha'uma
MONDAY	3:00 p.m. Short ceremony at the Museum Building in Tel Aviv, where Ben-Gurion proclaimed Israel's statehood in 1948, followed by march through downtown Tel Aviv to Malchei Israel Square.
TUESDAY	Reception at the Hilton Hotel Banquet in the Chagall Room at the Knesset

WEDNESDAY 3:30 p.m. Visit to Mt. Herzl

7:30 p.m. Holocaust Memorial evening with focus also on the issue of Soviet Jews

THURSDAY 7:30 p.m. Closing night, with brief speeches and special music

** Every morning from 8:30 a.m. to 12:30 p.m. there will be different seminars held at Binyenei Ha'uma.

Jerusalem Post coverage of the Second International Christian Zionist Congress by Melanie Rosenberg, reproduced courtesy of the *Jerusalem Post*.

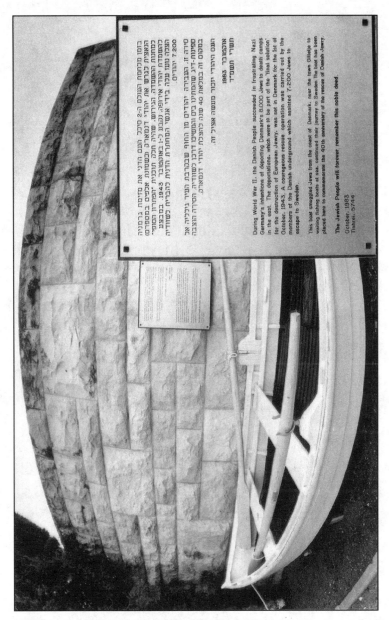

This small boat was used by the Danes to smuggle
Jews from Gillelje, Denmark, to fishing boats at sea,
on their way to the safety of Sweden.

Here are a few books written by Jewish survivors of the Holocaust. They say they owe their lives to those Christians who aided them in their fight for suvival and Jesus, the one they came to realize is the Jewish Messiah, through whom they were miraculously preserved.

This citation is presented by Yad VaShem to righteous Gentiles in honor of their commitment to save Jews during the Nazi Holocaust.

The entrance to the Garden of the Righteous Gentiles, which leads to the Yad VaShem Holocaust Museum in Jerusalem. The garden is filled with plaques and trees, to honor those Christians who saved Jews, at risk of their own lives from the Nazis.

Corrie Ten Boom, the loving old woman whose book, *The Hiding Place*, later became a film,[40] saved many Jews in her own personal "hiding place" behind a double wall in her home. Corrie was a wonderful Evangelical Christian who said she was willing to save Jesus' people, the Jews, from the Holocaust even if it meant her death. Even though she was relentlessly beaten by the Gestapo, she never turned in any of the Jews she was hiding. Recently, Corrie died and her tree was placed in the Yad VaShem Memorial Park in Israel.

Corrie Ten Boom's name plaque and tree.

The famous Christian Swedish diplomat, Raul Wallenberg, who some feel is still alive and incarcerated in Russia, saved 100,000 Jews. Dr.

---

[40]This film is now available on home video.

Bauminger describes this "angel of mercy":[41] "...Wallenberg rented 32 houses that he proclaimed a Swedish extraterritorial zone. Into these houses Wallenberg brought his 'protected Jews,' after having duly provided them with forged papers in the name of the Swedish Embassy and the Red Cross."[42]

Bauminger went on to tell how Wallenberg hid the Jewish children in "churches or private Christian homes," and that: " 'All this was done by a courageous man who had the strength of his convictions to act according to his conscience and beliefs. As in the case of King Christian of Denmark, Wallenberg's deeds once more bring to mind the poignant thought: how much greater could have been the number of survivors in the lands of extermination, had there been others like him....' "[43]

---

[41] Bauminger, Arieh L. *The Righteous,* Third Edition. Jerusalem: Yad VaShem Martyrs and Heroes Remembrance Authority, © 1983, p. 79, used by permission.
[42] Ibid.
[43] Ibid, p. 81. Attorney General of Israel at the Eichmann trial.

The Wallenberg Memorial, built to honor the man who saved 100,000 Jews from the Holocaust.

" '...Only the church stood squarely across the path of Hitler's campaign....I am forced to confess that what I once despised I now praise unreservedly.' " [44] "I am a Jew, but I am enthralled by the luminous figure of the Nazarene....No one can read the Gospels [of the New Testament] without feeling the actual presence of Jesus. His personality pulsates in every word. No myth is filled with such life."[45]

Albert Einstein

Einstein remembered on Israeli currency and stamp.

---

[44] *The Evening Sun*, Baltimore, April 13, 1979.
[45] Arthur W. Kac, *The Messiahship of Jesus*, p. 36. Kac's source was *The Saturday Evening Post*, Oct. 26, 1929. [ ] mine.

Israeli's guard their border.

The Golden Gate, in Jerusalem, where
the Messiah will enter one day soon.

"These men betrayed their pure Aryan Blood to the dirty superstitions of <u>the Jew</u> Jesus—superstitions as loathsome and ludicrous as the Yiddish rites of circumcision.... Christianity only added the seeds of decadence such as forgiveness, self-abnegation,...and the very denial of the evolutionary laws of survival of the fittest."[1] ADOLF HITLER

"Salvation is of <u>the Jews</u>.... I am the way, the truth, and the life: no man cometh unto the father, but by me...I say unto you, Before Abraham was, I am."

JESUS, John 4:22; 14:6; 8:48 KJV

Hitler's forthright lies and statements of hate against the Jews and Jesus shed insight into the truth. The truth is that the Jews and the Jewish teachings of Jesus have secured freedom for many nations of the world to this present day. This can be seen in Hitler's accusation, "Had Charles Martel not been victorious at Poitiers—already, you see, the world had fallen into the hands of the Jews, so gutless a thing was Christianity! Then we should in all probability have been converted to Mohammedanism, that cult which glorifies heroism and which opens the seventh Heaven to the bold warrior alone. Then the Germanic races would have conquered the world. Christianity alone prevented them from doing so."[2] Therefore the Jews and Evangelical Christians can glory in having preventing a Hitler Germanian conquest!   PHILIP MOORE, 1998

APPENDIX 2
HITLER'S ACCUSATIONS AGAINST THE JEWISH PEOPLE ARE FALSE

Hitler hated the Jewish people and sighted several reasons as to why he was dedicated to the destruction of the chosen people of God.

---

[1] Trevor Ravenscroft, *The Spear of Destiny,* York Beach, Maine: Samuel Weiser, Inc. © 1973. pp. 49, 70, bold mine., used by permission

[2] *Hitler's Secret Conversations 1941-1944*, New York: Farrar, Straus and Young, © 1953. p. 542, translated by Norman Cameron and R.H. Stevens, used by permission.

However, his "reasons" are categorically untrue and unfounded! For example in 1925 Hitler wrote in his book, *Mein Kamf:*[3]

"...while the Zionists try to make the rest of the world believe that the national consciousness of the Jew finds its satisfaction in the creation of a Palestinian state, the Jews again slyly dupe the dumb *Goyim.* It doesn't even enter their heads to build up a Jewish state in Palestine for the purpose of living there; all they want is a central organization for their international world swindle, endowed with its own sovereign rights and removed from the intervention of other states: a haven for convicted scoundrels and a university for budding crooks...It was and it is Jews...always with the same secret thought and clear aim of ruining the hated white race by the necessarily resulting bastardization, throwing it down from its cultural and political height, and himself rising to be its matter.

"For a racially pure people which is conscious of its blood can never be enslaved by the Jew...in politics he begins to replace the idea of democracy by the dictatorship of the proletariat.

"In the organized mass of Marxism he has found the weapon which lets him dispense with democracy and instead allows him to subjugate and govern the peoples with a dictatorial and brutal fist.

---

[3] Mein Kamf is German for my struggle, the title of the book which he wrote while in prison.

"He works systematically for revolutionization in a twofold sense: economic and political.

"Around peoples who offer too violent a resistance to attack from within he weaves a net of enemies, thanks to his international influence, incites them to war, and finally, if necessary, plants the flag of revolution on the very battlefields.

"In economics he undermines the states until the social enterprises which have become unprofitable are taken from the state and subjected to his financial control.

"In the political field he refuses the state the means for its self-preservation, destroys the foundations of all national self-maintenance and defense, destroys faith in the leadership, scoffs at its history and past...Culturally he contaminates art, literature, the theater, makes a mockery of natural feeling...Religion is ridiculed, ethics and morality represented as outmoded, until the last props of a nation in its struggle for existence in this world have fallen.

"Now begins the great last revolution. In gaining political power the Jew casts off the few cloaks that he still wears. The democratic people's Jew becomes the blood-Jew and tyrant over peoples. In a few years he tries to exterminate the national intelligentsia and by robbing the peoples of their natural intellectual leadership makes them ripe for the salve's lot of permanent subjugation.

"If, with the help of his Marxist creed, the Jew is victorious over the other peoples of the world, his crown will be the funeral wreath of humanity and this planet will, as it did thousand of years ago, move through the ether devoid of men."[4]

Believe it or not there are people to this day that still read and believe the claims of this book that Hitler wrote almost three quarters of a century ago. Neo Nazis, etc. I had no trouble in walking into my local Oxford Book Store and pulling a copy off of the shelf in 1996. Hence, I feel it is a necessary task to dispel of this myth and expose the untruths of Hitler's writings!

I lived in Israel for many years during the 1980's and 1990's. This wonderful state, which was founded in 1948, three years after Hitler shot himself, is a reality and is presently inhabited by about 4 million Jews. As you will remember Hitler wrote, "The Zionists try to make the rest of the world believe that the national consciousness of the Jew finds it's satisfaction in the creation of a Palestinian state, the Jews again slyly dupe the dumb *Goyim*. It doesn't even enter their heads to build up a Jewish state in Palestine for the purpose of living there."[5]

Goyim is a Hebrew word and refers to non-Jews. Hitler should have spoken for himself because Israel

---

[4] Adolf Hitler, *MEIN KAMPF*, Boston, Mass: The Houghton Mifflin Co. © 1943, 1971, pp. 324-26, 65, original © 1925 by Verlag Frz Eher Nachf, G.N.B.H., used by permission.
[5] Ibid.

is a state and is cherished by many Jews who see this country as their national consciousness. During my years of living and communing with the Israel people this *Goy*[6] witnessed these truths personally! Israeli is, in no way, a haven for budding crooks who swindle the world. Likewise Hitler's statements regarding Jews promoting the destruction of the white race are unfounded. The Ashkenazim[7] Jews are white themselves.

Despite Hitler's claim, Jews have contributed to all fields including those of art, literature and theater—just read your history books. The evangelical fundamental Christian writer, John Phillips, in his book *Exploring the World of the Jew* documents immense accomplishments achieved through out history by the Jewish people which have been for the betterment of **all** people. Phillips documents:

BRITAIN AND SUEZ CANAL

"One of the keys to Britain's success as a major world power was her control of the Suez Canal. The canal had been built by France. Britain contributed nothing to it, had no part in its construction, and bought none of its original stock. But in 1875 news filtered out of Egypt that the bankrupt khedive, Ismail Pasha, was putting up his shares for sale. It

---

[6] Hebrew singular for gentile/non-Jew i.e. myself.
[7] Jews of central and eastern Europe, or their descendants, *Random House College Dictionary*.

was simple imperial common sense that any nation that controlled the canal could control the Middle East, India and the Far East as well. It was in the best interests of both Britain and France to buy up the khedive's shares.

"The news reached Lord Beaconsfield, the British Prime Minister, but Parliament was in recess. By Monday morning, and by the time the slow machinery of British democracy had creaked through all the pros and cons, haggles over the details, and counted up the cost it would be too late; the French would have snapped up the shares. Beaconsfield could not wait for all that. Deciding that a bold move was best, he called the bank of England, borrowed the great sum needed on his own signature and bought out the khedive. When Monday came he presented the government and the furious French with one of history's great scoops. He had bought the Suez and guaranteed the growth of the British Empire. And **who was Lord Beaconsfield?** He is better known, perhaps, as **Benjamin Disraeli, a Jew.**

A JEW SAVES THE BRITISH EMPIRE

"Forty years later the empire had its back to the wall in a desperate struggle with Germany, then news came that shocked the War Office-there was no more cordite in the country for the manufacture of gunpowder, and the war was as good as lost. Lord Balfour, Prime Minister of Britain, turned to a brilliant young chemist. Could he devise some sort of synthetic cordite? It would have to be cheap and readily available. And it was needed in a desperate hurry. The chemist was sure that he could, and came up with a formula for making the needed chemical from horse chestnuts-abundant everywhere in the British Isles. In so doing he gave the British Empire a lease on life for another generation. We have met **this chemist** before. He **was Chaim Weizmann, a Jew.**

COURT JEWS IN EIGHTEENTH CENTURY EUROPE

"In the seventeenth and eighteenth centuries Jewish financial genius was so fully recognized by European monarchs that they realized they could not get along without Jewish counselors at court. Thus emerged the 'court Jew' entrusted with the financial affairs of the kingdom, authorized to raise loan, suggest taxes, control currency, and keep things solvent. The court Jews made it possible for kings to become independent of this barons and helped bring Europe into the modern age. The coming the court Jew heralded the approach of capitalism as a means of creating wealth and of carrying on the business of the world.

* * *

THE JEWISH BANKER

"The science of astronomy is greatly in debt of the Jews, who brought Arabic learning to the West. They translated and edited the great Arabic, Latin, and Spanish works, and the works of the great Greek astronomers. Sir William Herschel, A Jew, discovered the planet Uranus, the first planet to be discovered in modern times. For this achievement he was appointed Astronomer Royal of England. He went on to catalog hundreds of stars and thousands of nebulae. It was he who discovered the binary character of double stars and who determined the sun's motion in space. William Beer, a German Jew, was the first man to map the mountains of the moon. Fritz Cohn calculated the orbits of the planets. Albert Michelin, a Jew, determined the velocity of light. In fact, so accurate were his calculations that even with today's sophisticated instruments his figures have been shown to be only four kilometers a second off. Einstein on several occasions acknowledged his indebtedness to Michelin....There is not a branch of medicine in which Jews have not been leaders and pioneers. Jonas Salk developed the vaccine that has largely stamped out polio. Nobel winner Selman Abraham Waksman discovered the antibiotic streptomycin, now a common weapon against a variety of diseases. The American Medical Association (formerly the National Medical Association) was founded by a Jewish ophthalmologist, Isaac Hays. Joseph Goldberger laid the foundation for the science of nutrition, Simon Baruch was the first doctor to identify syphilis was developed by August von Wasserman, and Paul Erlich and another Jew discovered its cure.

JEWS IN MANY FIELDS

"Finance, astronomy, medicine—those fields only begin to introduce the subject of the world's debt to the Jew. Only 3 percent of the population for the United States is Jewish, yet Jews make up 80 percent of the country's professional comedians. Milton Berle, George Burns, David Brenner, Sid Caesar, Joan Rivers, David Steinberg, and Abe Burrows are all Jewish. The greatest state actress of all time, Sarah Bernhardt,[8] was Jewish.

---

[8] With regards to Hitler's comment that Jews "contaminate art, literature [and] the theater" we note that before he came to power in Germany, Max Rheinhardt reigned in the theater while Lotte Lehen, Joseph Zigeti and Arthur Schnabel, all Jews, were in the music headlines of the world. Modern American stage life was revolutionized by the Frohman and Shubert brothers, Abraham Erlander, and David Belasco. The Jews founded early experimental theaters, examples are: the theater Guild and the Group Theater. Plays of George S. Kaufman, Lillian Hellmand, Arthur Miller, Elmer Rice, Glivvord Odets, Sidney Kinglsley, and Irwin Shaw gained international recognition. Yesterdays American movie industry was practically founded by Jews. Most of it's best directors, actors and script writers have been Jews. The modern musical comedy became a world art form via the genius of Richard Rodgers and Oscar Hammerstein II. The tunes of Sigmund Romburg, Irvin Berlin, Jerome Kern and George Gershwin achieved semiclassical status. Benny Goodman made jazz respectable through Carnegie Hall. America won fame on the concert stages the world over through performances of such naturalized Jews as: pianists Alexander

"The Jews have been the world's foremost inventors. The microphone, the gramophone, and the internal combustion engine all originated in the mind of a Jew, Emile Berline. The calculating machine was invented by Abraham Stern. Herman Jones invented synthetic rubber. Petroleum, the basic energy source of the modern world, owes its discovery and distillation to Abraham Schreiner. Atomic research was largely the work of Jews, notably Michelin and Einstein, closely followed by J. Robert Opperheimer. Otto Lilenthal, a German Jew, made history's first successful attempts at glider flying, and his findings inspired the Wright brothers to go on and achieve fame. Marconi did not invent the radio; he simply exploited the work of a German Jew, Heinrich Hertz, who discovered the functions of radio waves. Alexander Graham Bell was not the first to invent the telephone; a German Jew, Johann Reis, was demonstrating a telephone in Europe years before Bell took out the patent on his.

"The Jews have not been the world's only benefactors, researchers, inventors and pioneers. The point is that, out of all proportion to their numbers, the Jews have put the world in their debt. Perhaps no book has done more to shape the

---

Brailowsky, Vladimir Horowitz and Arthur Rubenstein. Violinists Mischa Elman, Efrem Zimbalist, Jascha Heifetz, Isaac Stern and Nathan Milstein; and cellist Gregor Piatigorskyu. The world will never forget Serge Koussevitzky, conductor of the Boston Symphany Orchestra and founder of the Berkshire Festival. Jewish conductors Brumo Walter and Fritz Reiner are familiar to those who love classical music. As is U.S. born conductor Leonard Bernstein and violinist Yehudi Menuhin.

destinies of mankind than has the Bible, needless to say, was given to the world by God through Jews."[9]

Another Evangelical author, Grant Jeffrey, who loves Israel and is world famous, pointed out, only last year that, "Despite the small size of the Jewish population, the Jewish contribution to Western and Eastern society is unparalleled by any other comparably sized group. There are approximately six billion people alive in the world today. Of these, only eighteen million (less than one-half of 1 percent of the world's population) are Jews. There are hundreds of equally small population groups throughout the planet that are absolutely unknown to anyone but their closest neighbors.

"However, the contributions of the Jewish people to modern culture is overwhelming. A recent estimate calculated that more than 12 percent of the Nobel prizes have been awarded to Jews in the fields of medicine, mathematics, chemistry, and physics. The contribution of the Jewish people to the fields of arts, music, literature, and religious writing is outstanding in its quality and quantity....However, the greatest Jewish influence on the history of mankind came from the lives, teachings, and actions of two Jews—Moses and Jesus of Nazareth. The Jews are finally looking at the life and teachings of Jesus and acknowledging that His influence on the nations has been both powerful and beneficial. They

---

[9] John Phillips, *Exploring the World of the Jew*, Chicago: The Moody Bible Institute of Chicago, © 1981, pp. 121-2, 125-9, [ ] mine, used by permission.

realize that the terrible atrocities and persecutions of the medieval period and the Holocaust were not based on genuine Christianity but were a perversion of evil produced by sinful men who, by their actions, rejected the teachings of Jesus."[10]

With respect to Hitler's claim of the Jews ridiculing religion and morality and destroying the state through the creed of Marxism all I can say is that many of my Jewish friends and all Jews for Jesus i.e. My Messianic Jewish friends uphold ethics, despise Marxism and believe in biblical morals. There is no way you can say that **all** Jews are immoral Marxist and **all** non-Jews are ethical thinking moralist. The answer to the liberals who espouse Marxism, if you don't believe in Marxism, which I do not, is to vote them out of office at the poles, not kill the opposition, be they Jew or non-Jew. That is democracy! Moral conservatism can thrive through the people's democratic choice in the voting booth. However, Hitler is on record as despising democracy. On the subject of morality and the Jews we recall a comment made by the second[11] most famous Jew of the time ever to live, Albert Einstein, wrote, "The most important endeavor is the striving for morality in our actions. Our inner balance and even our very existence depend on it.

---

[10] Grant Jeffrey, *The Handwriting of God*, Toronto, Ontario: Frontier Publications, Inc., © 1997, p.187, used by permission.
[11] The first was Jesus.

Only morality in our actions can give beauty and dignity to life."[12]

---

[12]Alice Calaprice, ed., *The Quotable Einstein,* Princeton, New Jersey: Princeton University Press and The Hebrew University of Jerusalem, © 1996, p. 209, used by permission.

Regarding the Lord God, Einstein also said, " 'I believe in Spinoza's God who reveals himself in the harmony of all that exists'...[from a] telegram to a Jewish newspaper, 1929, Einstein Archive 33-272 (Spinoza reasoned that God and the material world are indistinguishable; the better one understands how the universe works, the closer one comes to God)." Ibid p. 147, [ ] mine.

Baruch de Spinoza was a Jewish philosopher of 17th century who believed in Jesus. See Chapter 13 of my book *The End of History- The Messiah Conspiracy* for further evidence.

In a letter dated September 2, 1945, Einstein wrote to his teacher, Oberlehrer Heinrach Friedmann, "I often read the Bible..." Abraham Pais, *Subtle Is The Lord, The Science and Life of Albert Einstein*, New York: Oxford University Press © 1996, used by permission.

Einstein's friend, Friedrich Dürrenmatt, also wrote, "Einstein was prone to talk about God so often that I was led to suspect he was a closet theologian." Friedrich Dürrenmat, *Albert Einstein: Ein Vortrag*, Zurich: Diogenes-Vertag Cop. © 1979 p. 12, used by permission.

Professor Popkin of UCLA enlightens us: "Einstein wept with joy when he heard [the evidence of Professor Yahuda's observations in Isaac Newton's astronomical calculations that proved] that one could establish the accuracy of the Bible on the basis of historical and philological research." James E. Force and Richard H. Popkin, eds. *Essays on the Context, Nature, and Influence of Isaac Newton's Theology*, Boston Kluwer Academic Publishers, © 1990, p. 112, bold mine, used by permission.

Einstein once told a news reporter: "I am a Jew, but I am enthralled by the luminous figure of the Nazarene....No one can read the Gospels without feeling the actual presence of Jesus. His personality pulsates in every word. No myth is filled with such life." *The Saturday Evening Post*, October 26, 1929.

Other interest of Einstein in God can be seen in his study of the planets and calculations of the orbit of Mercury. "The orbits of the planets are exact in a sense with the exception of Mercury–it's orbit shifts slightly every year. Martin Klein of Harvard University notes, "It's [the Mercury shift] a very small number previously totally unexplained now here on the basis of this theory which he [Einstein] had invented...out of his view of how God would have had to make the universe, to make it right, he's able to calculate

The Nazis made fun of Einstein and what they called "Jewish science" and "Jewish physics." For example one German author wrote in *German Physics*, "Jewish physics can best and most justly be characterized by recalling the activity of one who is probably its most prominent representative, the pure-blooded Jew, Albert Einstein. His relativity theory was supposed to transform all of physics, but when faced with reality it did not have a leg to stand on. In contrast to the intractable and solicitous desire for truth in the Aryan scientist, the Jew lacks to a striking degree any comprehension of truth." [13]

Einstein's special and general relativity theories have been strengthened and supported through experiments to the year of 1998 and I believe will continue. Leaonard's Nazi view of 1936 is the hilt of ignorance!

The Nazis burned Einstein's books and he received death threats from them which lead to his leaving Germany for the United States in 1932.

---

this very real small effect and get a right answer. That could give you palpitations." Video, *Einstein Revealed*, Nova, Boston, © 1996 [ ] mine.

Abraham Pais of Rockefellar University commented on his calculations saying, "**And I believe that at the moment Einstein said, 'I don't care what the world will say, I am right, because the Lord has told me—calculate the perihelion motion of Mercury and you will see,' and he did, and it came out.**" Ibid.

Einstein had said, "When I found that my calculations predicted the motion of Mercury exactly something snapped inside me, the feeling was so extreme, I couldn't work for days, I was beside myself. In all my life I never felt such joy." Ibid.

[13]"Philipp Lenard, *Deutsche Physik,* Munchen: JF Lihmann © 1936 p. 50, used by permission.

Einstein in Palestine (left) in 1923 promoting the Zionist cause (a Jewish return to create the state of Israel).

Hitler's remark on the ether (a hypothetical substance once supposed to occupy all space) intrigues us, in that the ether does not exist, yet it has not yet been removed from his book. Einstein was the first to propose this.[14] Because experiments showed that light was not slowed by this "ether" which was thought to blow by the earth (as it traveled around the sun) at a rate of 20 miles per second as an outer space wind that supposedly made light behave.

Einstein[15] convinced President Roosevelt to pursue the A-bomb. Had Hitler favored the Jew,

---

[14] Einstein wrote in his famed paper entitled, "The Electrodynamics of Moving Bodies" in 1905 that, "The introduction of a luminferous aether will prove to be superfluous."

[15] Very early on *Time* Magazine called Einstein, "The father of the bomb." *Time,* July 1, 1946 p. 52. He categorically denied this insisting that his part in it's discovery was indirect. To sumise his truthful claim and to illustrate how the bomb was developed in 1945 we note: In 1905 Einstein completed works on the quantum theory of light, which involved lights particle nature and his works on the existence of the atom. At that time he also applied his theory of special relativity involving time, space and motion, to mass & energy and concluded that the energy contained in a particular object is equal to it's mass times the speed of light squared. An unbelievable amount. This was expressed in his well known equation of $E=MC^2$ (Einstein realized that the mass of all matter is essentially energy in another form. In $E=MC^2$ the E stands for energy measured in ergs, M for mass in grams and C for the speed of light measured in centimeters per second. He understood that every pound of matter contained the energy of the exploding force of 14 million tons of TNT). Later on the basis of this equation it was realized by others that the possibility of release of this immense energy through the destruction of uranium 235 might be possible after chain reactions were discovered and correctly interpreted. On this premise the Atom bomb was sought by German scientists, in the 1930s.

Einstein said of the media's accusations which later included *Time* Magazine's statement quoted earlier, "I do not consider myself the

perhaps he would have beat us to the bomb and won the war. Hitler was truly the cause of his own destruction. If Hitler had taken what he read in the Bible seriously instead of claiming:

"It is a great pity that this tendency towards religious thought can find no better outlet than the Jewish pettifoggers of the Old Testament. For religious people who, in the solitude of winter, continually seek ultimate light on their religious problems with the assistance of the Bible, must eventually become spiritually deformed. The wretched people strive to extract truths from these Jewish chicaneries, where in fact no truth exist. As a result they become embedded in some rut...unless they posses an exceptionally common sense mind, degenerate into religious maniacs.

"It is **deplorable that the Bible should have been translated into German**, and that the whole

---

father of the release of atomic energy. My part in it was quite indirect. I did not, in fact, foresee that it would be released in my time. I believed only that release was theoretically possible. It became practical through the accidental discovery of chain reactions, and this was not something I could have predicted. It was discovered by Hahn in Berlin, and he himself misinterpreted what he discovered. It was Lisa Meitner who provided the correct interpretation..." "Einstein on the Atomic Bomb," *The Atlantic Monthly*, November 1945, p. 44. On August 12, 1945 Einstein told a *New York Times* Reporter, "I have done no work on [the Atomic bomb], no work at all."

In order to liberate atomic energy from matter, which Einstein's theory of relativity indicated existed therein the discovery of the neutron by James Chadwick (in 1932) was essential.

When accused that special relativity was the guilty party with respect to nuclear fission in the A-bomb Einstein wrote in a letter to Jules Isaac on February 28, 1955, "There was never even the slightest indication of any potential technological application."

of the German people should have thus become exposed to this **Jewish mumbo-jumbo**. So long as the wisdom, particularly of the Old Testament, remained exclusively in the Latin of the Church, there was little danger that sensible people would become the victims of illusions as the result of studying the Bible. But since the Bible became common property, a whole heap of people have found opened to them lines of religious thought which—particularly in conjunction with the German characteristic of persistent and somewhat melancholy meditation-as often as not turned them into religious maniacs....As a sane German, one is flabbergasted to think that German human beings could have let themselves be brought to such a pass by Jewish filth and priestly twaddle, and that they were little different from the howling dervish of the Turks and the Negroes, at whom we laugh so scornfully. It angers one to think that, while in other parts of the globe religious teaching like that of Confucius, Buddha and Mohammed offers an undeniably broad basis for the religious-minded, Germans should have been duped by a theological exposition devoid of all honest depth.

"When one seeks reasons for these phenomena, one is immediately struck by the extent to which the human brain reacts to external influence....we must do everything humanly possible to protect for all time any formity, regardless of whether it be religious mania or any other type of cerebral derangement."[16]

Hitler might have realized that the **Jewish** Messiah, Jesus, will be returning to bring peace and create a world free of war where harmony and true happiness will exist. However, Hitler saw himself as the strong man Savior Messiah of the German race and condemned himself to suicide and an eternity in Hell![17]

Hitler's goal was to conquer and rule the world. Jesus said, "For what is a man profited, if he shall gain the whole world, and lose his own soul? Or what shall a man give in exchange for his soul? For the Son of man shall come in the glory of his Father with his angels, and then he shall reward every man according to his works."[18]

In my 1200 page work, *The End of History-Messiah Conspiracy*, I show in great detail that despite history's leaders, hatred and persecution of the Jews and Israel, while no people is perfect, that God has an important purpose and plan for his

---

[16] H.R.Trevor Roper, *Hitler's Secret Conversations 1941-44,* New York: Farrar, Straus and Young Inc. © 1953, pp. 416-17, used by permission.

[17] Many liberal theologians and some Rabbis scoff at the concept of an eternal Hell. (See my work, *Nightmare of the Apocalypse*, Appendix 2- "The Reality of the Ancient Jewish Acknowledgment of Hell, Covered Up Until Now.") We ask ourselves, "What do these theologians want? Do they want Hitler to go free, with no eternal punishment for his millions of murders and the Jewish holocaust?" Reprehensible isn't the word. If you believe there is no Hell, think about it, you believe in Hitler going free, escaping for eternity?

[18] Matthew 16:26-27.

chosen people, whom we should value as our cherished friends.

In his dealings with his beloved chosen, the sons and daughters of Abraham, Isaac and Jacob, God will in the future bring forth the revelation of redemption and eternal life on this planet as the New Testament has foretold.

"For all creation is waiting patiently and hopefully for that future day when God will resurrect his children....For we know that even the things of nature, like animals and plants, suffer in sickness and death as they await this great event. And even we Christians, although we have the Holy Spirit within us as a foretaste of future glory, also groan to be released from pain and suffering. We, too, wait anxiously for that day when God will give us our full rights as his children, including the new bodies he has promised us—bodies that will never be sick again and will never die....Does this mean that God has rejected his Jewish people forever? Of course not! His purpose was to make his salvation available to the Gentiles, and then the Jews would be jealous and begin to want God's salvation for themselves. Now if the whole world became rich as a result of God's offer of salvation, when the Jews stumbled over it and turned it down, think how much greater a blessing the world will share in later on when the Jews, too, come to Christ....And how wonderful it will be when they become Christians

[Messianic believers in their Messiah]![19] When God turned away from them it meant that he turned to the rest of the world to offer his salvation; and now it is even more wonderful **when the Jews come to Christ. It will be like dead people coming back to life**. And since Abraham and the prophets are God's people, their children will be too. For if the roots of the tree are holy, the branches will be too....I want you to know about this truth from God, dear brothers, so that you will not feel proud and start bragging. Yes, it is true that some of the Jews have set themselves against the Gospel now, but this will last only until all of you Gentiles have come to Christ—those of you who will. And then all Israel will be saved. Do you remember what the prophets said about this? 'There shall come out of Zion a Deliverer....' " (The New Testament book of Romans 8:19-23; 11:11-12, 15-16, 25-26 *The Living Bible,* [ ] mine).

I believe this beautiful biblical description of God's earth in redemption may occur before the year 2040.

---

[19]*The Living Bible* beautifully simplifies the more difficult renderings of certain English translations of the New Testament. However, when it says Christians, it may confuse some Jews who do not realize that the word Christian does not designate a religion foreign to Judaism. This word is derived from the Greek *Christos*, which means "Messiah"—in Hebrew *Meshiak*—which the Jewish Bible (our Old Testament) predicts of our true faith. *Ian* simply means "one who follows Christ," i.e., Messiah!

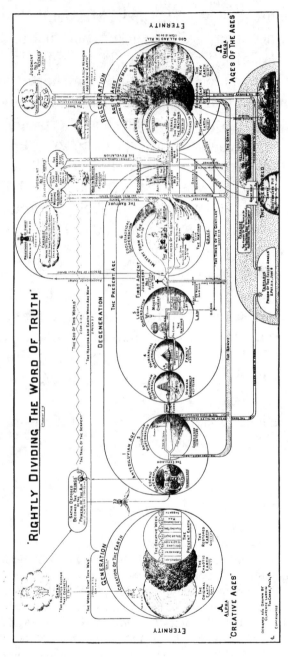

Courtesy Clarence Larkin Estate.

"The **heaviest blow** that ever struck humanity **was the coming of Christianity**...evolution[1] was in the natural order of things." [2]

ADOLF HITLER, 1941

"Was it not the Germans who when the Roman Empire **had been rotted inwardly by Jewish Christianity** and a declining population, had conquered and inherited it? The Germanic Middle Ages had indeed been frustrated by the "Christian" Renaissance, the rise of the plutocratic capitalist civilization of Western Europe but now that that plutocratic capitalist civilization was in its turn decaying, might not the German reawaken and, awakened, resume and redirect their splendid mission? The old German Emperors, for good technical reasons, had looked south to Italy; the new German Reich, for similar reasons, must look east. Might it not, even now, by some heroic effort, wrest from the Russians their dominion and impose upon the Heartland a German instead of a Russian Empire? It is true, the Russians were more numerous; but had not minorities often before, by skill and determination, conquered and enslaved great nations?... Christianity, with its disgusting equalitarianism, would be exterminated.....he [Hitler] had also read *The Protocols of the Elders of Zion*,[3] the intellectual justification of his anti-Semitism, and Houston Stewart Chamberlain's *Foundations of the Nineteenth Century*, the avowed and recognizable basis of his racial doctrines." [4]

Oxford scholar, H. TREVOR ROPER, 1953

Hitler considered civilization "rotted by **Jewish Christianity**" because it's biblical principles of free capital and high morals allowed people to rule themselves and to be free without an elite dictatorship. Since Hitler saw national socialism as the elite ruling aristocracy of the world to come, with himself at the helm as it's Führer, is it any wonder he hated our form of government-democracy based on Judeo Christian values. Dismissing his statement falsely connecting Bolshevism with Christianity we emphasize that the Jew and his second coming Messiah, the hope and promise of "Jewish Christianity" will indeed be the answer to all of the present woos of Christianity and this certainly is not more than 40 years from our time.   PHILIP MOORE, 1998

APPENDIX 3
HITLER'S ATOMIC BOMB ALMOST ELIMINATED THE JEW FROM THE EARTH

An A&E segment of *Biography*, hosted by Peter Graves, entitled "The Fatal Attraction of Adolf

---

[1] See my work, *The End of History- Messiah Conspiracy*, Appendix 3, for supporting evidence indicating evolution is untrue.

[2] H.R. Trevor-Roper, Introductory Essay on the Mind of Adolf Hitler to *Hitler's Secret Conversations 1941-44*, pp. 6-7, underline mine, used by permission.

[3] To better understand this forged Anti-Jewish document and how Hitler used it to ride to power through creating nation wide hatred of the Jews, see our Appendix 5.

[4] Introduction to Ibid p. XVII, XIX, XXV, underline mine.

Hitler" which aired on November 13, 1991 interviewed a member of the Hitler youth, Wilhem Huebner, who was patted on his cheek by Hitler only days before he committed suicide in his Berlin bunker. Huebner was asked, "Didn't you realize at the time that the war was lost?" His answer was, "No, not at all, we boys still fought and we heard **rumors** that the Führer somehow had **a secret weapon** in reserve."

This author believes this "secret weapon" was the Atomic[5] bomb. It was first exploded in a U.S. test on July 16, 1945 near Alamogordo, New Mexico,[6] only ten weeks after Hitler died. The bomb was kept from his hand because of our allied, clandestin bombing of his heavy water plant in Norway. This delayed his developing the bomb before we did. This was, until recently, one of the best kept secrets of modern history. No one, it would seem, wanted to admit just how close Hitler came to conquering earth and destroying the Jewish people.

* * *

---

[5] The Greek term atoms ατομος (meaning "that which can not be cut") since the innovation of the atom bomb, whereby atoms are split, is now proven false. The neutron, a chargless particle which was unknown to the Greeks, is not repelled by the atom thus it enters with ease. Once inside it splits the atom and atomic energy is released.

[6] On August 6 "the little boy" Atomic bomb was dropped on Hiroshima and August 9 "the fat man" Atomic bomb destroyed Nagasaki.

The Japanese present gifts at the signing of the tripartite pact between Germany, Italy and Japan.

As this manuscript was in the final stages of being readied for publication, a friend of mine, G. A. Bennett, informed me of a recent book entitled, *Japan's Secret War- Japan's Race Against Time to Build it's Own Atomic Bomb*. It's author, Robert Wilcox, has used the freedom of information act to obtain U.S. government files which proved Hitler and Japan were near completion of the bomb and that only days before Germany surrendered in May 1945, a German U-boat (U-234) left Hamberg carrying large portions of heavy water and uranium (see page 156 *Japan's Secret War*). The boat was to dock in Japan and it's contents were to be quickly assembled and used to secure a Japanese/German victory at the end of WWII. On the back cover of Wilcox' book, Lawrence McQuillan of UPI commented, "In a fascinating look at what **might have been**, Robert Wilcox details just how close Japan came to successfully building an Atomic bomb of its own and radically altering world history."[7]

Lieutenant General Takeo Yasuda, the Director of Japan's Army Airforce Technical Research Institute Research, has said, regarding the joint Nazi Japanese bomb project, "Japan is a small country, so it is limited. We cannot make as many airplanes as America. So we cannot win the war by doing the same things as she does. To win a war, we needed something special, like an Atomic bomb."[8]

* * *

---

[7] Robert Wilcox, *Japan's Secret War- Japan's Race Against Time To Build It's Own Atomic Bomb*, New York: Marlowe & Co. © 1995 p. back cover, bold mine.
[8] Ibid, p.52.

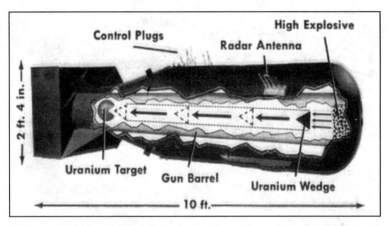

The "Little Boy" Atomic bomb obliterated Hiroshima, Japan August 6, 1945. Over 93,000 persons were dead on impact. At the end of that year deaths totaled 140,000.

Hiroshima after the blast.

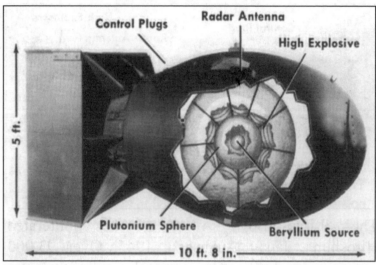

The "Fat Man" Atomic bomb demolished Nagasaki, Japan, August 9, 1945. Over 41,000 persons were killed.

Nagasaki

Crater blasted by a Hydrogen bomb in the Nevada dessert in 1962. In the hydrogen device an Atomic bomb is used to detonate the H-bomb. The first atomic bomb dropped on Japan destroyed four square miles. However, the cloud of the H-bomb after the explosion spans more than 100 miles.

In 1954 the U.S. test detonated a twelve megaton[9] Hydrogen bomb called the "Bravo" which showered down radio active fallout over an area of 7,000 miles. This bomb had an explosive force 1,000 times greater than the Atomic bomb that destroyed Hiroshima. A bomb like this could easily exterminate over 100 million people if used in a well populated area.

---

[9] Megaton means millions of tons of TNT.

In 1961 the Russians[10] exploded a 58 megaton Hydrogen weapon which made the "Bravo" look like child's play. China and France followed with the H-bomb testing in 1967-68.

Production of Hydrogen weapons quickly followed the advent of the Atomic ones because they required Atomic force to be detonated.

One can only imagine what would have happened if Hitler had become the first with the bomb as his scientist[11] were so close to it as we will

---

[10]Emile Klaus Fuchs, a German scientist, who participated in the research of thermal nuclear weapons admitted, "He had transmitted classified information to the Soviet Union." Colliers Encyclopedia, Volume 17, New York, NY: © 1997, P.F. Collier, A division of New Field, Pub., Inc. p. 756, used by permission..

Fuchs, having given critical atomic secrets to the Russians, "....was not Jewish He was a member of the Communist party at Kiel University," Toney Hey and Patrick Walters, *Einstein's Mirror,* New York, NY: Cambridge University Press © 1997, p. 157, used by permission.

Hey and Walters also pointed out that "In 1933 he arrived in England and became Nevill Mott's first Ph.D. student in Bristol. He was recruited by Peierls for the British bomb program, and followed Peierls to Los Alamos. From 1942 to 1950 Fuchs passed on very detailed information, not only about the uranium and plutonium bombs, but also about the 'Super'-Teller's hydrogen bomb project....Joe-I, the first Russian atomic bomb exploded in 1949, was a direct copy of [America's] Fat Man [Atomic bomb]." Ibid. p. 158 [ ] mine.

[11] The 1997 edition of *Collier's Encyclopedia* notes of this "As early as 1934, the American Association for the Advancement of Science discussed the possibility of making nuclear weapons. However, at that time, Einstein himself doubted the possibility of initiating a chain reaction by which large amounts of energy might be released.

In 1939, the key to the problem was found **by four scientists working in Berlin, Otto Hahn, Lise Meitner, Fritz Strassmann, and Otto Frisch**. [These were Jews, Meitner was a Jewish Christian.] They found, that a neutron, when introduced into a uranium nucleus by radioactive bombardment, split the nucleus into two nuclei, barium and krypton, with a very great release of energy." *Collier's Encyclopedia* Volume 17, p. 753 [ ] and bold mine.

show. Hitler, of course, would not have allowed anyone else to develop similar weapons (which could be used against him) and would have exercised ultimate power over the world for the rest of his life. In a 1991 PBS documentary entitled, *Albert Einstein- How I See The World,* Eugene Wigner of Einstein College commented, "We were very worried that the Germans will develop atomic weapons. We wanted therefore to interest the United States to develope nuclear weapons so that Hitler should not be the only one to possess them."[12]

After 1939 Nuclear scientist involved in the early innovations of the A-bomb were brought to the United States. Among them were: Enrico Fermi of Italy, Niels Bohr of Denmark and Leo Szilard, Eugene Wigner and Edward Teller of Hungary. These scientists, as well as many Americans in this field, were impressed by the discovery of Hahn, Meitner, Strassmann, and Frisch, and they understood immediately the possibilities of exploiting it to create a nuclear weapon. The first overtures for U.S. Government support were made by Fermi to the Navy Department, but Navy officials showed little interest. **The Germans had grasped the implications of the fission discovery and had launched an intensive study of the subject.** In July 1939 several scientists prevailed on Einstein to write a letter to President Franklin D. Roosevelt, pointing out that the nuclear chain reaction made a nuclear bomb theoretically possible. Roosevelt set up a committee to look into the matter. The committee confirmed the potential of nuclear weapons and recommended that further research be supported by government funds." Ibid. p. 754.

[12] "Albert Einstein - How I See The World," a production of VIP Video Film Producers Ltd. and Lumen Productions in association with WNET/13 © 1991, VIP Film Producers International Ltd. English is Wigner's.

The ships at the base of this underwater atomic test explosion show its proportional size.

Hitler would have had time to set up crematoria and gas chambers world wide and exterminate the Jews and vast segments of "the inferior races," all but the Aryan people, as was his plan. His political ideal was "a world without Jews." Believe it or not, plans before Hitler's death were already being implemented to exterminate the Jews in the Middle East. Gas chambers and crematoria were under construction in that part of the world. Mufti Haja Amir Le-Husseini (cousin of today's Arafat) had met with Hitler and anticipated his break through to the Middle East. For details read the rare book, *The Mufti and The Führer*, by Joseph B. Schecktman. On page 207 of this book a letter of Freiherr Von Weizsaeeker written at the request of Hitler to the Mufti is reproduced. Part of it reads, "The Germans and the Arabs have common enemies in...the Jews; and are united to fight against them."

Mufti Haj Amin al-Husseini & Adolf Hitler in 1941.

HEAVY WHAT? ATOMIC!

In April of 1996 Prime Minster Peres of Israel, after being briefed on intelligence, regarding Arab endeavors to obtain advanced nuclear weapons made the statement, "It is the first time in history that an evil and malicious movement, covered by a religious lining, may acquire these terrible weapons. Imagine what would have happened if Hitler had a nuclear bomb."[13]

---

[13] ABC News Magazine, *Night Line,* April 29, 1996. This statement was made in response to a comment that Colonel Quadafi made

It is often overlooked that if we had not located and kept destroying Hitler's heavy water plant and heavy water shipments,[14] Hitler probably would have developed and assembled the bomb before the U.S.

Einstein in an August 2nd letter of 1939 to Roosevelt noted that Germany had "stopped the sale of uranium." Our point is had Hitler beat us to the bomb we would all be speaking German today—those of us left that is.

Just imagine having a few Hiroshima type A-bombs exploding in America. We would have had to surrender! Hitler would have confiscated our wealth, **murdered our Jewish citizens** and occupied the United States for—who knows how long? Is it any wonder why Albert Einstein wrote, "When I signed that letter to President Roosevelt advocating that the atomic bomb should be built...we all felt that there was a high probability that the **Germans...might** succeed and use the atomic bomb **to become the master race**."[15]

Professor Tony Haye and Patrick Walter, in their 1997 book, *Einstein's Mirror,* documented that,

---

regarding recent Arab endeavors to obtain the bomb with the intention of using it on Israel.

In the 1997 edition of *Collier's Encyclopedia*, it was noted that, "Inspections carried out by the United Nations Special Commission and the IAEA in Iraq after the end of the Persian Gulf War (1990-1991) revealed that Iraq...was within two to three years of having an operational nuclear weapon." Ibid. p. 757.

[14] Heavy water—D_2O—deuterium oxide, is an essential ingredient for the atomic bomb in that it acts as a modulator to control the energy of the neutrons in a chain reaction.

[15] Quoted from a letter to Linus Pauling which was recorded in Pauling's diary, bold mine.

"......the U.S. bomb program had stagnated in bureaucracy and committees. Perhaps because the threat of Nazi domination seemed more real to them, it was two physicist refugees in England who made the crucial next step. At Birmingham University in March 1940, Otto Frisch asked Rudolf Peierls the question: 'Suppose someone gave you a quantity of pure 235 isotope of uranium–what would happen?' Peierls had developed a formula to calculate critical masses, so they put in the numbers for U235. They were amazed at how small a mass was needed:

"We estimate the critical size to be about a pound, whereas speculations concerned with natural uranium had tended to come out with tons'....Could such a chain reaction lead to an explosion?...The chain reaction has to proceed very quickly, otherwise the pressure caused by the fissioning atoms will push the uranium atoms too far apart for the chain reaction to continue. Peierls made a rough estimate...assuming that fast neutrons also caused U235 to fission. His calculation showed that some eighty links of the chain would be generated before the pressure blew the uranium apart. This meant that a pound or so of uranium would release the equivalent energy of thousands of tons of ordinary explosive–the kiloton bomb had arrived. They were in awe of their own results. Separation of tons of U235 was not a practical proposition: separation of a few pounds was....Frisch and Peierls wrote up their discoveries in a two-part report, known later as the 'Frisch-Peierls Memorandum.' Since they did not dare give it to a secretary, Peierls had to type the report himself. The memorandum is an amazingly farsighted document, with the second, less technical part written in such direct and simple language that not even the politicians or the military could fail to grasp its message. After pointing out that the explosion would be large enough to destroy 'the center of a big city,' the authors went on to explain the implications of the radioactive contamination such a bomb would cause.

"Peierls and Frisch ended their report with a bleak warning about a possible German bomb:

" 'Since the separation of the necessary amount of uranium is, in the most favorable circumstances, a matter of several months, it would obviously be too late to start production when such a bomb is known to be in the hands of Germany, and the matter seems, therefore, very urgent.' "

"Frisch and Peierls were right to be worried. After the war was over, it was discovered that in December 1939, Heisenberg had written a report for the German War Office in which he concluded that 'enriched uranium' with more than the normal percentage of U235 was 'the only method of producing explosives several orders of magnitude more powerful than the strongest explosives yet known.' "[16]

Hey and Walters also note that: "Kurt Diebner of the German Army ordnance said...'It was the elimination of the heavy water production in Norway that was the main factor in our failure to

---

[16] Toney Hey and Patrick Walters, *Einstein's Mirror,* New York, NY: Cambridge University Press © 1997, pp. 154-56, used by permission.

achieve a self-sustaining atomic reactor before the war ended.' "[17]

In Anthony Cave Brown's book, *Bodyguard of Lies*, published by Bantam the cover is prefaced, "The never-before story of allied espionage in World War II. The hidden war of spies, code-breakers and double-agents—The **secrets** of the **greatest clandestine operation in history**... revealed for the first time in this truly extraordinary bestseller."

The hidden story of Hitler's heavy water storage plant in Norway is told. Had Hitler's plant not been disabled and his heavy water not destroyed (as it was being shipped for completion of his A-bomb) by the allied underground there would be no Jew on earth today. There would solely exist a pagan Aryan race and the Old and New Testament would have been shown to be untrue, in that God's promises of Jewish preservation would have failed.

The book tells us that, "....the Allies had not ignored the possibility that the **Germans might possess** the war's one decisive weapon—**the atomic bomb**. Would Hitler be able to unleash an atomic bomb on, or even before, D-Day? No one in London or Washington really knew. It was theoretically possible; the Germans were known to be advanced in nuclear fission; in 1939 they had begun a vigorous program to build such a weapon. At the same time, British intelligence undertook a vigorous program of it's own to discover the nature and extent of German research, and to look for the means, if possible, to neutralize it. There was as an

---

[17] Ibid. p. 152.

extreme urgency to MI-6's task, and the way in which it was performed would become one of the most remarkable feats of the war.

"The first 'break' for MI-6 came in 1939 when the Oslo Report revealed that the Germans were, in fact, actively engaged in atomic research. Then it was discovered that their research was dependent upon the use of heavy water—deuterium oxide, which required enormous amounts of electrical power to make, and was being produced only at the Vemork plant in Rjukan, a small town under the Hardanger plateau of South Norway. With the conquest of Norway, the Germans had taken possession of the plant and gained easy access to its production of heavy water.

"Menzies and his service had little technical knowledge of the eerie subject of atomic physics, save that it might breed the deadliest weapon the world had ever known. But if there was a weak link in the Germans' research and development program, it was in Norway. Therefore, Menzies put Lieutenant Commander Eric Welsh, the chief of the Norwegian country section of MI-6, in charge of the intelligence attack. Welsh was an officer with a considerable layman's knowledge of science, and he had an even greater knowledge of Norway. He had managed a chemicals and paint factory there for several years and had married a Norwegian. He knew the geography of Rjukan, he knew many of the personalities there, and in his mind's eye he knew how men might be got in to blow the place up.

"The need for an attack became acute when, in October 1941, the "Princes"—the underground secret intelligence service in Denmark—sent a telegram to MI-6 saying that Niels Bohr, the Danish physicist who was something of a confessor to the international scientific fraternity engaged in atomic research, had received a visitor from Germany, **Professor Werner Heisenberg, a leading figure in the German program to develop the atomic bomb, had come to ask** Bohr a very difficult question. **Was it morally correct**, Heisenberg wished to know, **for a physicist to engage in the construction of such an absolute weapon,** even in wartime? Bohr responded with a question of his own. Did Heisenberg mean to imply that the Germans believed such a weapon to be feasible? Heisenberg said, sadly, that such was the case. The conversation left Bohr deeply shocked; he warned the Princes and they warned London. He was, said Bohr, convinced that **Germany was on the threshold of obtaining the atomic bomb,** and that belief was sufficient to compel London to take decisive action.

"MI-6 turned to Professor Lief Tronstad, a chemist in his late thirties who had helped build the heavy water plant it Rjukan. Tronstad had become chief of the Norwegian government-in-exile's Section IV—the secret service—and under him there was an agent who was a native of Rjukan, Einar Skinnerland. On March 29, 1942, Skinnerland was parachuted onto the wild and desolate Hardanger plateau above Rjukan to establish an intelligence post. He soon made contact with the Vemork plant's chief engineer, Jomar Brun; and Brun reported that the Germans were increasing the plant's production of heavy water. Skinnerland transmitted that information to London by secret writing through Stockholm, and he was then instructed to obtain detailed drawings and photographs of the plant, together with the surrounding countryside. With Brun's help, he gathered the necessary information, microphotographed it and smuggled it out in a tube of toothpaste to Stockholm. When it reached London it was carefully studied at MI-6, and Menzies approached the Joint Intelligence Committee with a proposition that the Vemork plant be destroyed as a matter of urgency. The JIC agreed, and plans were made for what came to be called 'Operation Freshman.'

"It was a bold operation. Two teams of paratroopers—forty men in all—were to land by gliders on the Hardanger plateau, and from Skinnerland's base, they were to storm and destroy the Rjukan plant in a swift and violent *coup de main.* Freshman's advance party landed as planned on October 18, 1942, just as Brun arrived in Britain after a fugitive's journey from Rjukan to Stockholm, where he was hidden in the bomb bay of a Mosquito and flown to London. He gave the Freshman teams a personal briefing on the weather, the German guards, the positions of the machine-gun posts, and the best routes down from the plateau into the gorge where the Vemork plant sat on an outcrop over a deep and powerful stream. But the Freshman teams would never reach the plant. Their gliders crashlanded in heavy weather over Norway. The survivors were quickly rounded up by German ski patrols, the injured were killed, and the rest, after interrogation, were shot, although they were in British army uniform. The Germans realized that the paratroopers' target was the heavy water plant at Rjukan. The result was inevitable; defenses were strengthened around the plant.

"There was considerable despair in London at the failure of Freshman. But the plant could not be left intact; its destruction was an imperative, and Colonel Jack Wilson, the chief of SOE's Norwegian country section, was authorized to mount a second attack—'Gunnerside.' The operation was well planned; from Brun's data, a large model was built not only of the plat but also of the surrounding terrain. Wilson selected his men from among volunteers from the Royal Norwegian Army. Their training was lengthy and thorough, and to ensure that none but the principals knew about Gunnerside, the men practiced at Station 17, a special training school in Scotland which had been cleared of all other agents. Their main target would be the eighteen stainless steel high-concentration cells at the Vemork plant, and the plan called for the Gunnerside party to land to a reception by the 'Swallows'—the new code name for the team that had preceded Freshman. But the condition of the Swallows was not short of desperate. They had gone to ground on the Hardanger plateau—an area of inaccessible terrain, mountain peaks, grinding glaciers, precipices, marshes, swamps, impassable streams—after the Freshman fiasco. They had long since exhausted their food; severe storms made it impossible for the RAF to parachute supplies, and the deep snow made it unusually difficult to live off the land. Yet Gunnerside could not succeed without the Swallows.

"Gunnerside was launched on February 16, 1943, although no one was sure what the men would find when they were parachuted in near Kkrykenvann, about 28 miles across country from the Swallows' hideout. The party landed safely, and at first the weather was in their favor; the squalls, which could lift men from their feet and hurl them bodily across the frozen snow, had died down. Then a blizzard broke out and delayed their progress, but finally, as they approached Lake Kalungsjå, they sighted two of the Swallows. They looked like the men in the famous painting of Scott's last march through the Antarctic; and their condition was not so very different. Their long ragged beards were hung with icicles, the cold had made deep splits in their skin, they could barely hobble with frostbite—but they were alive.

"The men holed up in the Swallows' hideout, and by the late afternoon of February 26—a Friday—the Gunnerside party had moved forward to take up position in two woodsmen's huts on a hillside just north of Rjukan. From there they planned their attack. It was decided that the only way to get into the plant without alerting the guards was to descend into the gorge below the lip of the plateau, cross the swollen and semi-frozen torrent in the bed of the gorge, and then climb the 500-foot face to the outcrop on which the heavy water plant had been built—a formidable physical feat.

"The following evening the attack party skied to the lip of the plateau and began the descent into the gorge. The night was filled with the hum of the plant's turbines; and this, together with a rising wind, muffled their way to the bottom of the gorge. They crossed the stream, began the difficult climb up the other side, and finally reached a ledge about 400 yards from the plant. Threading through a minefield and staying out of sight of the German sentries, they found a basement door; two men got into the factory through a cable duct which Brun had described, unlocked the door and let the rest of the party in. They detained the only workman in the plant that Sunday morning—a Norwegian. Then they laid the charges on all eighteen cells which helped produce the heavy water.

"By 1 a.m. Gunnerside had finished its work; the fuses had been set and started. The men told the Norwegian workman to find a place of safety on one of the upper floors; and then they withdrew, scrambling down into the gorge and crossing the stream. As they began the climb on the other side, the charges exploded and the Germans woke up to the noise of the blast and the wail of an air-raid siren. Not a shot had been fired. The Germans never saw the Gunnerside attackers, who melted into the darkness and would escape on a 250-mile march across the Hardanger plateau into Sweden. But each one of the cells had been blown up and almost a ton of heavy water had been destroyed.

"When the results of the attack were analyzed in London, it was predicted that the German production of heavy water would be delayed by two years. As it was, the plant was restored by April of that same year and toward the end of 1943 the Germans were again able to begin tapping heavy water. By that time Niels Bohr was in London. He had been spirited away from Copenhagen by MI-6 with the aid of the Princes and he again warned of the dangers of a German atomic bomb. One November 16, 1943, the American high command ordered the 8th Air Force to make another attack on the Rjukan plant. Over seven hundred 500-pound bombs rained down upon the target and while the plant escaped, sufficient damage was done to the power system to make further production of heavy water impossible for some time. With that, Goering, who was the minister responsible for the German atomic program, deduced the time had come to evacuate the Vemork installations to Germany.

"News of the decision was quickly in London. On November 30, 1943, Einar Skinnerland, SOE's principal agent in Norway, radioed from his base at telmark that Vemork was to be evacuated to Germany. When this intelligence was examined at a meeting in London, it was decided that because Germany's available hydroelectric power was so limited and costly, the evacuation of the plant would present no immediate danger to the Allies. But there would be danger if the Germans successfully evacuated their existing stocks of heavy water. Skinnerland was instructed to make developments at Vemork his primary target.

"At the end of January 1944, Skinnerland was able to wireless that the heavy water consignment was ready for shipment to Germany. There were 14 tons of fluid and 613 kilograms of heavy water in various stages of concentration; the Germans had drawn off the lot and sorted it for shipment in thirty-nine drums stenciled with the words 'Potash Lye.' More-over, Skinnerland reported, the consignment and the route over which it was to be shipped were being guarded by special squads of Feldgrau and SS. London wirelesses back to inquire about the opportunities for preventing the shipment. But Skinnerland replied that if the British intended to do anything militarily they would have to act quickly; he had heard that the heavy water was to begin its journey from Rjuken in seven days. SOE acted hurriedly. Knut Haukelid, a member of Gunnerside who had remained behind in Norway, and Skinnerland were instructed to attack and destroy the shipment.

"....How could the heavy water be destroyed? Larsen thought it would be vulnerable to attack at only one point. The Germans, he revealed, intended to transport the heavy water in railway wagons from the plant down to the rail-ferry that crossed Lake Tinnsjö to Tinnoset. There, it would proceed by rail and road to Heröya for loading onto the ship for Germany, particularly deep—1300 feet at one point—and if the ferry was sunk, the cargo could never be salvaged. Larsen agreed to arrange it so the heavy water would be ready for shipment only in time to catch the ferry on Sunday morning, February 20, a day when it would be less crowded with Norwegian civilians than at any other time in the week; and Haukelid agreed to help Larsen escape to avoid certain execution for his part in the conspiracy....Haukelid calculated...that he would need 18 pounds of *plastique* shaped into a sausage

12 feet long. This he made, and put it into a sack. He also made two fuses with ordinary alarm clocks, tested one, found it worked, and then he and his men retired to their mountain hideout.

"Meanwhile, both London and Berlin were taking extraordinary steps, the former to make sure that the heavy water did not reach Germany, the latter to see that it did. SOE wirelesses a second group in Norway, 'Chaffinch,' to attack the consignment if it got as far as Heröya. The RAF was ordered to lay on a mission to sink the ship taking the heavy water across to Germany—if the consignment got that far. At the same time an SS police company was moved to Rjukan, a squadron of Fieseler Storch reconnaissance aircraft was sent from Himmler's Special Air Group to fly anti-ambush patrols, and a large army detachment was assigned to guard the heavy water during its journey. SD agents detected that some plan was afoot to destroy the consignment; but they were not sure how and where the attack would be made. In consequence, the Germans decided to mount a special guard from Vemork down to the lake and, when the *Hydro* reached the far side, to split the shipment into two halves and send them by different routes and methods. Oddly, they undertook no precautions of a special nature aboard the *Hydro* itself.

"At 11 p.m. on February 19, the night before the consignment was to arrive, Haukelid and two of his men went down to the quay and boarded the *Hydro*; the boat was alongside overnight and her crew was having a party. There were no German guards aboard, but there were Norwegian watchmen. One of them stopped Haukelid and his companions as they entered the passenger saloon, but Haukelid explained that they were on the run from the Gestapo and asked for his help. The watchmen showed them the door into the binges, and Haukelid went down with one of his men, leaving the other to guard the door. Once in the bilge's, they made their way along the flat bottom to the bow, and there, deep in filthy water, they laid the charge with an electric detonator and timed the fuse. By 4 a.m. that morning the job was finished, and Haukelid and his men left the Hydro. If all went well, at 10:45 the following morning the Hydro and its cargo would be on the bottom of Lake Tinnsjö.

"Haukelid collected Larsen and the two men immediately began their flight, traveling by car and skis to Kongsberg, where they would board a train for the first stage of their journey to Sweden. Just as they were buying their tickets, the train from Oslo pulled in and the SS police chief of Rjukan, a certain Muggenthaler, stepped out. He had been called back from a weekend in the capital to superintend the movement of the heavy water.

"At 8 a.m. that Sunday—February 20, 1944—the ferry train left the Rjukan sidings with two wagons laden with drums containing the heavy water. Guards were posted at 30 yard intervals on either side of the track, and the Fieseler Storchs flew overhead. The train itself was guarded by SS men, and Muggentaaler rode on the locomotive by 10 a.m. the wagons had been anchored to the *Hydro's* deck, and the ferry set out on schedule with fifty-three

people aboard. Then, exactly at 10:45 a.m., the ferry
shuddered under the impact of a violent "knock.'
The exploding *plastique* ripped a hole in the *Hydro*,
and it began to settle by the bow...Within five
minutes the *Hydro* had sunk....With that explosion,
Germany's hopes of building an atomic bomb in
time for use in the Second World War ended. It was
a major triumph for Britain in the secret war. For as
Dr. Kurt Diebner, one of the main figures in the
Reich's research and development program,
acknowledged after the war, '...it was the
**elimination of German heavy water production
in Norway** that was the main factor in our failure to
achieve **a self-sustaining atomic reactor before
the war ended**.' The Allies had knocked out one
potential threat to the success of D-Day and even to
the eventual outcome of the war, although that fact
would not become known..."[18]

Hitler would continue to attempt to obtain the
necessary amount of heavy water and to build[19] his

---

[18] Anthony Cave Brown, *Bodyguard of Lies,* New York, NY: Bantam
Books, © 1975, pp. 370-77, used by permission, bold mine.

[19] A few days before Hitler committed suicide he launched a German U-
boat from Hamburg loaded with uranium and heavy water, which was
to dock in Japan. Japan had been working on the Atomic bomb in
conjunction with Hitler. Though this has been kept from the world's
eye, until Robert Wilcox published his book, *Japan's Secret War-
Japan's Race Against Time To Build Its Own Atomic Bomb*, in 1995.

In this book Wilcox used secret FBI documents he obtained
through The Freedom of Information Act to prove the claim of his title.
Of course Truman was briefed on Japan's progress and this was the real
reason he hit Japan twice, until they surrendered. On the back cover of
Wilcox' book, the *Washington Post* commented, "Truman...must have
been aware of Japan's nuclear capability as he deliberated about using
an American Atomic bomb." The *Washington Times* commented,

atomic bomb, until the day he learned his bunker would soon be under siege, though this would be unknown to most for decades. Fearful of the Russians capturing him alive and possible public mutilation of his body thereafter, he ordered his body burned and shot himself in the head little more than a day before his hideout was penetrated.

The question remains, What if Hitler had not turned against Stalin and the Russians who we will show from new findings were also murdering Jews. Would this have bought him the time he needed to beat America to the bomb? The answer would certainly seem a resounding 'yes!'

The "Fat Man" Atomic bomb, a day before it's fatal flight to Japan.

"...had Japan developed the bomb first, they would have used it ruthlessly." Ibid.

Jews pray at the Western Wall in Jerusalem.

Jerusalem—the eternal home of the Jew.

"Can you give me one single irrefutable proof of God?"
"Yes, your Majesty, the Jews."
                    MARQUIS D'ARGENS to Frederick the Great, 1779

APPENDIX 4
WHAT IF HITLER HAD
NOT TURNED AGAINST STALIN?
WHAT WOULD RUSSIA HAVE DONE?

A mid-1994 ABC television broadcast entitled, "What Really Happened to Adolf Hitler?" revealed that: "Stalin was obsessed with Hitler and had maintained a secret and jealously-guarded collection of Hitler's personal belongings. On his death bed, Stalin ordered that they be locked away forever...."[1]

In this broadcast, they displayed, for the first time, photographs of Stalin's collection of Hitler's personal effects. These included Hitler's watercolor paintings, his V.I.P. guest book, his boots, his

---

[1]"What Really Happened to Adolf Hitler?" June 13, 1994. Researchers: Klaas Jan Hindriks and Charles Barrand. Field producer: Walter Siegers. Executive in charge of production: David R. O'Dell. Senior series executive: J. Nicoll Durrie. © 1994, ABC/Kane Productions International, Inc. All rights reserved.

walking stick emblazoned with Nazi symbols, his violin with a carving of his head on the handle, and his dinner jacket.

Dutch journalist, Klaas Jan Hindriks said: "This is the first time in their [the Soviet authorities] life that they feel free to speak out. They never could do so out of fear. All those guys had pledged a solemn oath never to reveal what happened...."[2]

Klaas went on to emphasize that today, they are "for the very first time,"[3] coming clean.

The narrator continued: "General Michael Millstein was Deputy Head of Military Intelligence in the Soviet Army's Berlin operation....Hitler and Stalin had not always been enemies, but in 1941, eighteen months after signing a 'non-aggression treaty' with the Soviet leader, Hitler launched a treacherous and brutal surprise invasion of the Soviet Union."[4] General Michael Millstein said: "Stalin, I have always been certain, thought of Hitler as his ally. I'm sorry if you don't like what **I'm saying**. Stalin was certain he could accomplish great tasks with Hitler's support; with his ideas, his power, his army, his potential. Then **he hoped** the two of them would rule **the world together**."[5] The narrator concluded: "Stalin's failed ambition turned into an obsession for personal revenge on Adolf Hitler...."[6]

---

[2]Ibid. [ ] mine.
[3] Ibid.
[4] Ibid.
[5] Ibid. Bold mine.
[6]Ibid. In 1994, during the fiftieth anniversary of D-Day, new facts were revealed demonstrating just how close we came to losing World War II.

An Israeli artist sculpture of the Holocaust.

MORE EVIDENCE IN 1996

Many have always believed that communist Russia was Anti-Hitler and a friend of the Jews. However, recently new evidence has been released that shows the contrary. Soviet Russians, believe it or not, helped Hitler murder Jews during the Holocaust. This was also kept secret until the release of Soviet documents proving this in late 1996.

Carl Modig, the Washington-based museum's project director for the former Soviet Union said, "Some of the mass killings occurred very early on, and therefore the Russians knew about them very early on, but it was kept a secret...." [7]

---

[7] October 24, 1996, p. 4a, *Atlanta Journal Constitution*, "Russia yields secret files."

The *Atlanta Journal* article titled, "Russia yields secret files on W.W.II massacres." Also noted that, "the papers, until now locked in Soviet, then Russian archives, include field reports from observers behind German lines and documents from little-known war crimes trials held on Soviet soil. The defendants were both Nazis and Soviet citizens who helped them round up, guard and even kill Jews....' "[8]

In a May 1995 *New Yorker* article entitled "Explaining Hitler" by Ron Rosenbalm, one Allan Bullock who wrote *Hitler: A Study of Tyranny*[9] was interviewed. Rosenbalm asked Bullock if his life long study of Hitler had "resulted in a change in his view of the potential of human nature for evil."[10] A portion of his answer was "Never believe God is omnipotent."[11] i.e. all powerful. I was astonished in that I for one would never give in to Hitler and allow him the honor and privilege of changing my perception of and belief in God! I was also astonished by what appears to me to be Bullocks lack of faith—because God's messenger, Moses, in the biblical book of Deuteronomy forecast the Holocaust nearly 4,000 years ago![12]

---

[8] Ibid.

[9] Now a classic.

[10] "Explaining Hitler" by Ron Rosenbaum, *The New Yorker* May 1995, p. 70.

[11] Ibid p. 68.

[12] See my book, *Nightmare Of The Apocalypse,* Appendix 9, "They Escaped to Petra" and Appendix 10, "Saved, Saved From What?" for additional details on this prophecy.

"Very considerable pressure was brought to bear to dissuade Dr. Walter Johannes Stein, from revealing what is now presented as the content of this book, [*The Spear of Destiny*], but in the final issue he was not influenced in any way by such external persuasion, not even in this instance by Sir Winston Churchill himself who was insistent that the occultism of the Nazi party should not under any circumstances be revealed to the general public. The failure of the Nuremberg Trials to identify the nature of the evil at work behind the outer facade of National Socialism convinced him that another three decades must pass before a large enough readership would be present to comprehend the initiation rites and black magic practices of the inner core of the Nazi leadership....It was apparent to Dr. Stein that a decision had been made on the highest political level to explain the most atrocious crimes in the history of mankind as the result of mental aberration and the systematic perversion of instincts. It was thought expedient to speak in dry psycho-analytical terms when considering the motives for incarcerating millions of human beings in Gas Ovens rather than to reveal that such practices were an integral part of a dedicated service to evil powers."[13]

TREVOR RAVENSCROFT

THOUGH THE JEWS HAVE BEEN RELENTLESSLY PERSECUTED, THEY HAVE NEVER BEEN CONSUMED— REMEMBER MOSES' BURNING BUSH?

We should emphasize that from the moment God created the Hebrew race, Satan has attempted to destroy it,[14] even though the Bible foretells that they will never be destroyed (Malachi 3:6; Psalm 137:5).

---

[13] Trevor Ravenscroft, *The Spear Of Destiny,* York Beach, Maine: Samuel Weiser, Inc. © 1973, pp. XIII-XIV, [ ] mine, used by permission.

[14] Satan's prime purpose in attempting to destroy the Hebrew race was to prevent the Messiah's birth, thus preventing mankind's redemption. Recent attempts to destroy the people of God since the birth of Jesus are aimed at nullifying God's word because Satan knows the Bible foretells a future Messianic kingdom, which the Jews who believe in

We may recall the Jewish bondage in Egypt under the Pharaoh during the Exodus, the Babylonian attack upon Jerusalem in the seventh century BC, and the attempt by Haman to exterminate the Jews in Persia. We recall Athaliah, who tried to kill Joash, which would have destroyed the Davidic Messianic line. We also remember King Herod murdering all the Jewish male babies two years old and under. This is alluded to in Revelation 12:4, and was an attempt by Herod to kill Jesus, because he feared His kingdom would take precedence over his own.

This senseless slaying of Jewish children was also predicted in the Old Testament book of Jeremiah: "Thus saith the LORD; A voice was heard in Ramah, lamentation, *and* bitter weeping; Rachel weeping for her children refused to be comforted for her children, because they *were* not" (Jeremiah 31:15 KJV).

Jesus Himself (the most famous Jew), who rose from the dead and ascended into Heaven (Revelation 12:4), was murdered by Roman crucifixion. Satan used the Romans and tried to wipe out all traces of Israel and the Jews in 70 AD and again in 135 AD. And, of course, the worst time of all was between 135 AD and the 1940's, when

---

Jesus and the true born-again Christians will enjoy forever. If he could destroy the Jews before this occurred, it would lend him moral support, which would give him a hope of winning the battle of Armageddon, thus conquering God. However, the Hebrew prophets of the Old Testament and the book of Revelation of the New Testament indicate that Jesus wins. The believing Jews and true Christians will have their kingdom with Jesus, while Satan will lose for the last time and thereafter be cast into eternal judgment.

Jewish persecution culminated in Hitler's Holocaust, also foreseen by the Bible: "...among those nations you shall find no rest, and there shall be no resting place for the sole of your foot....your life shall hang in doubt before you; and you shall be in dread night and day, and shall have **no assurance of your life**. In the morning you shall say, 'Would that it were evening!' And at evening you shall say, 'Would that it were morning!' because of the dread of your heart which you dread, and for the sight of your eyes which you shall see" (Deuteronomy 28:65-67 NASB).

"HITLER" AND THE NAMES OF NAZI DEATH CAMPS ARE FOUND ENCODED IN THE HEBREW BIBLE

Some feel that the Hebrew Bible contains hidden predictive codes (written thousands of years ago), one of which describes in great detail, Hitler's horrible reign of terror in relation to the Jewish people. Grant Jeffrey notes: "Truly one of the most incredible of the hidden codes in their discovery of the words Hitler, Nazis and names of several of the actual death camps embedded within this text of the Book of Deuteronomy....The Hebrew text of this Deuteronomy 10:17-22 passage reads as follows. The word 'Hitler' in Hebrew (היטלר) is spelled out at a twenty-two letter interval.

Hitler — הִיטְלֶר

17 כִּי יְהוָה אֱלֹהֵיכֶם הוּא אֱלֹהֵי הָאֱלֹהִים וַאֲדֹנֵי הָאֲדֹנִים וְאֵל הַגָּדֹל הַגִּבֹּר וְהַנּוֹרָא אֲשֶׁר לֹא־יִשָּׂא פָנִים וְלֹא יִקַּח שֹׁחַד׃ 18 עֹשֶׂה מִשְׁפַּט יָתוֹם וְאַלְמָנָה וְאֹהֵב גֵּר לָתֶת לוֹ לֶחֶם וְשִׂמְלָה׃ 19 וַאֲהַבְתֶּם אֶת־הַגֵּר כִּי־גֵרִים הֱיִיתֶם בְּאֶרֶץ מִצְרָיִם׃ 20 אֶת־יְהוָה אֱלֹהֶיךָ תִּירָא אֹתוֹ תַעֲבֹד וּבוֹ תִדְבָּק וּבִשְׁמוֹ תִּשָּׁבֵעַ׃ 21 הוּא תְהִלָּתְךָ וְהוּא אֱלֹהֶיךָ אֲשֶׁר־עָשָׂה אִתְּךָ אֶת־הַגְּדֹלֹת וְאֶת־הַנּוֹרָאֹת הָאֵלֶּה אֲשֶׁר רָאוּ עֵינֶיךָ׃ 22 בְּשִׁבְעִים נֶפֶשׁ יָרְדוּ אֲבֹתֶיךָ מִצְרָיְמָה וְעַתָּה שָׂמְךָ יְהוָה אֱלֹהֶיךָ כְּכוֹכְבֵי הַשָּׁמַיִם לָרֹב׃

Hebrew text of Deuteronomy 10:17-22 Passage.

Beginning with the second last appearance of the Hebrew letter *bet* ב in this passage, researchers counted every thirteenth letter from left to right. To their amazement they discovered that the coded letters spelled out the phrase, 'b'yam marah Auschwitz,' which means, 'in the bitter sea of Auschwitz.' As they carried the counting forward another thirteen letters they came to the letter *resh* ר. From this resh, they counted every twenty-second letter from left-to-right. To their amazement they found the word הִיטְלֶר, 'Hitler,' the name of the greatest enemy of the Jews in history, the one who almost conquered the Western World in World War II. It was Hitler's satanic obsession against the chosen people that motivated him to create the Final Solution which ultimately slaughtered over six-million Jews and another six-million Poles and Russians in the murderous death camps in Eastern Europe, such as Auschwitz. Amazingly, the actual names of the Nazi concentration camps, 'Auschwitz' and 'Belsen,' were also encoded close to the word

'Hitler' and 'Berlin' in a cluster of letters hidden within the text of this passage in Deuteronomy.

"Scientists found that Deuteronomy 33:16 also contained a hidden message about the Nazi Holocaust. Beginning with the first Hebrew letter *mem* מ, they counted every two hundred and forthsixth letter from left to right and found that the coded letters spelled out the phrase, 'Melek Natzim,' which translates as the 'King of the Nazis.' Another group of nearby letters spelled out the phrase, 'laiv m'Laivi' which means, 'the heart from Levi,' referring to the Levites, one of the twelve tribes of the Jews. Incredibly, this same passage yielded another hidden code about the rise of Nazi Germany; the phrase 'kemi bait rah,' 'an evil house rose up.'

"One of the most fascinating of these Nazi codes appeared in Deuteronomy 32:52. Beginning with the appearance of the first letter *aleph* א, the researchers counted from left to right every six-hundred and seventy letters throughout the passage, and discovered the name 'Aik'man,' which is a Hebrew form of the name 'Eichmann.' Adolf Eichmann was a Nazi official who designed the Final Solution, the evil system of concentration camps used in the Holocaust. Eichmann and Hitler were among the greatest killers in history.

This whole series of hidden codes dealing with Nazi Germany ended in Deuteronomy 33:21 with a final astonishing code. Beginning with the letter resh ר that appeared in the word 'Yisrael,' researchers counted every twenty-second letter from left to right and found the tragic phrase 're'tzach alm' describing the terrible sufferings of the Jews during the Holocaust, which translated as 'a people cry murder, slaughter.' "[15]

NOT   WANTED !

This picture, drawn before the rebirth of Israel in 1948, quite accurately illustrates Moses' prophecy

---

[15]Grant R. Jeffrey, *The Signature of God.* Toronto, Ontario, Can: Frontier Research Publications, Inc., © 1996, pp. 209-211, used by permission.

This Hebrew encoding of prophesy, so to speak, has become a science of sorts which is being studied by Yale, Harvard, The Hebrew University of Jerusalem and the U.S. Department of Defense. The Israeli Rabin assassination is spelled out in the over 3,000 year old book of Genesis. See our documentation on Hebrew Bible codes which includes illustrations and enlargements of key letters showing equal space distances in *The End of History- The Messiah Conspiracy* page 427-28, 830-32 and 943-44; *Nightmare of the Apocalypse* page 14; *Eternal Security For True Believers- The Rabin Assassination Predicted* page 14-24 and A *Liberal Interpretation of the Prophecy of Israel- Disproved* inside front and back cover for examples. The odds of this phenomenon occurring by accident/chance in some cases run as h12-2igh as 50,000,000,000 to 1.

in Deuteronomy: "If you are not careful to observe all the words of this law which are written in this book...the LORD will bring extraordinary plagues on you and your descendants....you shall be left few in number, whereas you were as the stars of heaven for multitude....Moreover, the LORD will scatter you among all peoples, from one end of the earth to the other end of the earth....but there the LORD will give you a trembling heart, failing of eyes, and despair of soul" (Deuteronomy 28:58-59; 62-65).

This has been characteristic of nearly 2,000 years of Jewish dispersion from 70 AD through 1948 and even during that time period Jews were also exiled from Spain and England and massacred in Germany. Truly, God has ordained only one true safe home for his people, the Jews, and that is Israel.

Ezekiel, the Hebrew prophet of the Old Testament, predicted that after God's anger with His people was over He would bring them back to Israel in forgiveness and mercy. God said: "...the house of Israel went into exile for their iniquity because they acted treacherously against Me, and I hid My face from them: so I gave them into the hand of their adversaries, and all of them fell by the sword....'Now I shall restore the fortunes of Jacob, and have mercy on the whole house of Israel'...When I bring them back from the peoples and gather them from the lands of their enemies, then I shall be sanctified through them in the sight of the many nations. Then they will know that I am the LORD their God because I made them go into exile among the nations, and then gathered them *again* to their own land....And I will not hide My face from them any longer...." (Ezekiel 39:23-29 NASB).

Getting back to our subject at hand, Bullock also attempted to draw a line between Hitler and the Russians saying, "When the Russians committed atrocities—by God they had provocation."[16] As we can clearly see—Bullocks statement is not true in light of findings published in the *Atlanta Journal.* The Russian socialist in some cases were just as Anti-Semitic and cold blooded as the German National Socialist—though much of their murders were kept secret[17] until now.

In 1952 a whole host of Jewish writers and diplomats including: "Lev Kvitko, Perets Markish... Isaac Fefer and...Semyon Lozovsky"[18] were falsely accused and shot as spies! Was this not atrocious? Was this not without provocation? Since it was obvious that these people were not "spies!" What about those 15 million Yukranians Stalin starved as he was "reforming" them into communism?

Regarding the most atrocious plans of Stalin to kill all Russian Jews, John Phillips reminds us that:

"In early 1953, Stalin's secret police arrested nine 'terrorist doctors,' six of whom were Jewish, and charged them with plotting to murder Soviet leaders 'on orders from abroad'...The 'plot' by the Jewish doctors gave Stalin the weapon he needed to proceed against the Jews. The trial was given

---

[16] "Explaining Hitler" by Ron Rosenbaum, The *New Yorker*, May 1, 1995, p. 69.

[17] In a PBS special entitled, "Russia's War" which aired in 1997, it was noted that many thousands of Russian citizens were killed by the Russian government after they were liberated from Hitler's camps in 1945. This was done secretly. The program noted that Stalin's millions of murders were kept from the public eye while Hitler's murders were shown to all the world! Shouldn't Stalin's have been also? Wasn't Stalin just as evil as Hitler? Yes!

[18] "Jews Shot As Spies In The Stalin Era Secretly Cleared" *Jerusalem Post*, January 2, 1989.

continuous front-page, sensational coverage in the controlled Soviet press.

"Also in early 1953, Stalin read a statement in which he outlined to the assembled Politburo his plan for the extermination of all Russian Jews. The result of the trial of the doctors was a foregone conclusion. They would be publicly hanged in Moscow a few days later. That would be followed by three days of 'spontaneous' rioting against the Jews. The government would then step in and separate the Jews from the Russian people and ship them all to Siberia. But two-thirds would never arrive. They would be killed along the way by the enraged Russian people. The third who did arrive would die swiftly in slave labor camps. The proposal was received in dead silence.

"On March 5 Stalin was dead. He suffered a stroke and was removed from the earth."[19]

How dare A. Bullock say, "When the Russians committe atrosoties—by God they had provocation" and "Never believe God is omnipotent"! In my opinion Bullock should read and reread his history and Bible **before** making such statements and passing judgment on **Almighty God**.

According to Ezekiel, a prophet of the Old Testament, the Russians will one day in our not to distant future launch a devastating attack against Israel. However, this time, the Messiah will save Israel as he is recognized and accepted! For extensive documentation of this and the horrible hidden truth of Russian Anti-Semitism of the past

---

[19] John Phillips, *Exploring The World Of The Jew*, Chicago: Moody Press, © 1991, p.117, used by permission.

and the 'yet to occur' future Russian war against Israel see Chapter 19 of my book, *The End of History—Messiah Conspiracy* entitled, "Russia is Crushed in Gog."

HITLER'S GREED CAUSED HIS DEMISE

With this newly revealed information, (especially that which we quoted from the ABC special, "What Really Happened to Adolf Hitler?") We can see how compatible Stalin felt Hitler's socialism was to his. If Hitler, in his greed, had not attacked Russia, it is clear that the USSR and Germany would have become a Neo-pagan[20] world empire, destroying all Jews on Earth. However, the Bible says: "Thus saith the LORD, which giveth the sun for a light by day, *and* the ordinances of the moon and of the stars for a light by night, which divideth the sea when the waves thereof roar: The LORD of hosts *is* his name: If those ordinances depart from before me, saith the LORD, *then* the seed of Israel also shall cease from being a nation before me for ever. Thus saith the LORD: If heaven above can be measured, and the foundation of the earth searched out beneath, I will also cast off all the seed of Israel for all that they have done, saith the LORD" (Jeremiah 31:35-37 KJV).

---

[20]For documentation that Hitler hated true Christians and believed in the occult and paganism, see my book, *The End of History- Messiah Conspiracy*, chapters 13 and 14, where I show how he was influenced by occult books and "philosophers," some of which are still held in high esteem by most academic authorities.

The Jews will never be destroyed. Hitler blundered, bringing his empire and himself to an end, while the Jews live on! They are a prophecy in their own right. Their very existence, against impossible odds, testifies to the Bible's truth and divine origin.

The exhibition of the "eternal Jew" which also opened in Munich before the war was lost.

Recently, my Messianic Jewish friend, Paul Blicksilver, told me a horrifying story. He said that he had seen a documentary that illustrated one of Hitler's reasons for saving clothes, belongings and religious implements, such as prayer shawls, yarmulkes (*kepas*) and Torah scrolls of the Jews he was killing, was for use in the museum he had planned. The museum was to be opened at the end of the war and called "The Relics of an Extinct People." This morbid museum was never opened because Hitler lost—more evidence that God's preservation of the Jews is true, as taught in the Scriptures (Jeremiah 31). We thank God for this.

God told Abraham, "And I will make of thee a great nation, and I will bless thee, and make thy name great; and thou shalt be a blessing: And I will bless them that bless thee, and curse him that curseth thee: and in thee shall all families of the earth be blessed" (Genesis 12: 2-3).

Hitler cursed and killed the Jew and that which he did to the Jew: imprisoned, poisoned and burned—happened to him in the end! This seemingly all powerful Hitler who almost conquered the world found himself imprisoned in his own bunker. He poisoned himself with cyanide (the base of the Zyklon B gas he used on the Jews) shot his cranium off and ordered his body burned.[21]

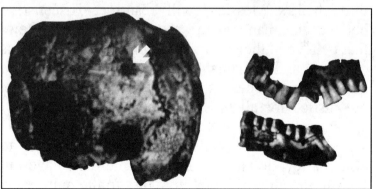

All that remains of the Führer are his teeth
and bullet pierced cranium.

---

[21] This is documented on pp. 230-4 of *The Last Days of Hitler* by the scholar Hugh Trevor Roper.

The New Testament words of Paul, "Be not deceived: God is not mocked; for whatever a man shall sow, that also shall he reap"[22] seem to apply here! Stalin and the Soviet Russian government after him possessed Hitler's bullet pierced cranium and many of his personal belongings retrieved from within and just outside the Berlin bunker. Truly Hitler and his "relics" were possessed by Stalin's own "private museum!"

Moses once told Pharaoh that his decrees of death to the first born of the Jews would become *his* judgment, and it did when the Angel of Death passed over. All of the Egyptian first born died but the Jews who had placed the blood of the lamb on the lentils and door posts (as God commanded in Exodus 12) were spared this judgment. Pharaoh's words were, "Moses God is God." Hitler's decrees have also become his fate!

When the Lord returns it will be universally known that Hitler will be in Hell forever and God, through His Messiah, will resurrect His just! I believe that many of the just will be faithful Jews that believe in their Messiah. I, unlike many millions of liberal and humanist minded theologians, have no question in my heart that God will be able to meet out justice for all those who have died unjustly. I speak as one who lost his father to gunfire for the senseless cold blooded desire of his murderer to obtain a few dollars. On issues of murder I have full faith in the God of Israel in regard to the murders in the holocaust and my dad. God will be just in the end and God help those who know the prophecies and yet doubt God!

---

[22] Galatians 6:7.

Photo of my father in a road side ditch where police found him murdered in LaGrange, Georgia.

Lewis Slaton

ATLANTA——I would like for your readers to join me in commending District Attorney Lewis Slaton for his alertness in solving a most heinous crime. The case involves the kidnapping and murder of Atlanta food distributor, Nick Moore, in August 1976.

The Georgia Bureau of Investigation, along with local agencies, spent many hours of hard work on this case covering numerous leads. We had reached the point where we had nothing promising when Mr. Slaton, after reviewing the case in his office involving Melvin Patrick Carroll who had been convicted in Atlanta of kidnapping Charles Pero, noticed the similarities between the facts in this case with those reported in the Moore case and promptly notified the GBI.

The investigation of Carroll as a suspect in the Moore case was given vigorous investigative attention, resulting in his conviction in Cobb County Superior Court, June 8, 1977, of kidnapping Moore. He still faces murder charges in Troup County where Moore was found with five bullet holes in his chest.

Had it not been for Mr. Slaton, it is doubtful that Carroll would have been developed as a suspect and we would still be working on an unsolved case.

B. E. PONDER
Director, GBI

Letter to the editor of the
Atlanta Journal-Constitution.

"FATHERLAND" ANYONE

What if Hitler *had* won the war? This was the subject of a recent HBO original production entitled, *Fatherland*, which was based on the 1992 novel by Robert Harris. In the film, set in 1964, Hitler reigns supreme over Europe, which is called "Germania." He is celebrating his seventy-fifth birthday. Hitler invites U.S. President Joseph P. Kennedy, Sr. to strike an alliance with him. Meanwhile, an American news reporter discovers, contrary to Hitler's claims, that all Jews were *not* resettled but instead, were murdered in internment camps. This secret is kept so well by Germany's powerful "Ministry of Information" that the world at large, including the German populous, was yet to realize Hitler's crime of Jewish genocide.

You might say that Jeremiah 31:36 is why the story is *fiction* and the Bible is true. God is keeping the Jew.

In the film, the reporter asked the mistress of the Nazi who smuggled the files (which proved what Hitler had really done to the Jews) to her: "So all the Jews were killed...there was no resettlement?"[23]

---

[23]*Fatherland*, the motion picture, based on the 1992 novel, *Fatherland*. Director: Christopher Menaub. Producers: Frederick Muller and Ilene Kahn. © 1994, Home Box Office, a division of Time Warner Entertainment Company. All rights reserved.

This idea of a victorious Hitler (due to the other side's premature desire for peace as an alternate history plot) was put forth in a 1966 episode of the popular TV series, *Star Trek*, entitled, "The City on the Edge of Forever." In *Star Trek* it was a prim and proper Edith Keiler, (played by Joan Collins), who persuaded F.D.R to stay out of the war. In the movie version of *Fatherland* it was the historical Charles Lindbergh, and those like minded, "who had argued against a war with Germany" which caused our withdrawal.

The reply by the one holding the secret government documents was: "I hardly think that after the war, there were enough left alive to resettle a half-acre."[24] The reporter also asked: "What does 'necessity of...removing the biological basis for Judaism once and for all' mean?"[25] As she read from the file anguishing and saying in horror, "They killed all the Jews."

Later an SS officer, once convinced after having seen the top-secret file of the evidence, sadly replied: "We killed an entire people." Most probably, this was what Hitler planned to do had he been victorious, murder all the Jews and try to keep it a world-wide secret. However, God had other plans and Hitler lost.

In the film, Hitler kills all the Nazis who participated in the Jewish genocide because they would have been able to expose him for his crimes. He did this in hopes of securing détente—to safeguard the cooperation of the United States regarding his on-going war with Russia.

I believe this is exactly what happened to the American prisoners of war held in Vietnam after the war was over. The POW's were secretly transported to the Soviet Union, held against their will for over twenty years without the world's knowledge, and killed in the early 1990's "for détente," which would not have succeeded otherwise.[26] Had Pat Robertson

---

[24] Ibid.

[25] Ibid.

[26] See my book, *The End of History- The Messiah Conspiracy*, Chapter 19, "Russia is Crushed in Gog," where we quote a *20/20* news magazine segment documenting that American MIA's from the Vietnam War were seen alive in the USSR years later! Some were found interred under Russian tombstones. Had the West realized what

been nominated and elected president in 1988, we probably would have seen some "Rambo" missions succeed—but he was not. Now it is too late—too late for forever because they are no more.

CONCLUSION

Soon, God will set up a Messianic kingdom. There will be much war[27] beforehand but afterward the Jews and Gentiles[*] who believe in the God of Israel and His Messiah will inhabit this kingdom forever where we will only know peace (see Isaiah 11:1-16; 65:17-25; Revelation 20-22). This future kingdom would not be possible if Hitler, or anyone for that matter, had succeeded in killing all Jews, Why?—because just prior to the kingdom's beginning, the New Testament book of Revelation testifies that one hundred and forty-four thousand Jews prepare the world to enter it! This is still in our future.[28]

Anyone who read the New Testament's final book, Revelation, during WWII, (even when it seemed as though Hitler would win in 1940-41), could clearly see that if this book was true, Hitler would have to loose because it is clear from passages contained therein that God loves the Jewish people and has special plans for the them. Certainly

---

Russia has done to our soldiers, public and world opinion would not have allowed for the tremendous aid given to the Russians between 1991 and the present.

[27]See my work, *The End of History—Messiah Conspiracy*, Chapters 26-30, for greater detail on the end time wars and coming kingdom.
[*] Non-Jews.
[28] See my book *The End of History—Messiah Conspiracy*, Chapters 23 and 29 for details on these subjects.

if the Old and New Testaments are God's word and if His word is true, Hitler's world could not be too. In my 1200 page work, *The End of History–Messiah Conspiracy* and in my forth coming book *Israel and the Apocalypse–Prophecies of Newton* I deal with the reasons wars are still allowed by the almighty. In fact I cover future wars predicted by the Bible which will involve the major spheres of power in our world today. I answer such questions as, "When will war end? and When will the Messiah come to end war?" This is the major objective of His second coming to earth to put an end to war and bring lasting peace! Most importantly we will review prophecies of his past including his first advent and illustrate why He was rejected when he walked the earth almost 2,000 years ago. Had he been received by his own, all wars from the first century to the present **would not have been**.

We will further investigate the cover up campaign as to how and why his identity as Messiah has been deviously and carefully explained away by an elitist group of Rabbis over 1,900 years ago in a town called Yavne. In the chapter entitled, "The Messiah Conspiracy," we display Hebrew documents which have recently been discovered to prove conspiracy.

Finally we will deal with the Apocalypse and Isaac Newton's literal interpretation of this coming era. The Apocalypse and the coming peace thereafter, whereby the Messiah is received by the Jews once they see Him win their victory in Israel's final war, will be the conclusion of world history. Thus, the world will finally realize forever peace for which man has yearned since Adam's fall in the garden of Eden! The wars the Bible predicted have been **real**. Therefore the culmination of Messianic peace it predicts will be **real**!

History Begins	Call of Abraham, the first Jew	Institution of Church replaces rejected king	Future after Second Coming
Adam to Abraham	*Abraham to Jesus*	*Jesus to present*	*1000 years of peace*
2000 years of general knowledge of God, the Fall and institution of sacrifice (Genesis).	2000 years of law. In this Dispensation, Jewish law is enforced.	Approximately 2000 years of Church, joined by many Jews and Gentiles through faith in the Jewish Messiah, Jesus.	Scriptures predict the 1000-year Jewish Messianic Kingdom of Jesus reigning on Earth, to be instituted by Jesus when He returns and is accepted by the Jewish people (Revelation 20).

God's timeline for the 7000 years known as the Millenial Dispensational Week. Very probably in the 2030's, when we are 2000 years from the time Jesus left (33 AD), the millenial kingdom will begin—peace on Earth!

"People set us down as the enemies of the Spirit. We are. But in a much deeper sense than the conceited bourgeois dolts ever dreamed of. What should I care for the Christian doctrine of the infinite significance of the individual spirit and of personal moral responsibility? I oppose it in icy clarity with the saving doctrine of the nothingness and total insignificance of the individual and of his continued existence only in the visible mortality of the blood of the race...I am liberating man from the demand of spiritual freedom and personal independence which only a few people can bear...A German Christianity is a distortion. One is either German or Christian." [1]   ADOLF HITLER, 1932

"The Nazis...denounced the Jews for having giving birth to 'such a sickness as Christianity.' "

Jewish Scholar, MAX I. DIMONT, 1962

"I have had more than one Rabbi tell me, 'Hitler was a Christian.' While attempting to dissuade me from sharing my faith, in Jesus as the Jewish Messiah, with my Jewish friends. The truth is, this is an improper claim, used to lay guilt trips on those who share their faith with Jews because it is not true. Hitler hated Christians and murdered many[2] of them also. True Christians love the Jewish people as Jesus commanded."   PHILIP MOORE, 1998

APPENDIX 5
THE PHILOSOPHICAL BASIS
FOR GERMAN ANTI-SEMITISM[*]
UNCOVERED AND EXAMINED

The significant reasons for Adolf Hitler's Anti-Semitism are often overlooked and pushed aside.

---

[1] See chapters 13-14 of my book, *The End of History- Messiah Conspiracy* and Professor Max I. Dimont's statistics which are quoted later in this appendix for documentation.

[2] See chapters 13-14 of my book, *The End of History- Messiah Conspiracy* and Professor Max I. Dimont's statistics which are quoted later in this appendix for documentation.

[*] Anti-Jewish Sentiment which results in hatred of the Jewish people.

These investigations are pursued to make way for novel inquiry or theories which, in all probability, sheds little light on the subject or reason for very long. For decades people have asked 'why?' This was the subject of a May 1, 1995 article in *The New Yorker* magazine entitled "Explaining Hitler." Since so many Jewish friends of mine have also asked me why I think Hitler hated the Jewish people, we will examine the inner workings of this evil man's mind with respect to the influence which was pressed upon him by *The Protocols of the Elders of Zion*, The writings of Houston Stewart Chamberlain and consequent "philosophical" predecessors.

Max I. Dimont outlines a specific trend in Anti-Semitism which was precipitated by "Race Philosophers." He tells us that: "...race philosophers made 'blood' the fount of grace, and the 'superman' supplanted the [New Testament] Gospels as a source of power...Count Gobineau...in his book *The Inequality of Human Races*, published in 1853.... held that blood of the Aryan elite was being diluted with the blood of a non-Aryan mass through the process of democracy. He does not mention the Jews. It is the middle and lower-class French he views with fear, for it is they who carry the taint of inferior blood, infecting the French aristocracy, which he claims was descended from Nordic Aryans. The French, at first, ignored Gobineau, but the Germans immediately embraced his theories. His book gained him the friendship of Friedrich Nietzche, creator of the concept of the superman.

"A whole school of apologists has recently arisen, making Nietzche the ethical successor to the humanists. Nietzsche, however, with all due regard for his nervous, brilliant prose, is the 'father' of Nazism, and his ethic is not the ethic of Torah and [New] Testament, but the limited code of the Nazi. 'Write with blood,' advises Nietzsche, 'and you learn that spirit is blood.' *In Beyond Good and Evil*, Nietzche also laid down the foundation for the morality of his superman with such maxims as 'You I advise not to work but to fight.'...His Superman is beyond good and evil, for, says Nietzsche, 'the falseness of an opinion is for us no objection to it...and we are fundamentally inclined to maintain that the falsest of opinions...are the most indispensable to us.' His philosophy led, indeed, to a complete defiance of Christianity, to a complete reversal of the teachings of [The New Testament] Gospel and Decalogue.

"Houston Stewart Chamberlain, an Englishman living in Germany, combined the social theories of Gobineau, the philosophy of Nietzsche, and anti-Semitism in his book *Foundations of the Nineteenth Century*, published in 1899 in German and in 1911 in English. In this work, Gobineau's supremacy of the aristocracy became Nordic supremacy race and blood were welded into a pseudoscientific sociology upon which the final Aryan-race and superman theories were fashioned. Like so many other racists, Chamberlain became a traitor to his country, defecting to the Germans during World War I.

"As the race theorists enlarged upon their philosophies, anti-Semites gave them practical application. Jewish history was vulgarized, distorted, and changed to fit the new needs. The first of these books to synthesize racism and anti-Semitism was Drumont's *La France juive*, published in 1886. It helped give people who entertained anti-Semitic feelings a reason for feeling the way they did."[3]

I personally made a trip to The Pitts Emory Theological Library in Atlanta, Georgia in January of 1998 to read Chamberlains book. I must admit his words of hatred towards the Jewish people were the most virulent I've read in many years. His lies and gross inaccuracies along with his diagrams, shown here, turned my stomach.

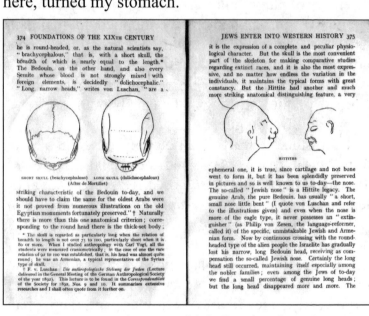

Diagrams and text which imply that Jews are members of an "inferior race". This greatly influenced Nazi decisions and helped precipitate the holocaust. Reproduced from Houston Stewart

[3] Max I. Dimont, *Jews, God and History*, New York: The American Library of World Literature, Inc., Signet Books © 1962 pp. 319-20, [ ] mine, used by permission.

Chamberlain's book translated in 1911, *Foundations of the Nineteenth Century.*

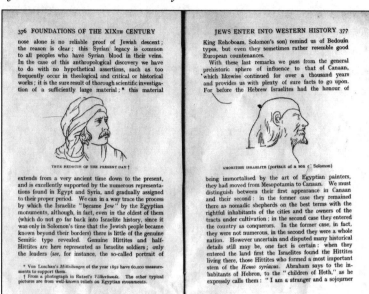

376 FOUNDATIONS OF THE XIXᴛʜ CENTURY

nose alone is no reliable proof of Jewish descent; the reason is clear; this Syrian legacy is common to all peoples who have Syrian blood in their veins. In the case of this anthropological discovery we have to do with no hypothetical assertions, such as too frequently occur in theological and critical or historical works; it is the sure result of thorough scientific investigation of a sufficiently large material; * this material

TRUE BEDOUIN OF THE PRESENT DAY †

extends from a very ancient time down to the present, and is excellently supported by the numerous representations found in Egypt and Syria, and gradually assigned to their proper period. We can in a way trace the process by which the Israelite "became Jew" by the Egyptian monuments, although, in fact, even in the oldest of them (which do not go far back into Israelite history, since it was only in Solomon's time that the Jewish people became known beyond their borders) there is little of the genuine Semitic type revealed. Genuine Hittites and half-Hittites are here represented as Israelite soldiers; only the leaders (*see*, for instance, the so-called portrait of

* Von Luschan's *Mitteilungen* of the year 1892 have 60,000 measurements to support them.
† From a photograph in Ratzel's *Völkerkunde*. The other typical pictures are from well-known reliefs on Egyptian monuments.

JEWS ENTER INTO WESTERN HISTORY 377

King Rehoboam, Solomon's son) remind us of Bedouin types, but even they sometimes rather resemble good European countenances.

With these last remarks we pass from the general prehistoric sphere of influence to that of Canaan, which likewise continued for over a thousand years and provides us with plenty of sure facts to go upon. For before the Hebrew Israelites had the honour of

AMORITISH ISRAELITE (portrait of a son of Solomon)

being immortalised by the art of Egyptian painters, they had moved from Mesopotamia to Canaan. We must distinguish between their first appearance in Canaan and their second : in the former case they remained there as nomadic shepherds on the best terms with the rightful inhabitants of the cities and the owners of the tracts under cultivation ; in the second case they entered the country as conquerors. In the former case, in fact, they were not numerous, in the second they were a whole nation. However uncertain and disputed many historical details still may be, one fact is certain : when they entered the land first the Israelites found the Hittites living there, those Hittites who formed a most important stem of the *Homo syriacus.* Abraham says to the inhabitants of Hebron, to the "children of Heth," as he expressly calls them : " I am a stranger and a sojourner

Hitler became indoctrinated with Chamberlain's material and another falsified document known to history as, *The Protocols of the Elders of Zion*. This horrific piece of literature claimed that the Jews were plotting to overthrow the world. A portion reads:

"We shall talk with the people on the streets and squares and teach them to take the view of political questions which at the moment we require. For what the ruler says to the people spreads through the country like wildfire, the voice of the people carries it on all four winds.

" 'We—the Beast always says 'We' for he is Legion-'shall create unrest, struggle, and hate in the whole of Europe and thence in other continents. We shall at all times be in a position to call forth the new disturbances at will, or to restore the old order.'

"Unremittingly we shall poison the relations between peoples and states of all countries. By envy and hatred, by struggle and warfare, even by spreading hunger, destitution and plagues, we shall bring all peoples to such a pass that their only escape will lie in total submission to our domination.

"We shall stultify, deduce, ruin the youth.

"We shall not stick at bribery, treachery, treason, as long as they serve the realization of our plans. Our watchword is: Force and hypocrisy!

"In our arsenal we carry a boundless ambition, burning avidity, a ruthless thirst for revenge, relentless hatred. From us emanates the specter of fear, all-embracing terror."[4]

Trevor Ravenscroft, in his interesting book, *The Spear of Destiny*, has well documented and shown to my satisfaction, beyond doubt, the details of how this falsified document called, *The Protocols of the Elders* [wise men] *of Zion* was used to create Anti-Semitism (hatred of the Jewish people) in Germany and thereafter worldwide.

We reproduce the following segment of his work to give credence to our agreement in Appendix 3 where we quoted the British Scholar, Trevor Roper noted that Hitler had read *"Protocols"* in his introduction to *Hitler's Secret Conversations* (also known as *Table Talk)* to illustrate the impact this horrifying document has had on world Jewry and why!

---

[4] Trevor Ravenscroft, *The Spear of Destiny*, York Beach, Maine: Samuel Wiser, Inc., ©1973, pp. 109-110, used by permission.

Ravenscroft has revealed that: "...Alfred Rosenberg....presented Adolf Hitler with a blueprint to total power—*The Protocols of the Wise Men of Zion.*

"The Protocols of the Wise Men of Zion purported to be a record of the proceedings of the World Congress of Jewry held in Basel in 1897 at which, it was claimed, plans were laid and resolutions carried towards achieving world domination.

"Rosenberg, a romantic of a sinister kind, had a mysterious story to tell about how a copy of the *Protocols* came into his possession. He claimed that a total stranger had presented him with it. 'The man, whom I had never seen before, came into my study without knocking, put the book on my desk and vanished without saying a word.'

"The *Protocols* proved to be an appendix to a work called *The Anti-Christ*. It was smitten by a degenerate Russian writer called Nilus, a rascally pupil of the great and profound Russian philosopher, Soloviev... After the first quick reading of the manuscript, Alfred Rosenberg knew the *Protocols* to be a forged document. He also knew that he was holding in his hands both political and racial dynamite, which, if used to advantage, might even become the key to his own personal success in a hostile world.

"Rosenberg, despite his Jewish antecedents, gained entry into the Thule Gesellschaft by showing the *Protocols* to Dietrich Eckart who proved wildly excited on reading the contents. The manuscript caused similar jubilation at a meeting of the Thule

Committee which was held to discuss the most effective way to publish the work.

"The Thulists decided not to associate the publication of the *Protocols* with their own occult movement, outwardly known for its vicious anti-Semitic feelings. An independent publisher, Ludwig Müller, of Munich, was chosen to put out the first edition of the work.

"*The Protocols of the Wise Men of Zion* had just the anticipated effect among German intellectuals who had been vainly searching for the scapegoat to explain the defeat of the Fatherland in the World War. At last they believed they had found the real explanation of how Germany had been stabbed in the back while her loyal soldiers were still fighting on French soil. The vile and loathsome Yiddish conspiracy had at last been unveiled.

"Edition after edition rolled off the press but the demand continued to increase. **Foreign publishers saw it as a great money spinner and the *Protocols* appeared in almost every country in the world. Everywhere it circulated people began to discuss the existence of an international network of Jewry secretly conspiring to control world capital and cunningly to manipulate even master-mind, world politics with the aim of dominating all life on the planet.** [Ravenscroft footnotes planet as follows:]

" 'In England the *Morning Post* published a whole series of articles which gave credence to the *Protocols. The Times,* more skeptical, demanded an immediate investigation to find out the truth, if any, of the serious accusations against the Jews'.....[5]

Ravencroft continues as he quotes an actual passage from protocols: " 'We [Jews] shall everywhere arouse ferment, strife, and enmity,' says...We shall unleash a terrible war on the world.... We shall bring the people to such a pass that they will voluntarily offer us the leadership through which we shall dominate the whole world.'

"The explanation of how the *Protocols* fell into non-Jewish hands was yet another cunning lie. Nilus maintained that a Jewish courier carrying the shorthand notes of the proceedings at the Basel Conference had been bribed to divulge them. For a large sum of cash he was supposed to have permitted agents of the Ocarina to make a copy of the notes before he himself delivered them for safe keeping to the archives of the 'Rising Sun' Lodge of the Freemasons in Frankfurt. The whole story was an obvious fabrication. Unfortunately, only too many people were only too willing to believe it. The *Protocols* aroused the wave of seething hatred for the Jews upon which Adolf Hitler rose to power."[6]

"William Shirer [In *The Rise and Fall of the Third Reich*] describes the first meeting between Adolf Hitler and Houston Stewart Chamberlain:

"It was on the Third Reich...that this Englishman's influence was the greatest. His racial theories and his burning sense of destiny of the Germans and Germany were taken over by the Nazis, who acclaimed him as one of the their

---

[5] Ibid, p. 106. [ ] mine.
[6] Ibid, pp. 106-8. [ ] mine.

prophets....It is likely that Hitler first learned of Chamberlain's writings before he left Vienna. In *Mein Kampf* He expresses the regret that Chamberlain's observations were not more heeded during the Second Reich.

"Chamberlain was one of the first intellectuals in Germany to see a great future for Hitler—and new opportunities for the Germans if they followed him. Hitler had met him in Bayreuth in 1923, and though ill, half-paralyzed and disillusioned by Germany's defeat and the fall of the Hohenzollern Empire—the collapse of all his hopes and prophecies! — Chamberlain was swept off his feet by the eloquent young Austrian.

" 'You have mighty things to do,' he wrote Hitler on the following day....' My faith in German-ism has not wavered for an instant, though my hope, I confess, was at a low ebb. With one stroke you have transformed the state of my soul. That in the hour of her deepest need Germany gives birth to a Hitler proves her vitality; as so the influences that emanate from him; for these two things—personality and influence—belong together....'

"The hypnotic magnetism of Hitler's personality worked liked a charm on the aging, ill philosopher and renewed his faith in the people he had chosen to exalt. This remarkable Englishman's seventieth birthday, on September 5th, 1925, was celebrated with five encomiums in the Nazi *Völkischer Beobachter,* which hailed his *'Foundations of the Nineteenth Century'* as 'The ...[Good News] of the Nazi Movement,' and he went to his grave 16 months later with high hopes that all he had preached...would yet come true under the...guidance of this new German Messiah.'

"Alfred Rosenberg,...of *The Protocols of the Wise Men of Zion,...* introduced the ex-Corporal [Hitler] with the hypnotic voice to the man who was chased by demons [The voice of Chamberlain].

"Chamberlain's teachings conceived Aryan blood to be the essential factor in the breeding of a future Master Race....Though the whole content of this discussion between the two men...has never been reported, it was the implication of Chamberlain's words which later inspired Rosenberg to write the racial...[guide] of Nazism: *The Twentieth Century Myth.* One thing is certain. Chamberlain convinced Hitler that [occult] religion and politics could be fused together to support the new image of the Herrenvolk.

"Chamberlain, whose clairvoyant faculties had mysteriously dispersed at the disastrous failure on the Western Front at the outbreak of World War I, was now seized anew with a strange excitement which mysteriously enkindled his former vision for the remaining years of his life."[7]

CHAMBERLAIN — A PERSONAL EXPERIENCE

In my reading of Chamberlain's book I personally found it to be both sickening and hilarious at the same time. The absurdity of Chamberlain's work can be seen in claims which, in today's scholastic world, can not possibly stand.

---

[7] Ibid pp. 147-8. [ ] mine.

These erroneous claims include: 1/ Jesus was not a Jew; 2/ The Jewish person's larynx are shaped different and this is why Jews alone can pronounce the guttural pronunciation of Hebrew and 3/ The Jews lineage from Abraham is 'forged.' To document what we have said we quote portions of Chamberlain's work. Chamberlain makes this statement:

"Whoever makes the assertion that Christ was a Jew is either ignorant or insincere."[8]

However, any fair reading of the Gospels regarding Jesus' observance of Jewish holy festivals and an examination of His genealogy prove conclusively He is Jewish.[9]

Chamberlain further wrote that: "In Judah and the neighboring lands Aramaic was spoken at the time of Christ; Hebrew was already a dead language, preserved only in the sacred writings. We are now informed that the Galleons spoke so peculiar and strange a dialect of Aramaic that one recognized them from the first word; 'thy language betrayeth thee' the servants of the High Priest cry to Peter.* The acquisition of Hebrew is said to have been utterly impossible to them, the gutturals especially presenting insuperable difficulties, so that they could not be allowed, for example, to pray before the

---

[8] Houston Stewart Chamberlain, *The Foundations of the Nineteenth Century*, London, New York: John Lane Company, © 1911, pp. 211.
[9] See Chapter 5 of my book, *The End of History- Messiah Conspiracy*, Volume 1, entitled "Which Prophecies did Jesus fulfill?" which proves His observance of Jewish custom and His fulfillment of Jewish prophecies regarding Messiahship. Also see Chapter 1 of my book, *Nightmare of the Apocalypse* for a thorough examination of His lineage.

people, as their "wretched accent made every one laugh." † This fact points to **a physical difference in the form of the larynx** and would alone lead us to suppose that a strong admixture of non-Semitic blood had taken place; for the profusion of gutturals and facility in using them are features common to all Semites."[10]   Chamberlain footnotes Semites as follows, "See, for example, the comparative table in Max Müller: *Science of Language,* 9th ed., p. 169 and in each separate volume of the *Sacred Books of The East.* How exceedingly difficult it is for such inherited linguistic marks of race to disappear altogether is well known to us all through the example of the Jews living among us; a perfect astery of the lingual sounds is just as impossible for them as the mastery of the gutturals for us."[11]

Chamberlain's evidence from such unreliable commentary is illegitimate and wholly without foundation. Furthermore recent findings show that Hebrew was not a dead language at the time Chamberlain claims.[12]

Chamberlain continues with his self styled irresponsible inaccurate words, accusing the Jews of falsifying the Bible as he writes, "The Israelite borrowed from the Canaanite the whole tradition of Prophets, as also the whole outward cult and the tradition of the sacred places.§ I need not discuss in detail what every one can find in the Bible (sometimes certainly obscured by so many strange-

---

[10] *Foundations of the Nineteenth Century,* Ibid pp. 208-9.
[11] Ibid p. 209. Bold mine.
[12] See my book, *The End of History–Messiah Conspiracy*, Volume 1, Appendix 1, "It's all Hebrew to Me."

sounding names that one needs an expert guide), namely, the great part played by the Hittites and by their relatives the Philistines in the history of Israel. Thrill the fusion was far advanced and the difference in names had disappeared, we find them everywhere, particularly among the best soldiers and how many **details in this connection must have disappeared after the later editing of the Bible by the Jews, who endeavored** to cut out all that was alien to them **and to introduce the fiction** of a **pure descent** from **Abraham!**"[13]

Once Hitler became thoroughly indoctrinated with the above and Chamberlain's other works which included a book he'd authored on Richard Wagner (Wagner was Chamberlain's mentor and father-in-law) Hitler decided to try his hand at eliminating the "inferior races." In Chamberlain's work on Wagner, Chamberlain reveals, "...he [Wagner] recognized the Indo-Germanic race as qualitatively the highest..."[14] It is a documented fact that Chamberlain was controlled by demons. William Shirer who wrote *The Rise and Fall of Third Reich*, which has become a classic on the subject of Nazi Germany said that, "Houston Stewart Chamberlain was given to seeing demons who, by his own account, drove him relentlessly to seek new fields of study and get on with his prodigious writing...he...wrote feverishly on a biological thesis:...Race and history....written in the grip of a terrible fever...as he says in his

---

[13] Ibid pp. 380-381.
[14] Houston Stewart Chamberlain, *Richard Wagner*, Philadelphia: J.B. Lippincott Company, © 1897, p. 130.

autobiography, *Lebenswege,* he was often unable to recognize...his own work..."[15]

Trevor Ravenscroft has also noted that General Von Moltke knew much about Chamberlain including the following: "....demons... drove him on into the feverish continuation of his work, leaving him later like an exhausted shell, frequently in near hysteria or on the point of collapse. Agents of the Abwehr keeping a close watch on Chamberlain had even reported seeing him fleeing from such invisible demons!....The General...had no doubt at all that Chamberlain was in the hands of demonic intelligences who sought to influence and disrupt the course of European history. Yet he could see no possibility of persuading the Kaiser that the Englishman might bring about the eclipse of the Hohenzollern Dynasty and bring Germany to defeat at the hands of her enemies....Konrad Heiden in his brilliant biography of Adolf Hitler, *Der Führer* comes astonishingly near to the truth when he writes: 'Chamberlain had learned from the great masters of world domination...who created, as he says, by order of the Persian King, the race-conscious Jewish people. To penetrate other nations, to devour them from within by superior intellect, bred in course of generations, to make themselves the dominant intelligence in foreign nations, and thus to make the world Jewish—this, according to Chamberlain, is the aim of the Jewish Race.' "[16]

---

[15] William L. Shirer, *The Rise And Fall Of The Third Reich- A History Of Nazi Germany,* A Touchstone Book, Simon & Schuster, Inc., New York, NY: © 1959, 1988, p. 105, used by permission.
[16] *The Spear of Destiny*, p. 119

This author, after reading Chamberlain's work, realizes how wrong Chamberlain was in virtually everything he comments on—including the above. As noted earlier from his diagrams and comments that Jesus was not Jewish—clearly Chamberlain was only a pawn whom demons sought to use to destroy the Jewish people because they are God's people, who one day will, with the Messiah, inaugurate world redemption.

The holocaust claimed 6 million Jewish lives and had Hitler not been stopped, world Jewry today would not exist. Truly 1/2 million[17] Jews lives were saved, mostly by Christians, as we have shown in Chapters 12-14 of *The End of History- Messiah Conspiracy* and we thank the Lord for this. Today true believers stand by ready to help the Jews should anyone attempt another holocaust. We love our Jewish friends.

DOES IT PAY TO HELP SOMEONE WHO WILL NOT BE ABLE TO PAY BACK AND THEN RESENT THAT FACT?

I for one love to give gifts and it is also fun to obtain something in return but for me "it is more blessed to give than to receive" as Jesus claims in (Acts 20:35). I feel so good afterwards yet I don't give for that reason at all. In Israel I have given out

---

[17] This number was used in the March 16, 1992 *Time* Magazine article entitled, "A Conspiracy of Goodness" which noted the reasons for the goodness of those who saved the Jews during the Holocast in Germany. In a book review on the works *Rescuers: Portraits of Moral Courage in the Holocaust* and *When Light Pierced The Darkness: Christians Rescue of Jews in Nazi -Occupied Poland*.

thousands of Bibles and Hebrew books about end time prophecy and Jesus. In the United States I give my Jewish friends Hanukkah presents and copies of my books. This makes me feel wonderful. However, all are not so thrilled to receive.

Once I gave a school teacher, who had a fascination with minerals, a giant geode, a few days later I got it back in the mail with a note which said "I can not accept a gift from you just as I can not accept anything else. I suppose you meant well but this has cost me some time and trouble to return...do not try to give me anything else." I was never so hurt in all my life. A few years later, she accepted my gift, but to this day she will not speak to me. I remember once she told me she didn't want to be friends with me as once we were so close. (She was like a mom when I was in my early teens). Because she felt she couldn't give me back what I needed. She didn't want to be obligated.

To this day I remember and truly wish I could be friends with this teacher although it has been nearly 30 years since I was her student. She was so warm and kind to me in my childhood but no matter how many of my own books or letters I send over the years[18] they are never answered. I still feel hurt when I am reminded of that stone cold silence which was so uncharacteristic of a once joyful, caring and very concerned warm person. Although I am hurt, I forgive her unconditionally—always. When superiority complexes, obligations and feelings of inability to repay others becomes a hang-up, it would seem demons take advantage and use

---

[18] Since 1995.

circumstances to gain a foothold to further their own interest. Whatever they may be![19]

I was shocked to discover, in my research on Anti-Semitism, that in Hitler's youth he was heavily befriended and given things - by who? Jews! M. Hirsh Goldberg, in his fascinating book, *The Jewish Connection*, has noted "Politics aside, Hitler had more reasons to like Jews than to hate them... Gestapo files clearly show Jewish art dealers befriended the youthful Hitler in Vienna when he was destitute and 'paid generously for his mediocre water colors.' Indeed, most of the paintings Hitler did sell were bought by Jewish dealers.

"During this period in his life, Hitler was also shown compassion by his landlady, a Jewish woman, who charged him only a small rent because of his situation. Once, to provide more space for Hitler and a friend, she even moved out of her own apartment.

"Another Jew who befriended Hitler at that time was a Hungarian old-clothes dealer who gave him a long black overcoat. In *The Rise and Fall of the Third Reich*, William Shirer relates that Hitler wore it so much that the shabby black coat hanging down to his ankles was still remembered by those who knew him then."[20]

Though Hitler rode to power on an Anti-Jewish platform and felt Jews were an inferior race, he didn't have to continue to murder them in the holocaust once he was dictator of Germany to

---

[19] Regardless of all - this teacher is always in my prayers.

[20] M. Hirsh Goldberg, *The Jewish Connection*, Briarcliff Manor, NY: Stein and Day, © 1976 pp. 376, used by permission.

remain dictator! He would have succeeded much more in his war effort, if he had left them alone. (At the end he was in bad need of soldiers. The Jews would have made good soldiers. He really didn't need to murder them and take their money.[21] For he had looted the national treasuries of all Europe and had an abundance of gold, an amount unsurpassed in history! General Patton found two billion dollars in gold bullion in one German salt mine alone).

Two billion dollars in sacked up gold bullion in
a salt mine close to Merkers, Germany.

---

[21] See the *Time Magazine* article entitled "Echoes of the Holocaust" February 24, 1997 which documents that Swiss bank accounts owned by Jews who were killed in the camps were mysteriously emptied and the records and account numbers were found to be non-existence when their children attempted to claim their parents earnings.

Perhaps it is possible Hitler had a deep inner feeling of unconscious obligation. He felt he could never repay so he hated them so much, he wouldn't stop killing them. Hitler realized Christianity (Jewish Messianism) was the "Jewish resultant faith and the fulfillment of Jewish prophecy" and hated Christians also, in much the same way and in using race as an excuse, murdered more Christians than Jews.

The Jewish Scholar Max I. Dimont has rightly pointed out that: "We must recognize the fact that Nazism was not just anti-Semitic but anti-human. Because Nazi beliefs of racial superiority had no basis in fact, Nazism was like a nightmare, unfolding without a past or future in an ever-moving present. Because none but German Aryans were qualified to live in the Nazi view, it stood to reason that everyone else would be exterminated. The chilling reality is that when the Russians overran the concentration camps in Poland they found enough Zyklon B crystals to kill 20 million people. Yet there were no more than 3 million Jews left in Europe. The ratio of contemplated mass killing was no longer 1.4 Christians for every Jew, but 5.3 Christians for every Jew. Nazi future plans called for the killing of 10 million non-Germanic people every year...The imagination of the rest of the Western world could not encompass such antihuman concepts, because the Western mind was still imbued with Jewish and Christian humanism and concerned with spiritual values, whereas in Germany these had been expunged by Nazism. If the Christian reader dismisses what happened in

Germany as something which affected a few million Jews only, he has not merely shown his contempt for the 7 million Christians murdered by the Nazis but has betrayed his Christian heritage as well. And, if the Jewish reader forgets the 7 million Christians murdered by the Nazis, then he has not merely let 6 million Jews die in vain but has betrayed his Jewish heritage of compassion and justice. It is no longer a question of the survival of the Jews only. It is the question of the survival of man."[22]

Hitler also feared he was part Jewish and as some have claimed, he indeed may have been. Might this be the reason for his own self destruction in the end? Again Mr. Goldberg astonished me when he wrote, "...Hitler's father was illegitimate, and the identity of Hitler's grandfather has never been established. Since Hitler made such an issue of everyone else's ancestry, it surely must have crossed his mind that his own family tree could come to haunt him. And haunt him it did, for he had reason to fear that his father's father was a Jew.

"During Hitler's rise to power, his half-brother supposedly threatened in a letter to divulge Hitler's Jewish ancestry. Toward the end of 1930, Hitler asked Hans Frank, who was at the time serving as lawyer to Hitler's political party, to investigate the basis for the threat. Frank, who became the Governor General of Poland when it was taken over by the Nazis, reported as part of his confession at Nuremberg that, when he looked into the matter, he

---

[22] Max I. Dimont, *Jews, God and History*, New York: The New American Library of World Literature, Inc., Signet Books © 1962 p. 389, used by permission.

was able to substantiate that Hitler's grandfather was Jewish. He said he discovered that Hitler's grandfather had been the son of a Jewish family called Frankenburger, living in Gratz, who had employed Hitler's grandmother as a maid. Frank said that he uncovered letters written by the Jewish family to Hitler's grandmother, Maria Anna Schicklgruber, who had become pregnant by the son, then nineteen, while working in their home, and that the family made regular payments to her during the first fourteen years of her child's life to help support him...Hitler was concerned about who his grandfather was and initiated searches to find out. According to [Dr. Walter] Langer Hitler knew of a study that had been made by the Austrian police and tried to get the incriminating evidence. But Austrian Chancellor Dollfuss had hidden the report, so Hitler never found it.

"Robert Waite puts the whole issue into stark perspective in his Afterward, saying, "The point of overriding psychological and historical importance is not whether it is true that Hitler had a Jewish grandfather; but whether he *believed* that it might be true. He did so believe, and that fact shaped both his personality and his public policy...according to Hitler's own perverted racial concepts, which searched back through generations for Jewish ancestors, he would have been tainted with Jewish blood."[23]

---

[23] *The Jewish Connection*, pp. 113-14.

"Say not a Christian e'er would persecute a Jew; A Gentile might, but not a Christian true. Pilate and Roman guard that folly tried. And with that great Jew's death an empire died!"[1]

WILL HOUGHTON, past president of Moody Bible Institute

"...for the first time in more than 2000 years Jerusalem is now completely in the hands of the Jews gives the student of the Bible a thrill and a renewed faith in the accuracy and validity of the Bible...."[2]   L. NELSON BELL, Billy Graham's father-in-law, speaking for the Evangelical Christians on July 21, 1967, hailing Israel's Six Day War victory

"Your [Christian] sympathy, solidarity and belief in the future of Israel—this to us is tremendous. We consider you part of the fulfillment of the prophetic vision expressed by Zechariah in Chapter 14. Your presence here will always remain a golden page in the book of eternity in heaven. May the Lord bless you out of Zion."[3]

Chief Rabbi of Jerusalem SHLOMO GOREN, 1980

"Indeed, the manifestation of growing support from our Christian friends all over the world was a source of encouragement to me and my colleagues."[4]

Israeli Prime Minister, MENACHEM BEGIN, 1983

APPENDIX 6
CHRISTIAN ZIONISTS (LOVERS OF ISRAEL)—PAST AND PRESENT

Do true born-again Christians really love Israel? Can we be sure Christian Zionism is not just a lot of talk? How? By putting our money where our

---

[1] Elwood McQuaid, "The Biblical Injunction." *Israel My Glory,* Apr.-May 1993, p. 6, © used by permission.

[2] Dan O'Neill and Don Wagner, *Peace or Armageddon.* Grand Rapids, MI : Zondervan Publishing House, © 1993, p. 81, used by permission. O'Neill and Wagner's source was *Christianity Today*, July 21, 1967.

[3] "The Press of Israel on the International Christian Embassy Jerusalem," Jerusalem: International Christian Embassy.

[4] Ibid.

mouth is.   At the 1990 Christian Feast of
Tabernacles held at the Benyenei Ha Uma
Auditorium in Jerusalem, where 5000 Christians
from many different nations came to express their
support for the State of Israel, Prime Minister
Yitzhak Shamir was presented with a check for one
million dollars to help Soviet Jews come to Israel.
Many Israelis were amazed to see that Christians
could love Israel so much. Being born-again is just
what it means.

A representative of the International Christian
Embassy presents Israeli Prime Minister Yitzhak
Shamir with a check for one million dollars to help
Russian Jews emigrate to Israel.

ALL PROTESTANTS ARE NOT TRUE-TO-THE-BIBLE SUPPORTERS OF PROPHECY AND ZIONISM

Before we list the true believers who have extended a helping hand to Jews throughout the ages, we would like to emphasize that many "Protestant" reformers who emerged from Catholicism, either mistreated the Jews,[5] or worse, killed Christian Zionists.[6] The true believers, the

---

[5]For an illustration of this, see Martin Luther's anti-Semitic publication, *Concerning the Jews and Their Lies*, written in 1544. For English excerpts of this see Regina Sharif, *Non-Jewish Zionism*, p. 21; and Hal Lindsey, *The Road to Holocaust*, p. 23.

[6]Regina Sharif documents the persecution of these Christian Messianic Zionists by Lutheran and Calvinist sects. She writes: "On the Continent messianic hopes were voiced by...the Anabaptists...but Lutheran and Calvinist official churches ruthlessly persecuted them as disruptive heretical forces....In Holland and Switzerland, a few messianic sects survived at the price of adopting a certain measure of conformity. In Germany, they were stamped out when Lutheranism had achieved a position of equality with Catholicism to form an alliance with the established order." Regina Sharif, *Non-Jewish Zionism*, London: Zed Press © 1983, p. 17, used by permission.

Several eyewitness accounts of this persecution of true believers are recorded in John T. Christian's book. He documents: "Henry VIII was already interested in the extermination of the Baptists, and his zeal extended to foreign lands. He extended his help in exterminating the Baptists in Germany....The Baptists died with the greatest fortitude. Of them Latimer says: 'The Anabaptists that were burnt here in divers towns in England...went to their death, even intrepid, as ye will say, without any fear in the world, cheerfully....'...In October, 1538, the king appointed a Commission composed of Thomas Cranmer, the Archbishop of Canterbury, as President...to prosecute the Anabaptists. ...the books of the Baptists were burnt wherever they were found....'...Anabaptists, and the like, who sell books of false doctrine, are to be detected to the king or Privy Council'....All strangers who 'lately rebaptized themselves' were ordered from the kingdom, and some Baptists were burnt at the stake....In the reign of Edward VI

millennial Zionists or pre-millennialists, as they are sometimes called, have a virtually sterling record in their love and support of the Jew, as they adopt the New Testament commands in this respect. The command of love toward the Jew is one of the most important facets of their faith and loyalty to Jesus! These were and are Christians who believed the Jews would return to Israel before Jesus returns to set up a 1000-year (millennial) kingdom (Matthew 19:28).

Hal Lindsey, in his well-known book, *Road to Holocaust*, defines the Christian pre-millennial faith: "One of the fundamental elements of a Premillennialist's faith is that God has bound Himself by unconditional covenants to the Jews and that even though they are currently under His discipline He will punish anyone who mistreats them. As God swore to Abraham and reconfirmed to his successors, **'I will bless those who bless you, and whoever curses you I will curse**....' "[7]

Lindsey goes on to show that the original church of Jesus' day taught and authorized these beliefs: "...the early Church...firmly believed that Israel was yet to be redeemed as a Nation and given her unconditionally promised Messianic Kingdom.

(1547-1553) the laws against the Baptists were enforced, and the two persons burned at the stake in this reign were Baptists....criminals were pardoned, but to be a Baptist was a grave crime." John T. Christian, A.M., D.D., LL.D., *A History of the Baptists: Together With Some Account of Their Principles and Practices*, Nashville, TN: Sunday School Board of the Southern Baptist Convention © 1922, Vol. I, pp. 191-193, 196.

[7] Hal Lindsey, *The Road To Holocaust*, New York: Bantam Books Inc. © 1989, The Aorist Corporation, Inc., p. 2. Used by permission.

They [the early Church until Augustine] believed that this theocratic kingdom would be set up on earth by Christ at His Second Coming, and that it would last for a thousand years. This teaching was called the doctrine of Chiliasm. (Chilias [χιλιας] is the Greek word for one thousand. The term chiliasm meant the belief in a literal one thousand year Messianic Kingdom on earth.)"[8]

Many of these individuals who espoused Chiliasm wrote books on the return of Jewry to Israel hundreds of years before it began to occur. Later, during the Holocaust, they saved Jews and Jewish children, at the risk of their own lives.[9] Indeed, some died in this service[10] when they were caught by the Nazis and murdered for helping Jews escape Hitler.

Lindsey further details: "Premillennialists believe that Christ will return to the earth with a cataclysmic judgment of the whole world. He will then separate the surviving unbelievers from the believers, casting the unbelievers off the earth directly into judgment (Matthew 25:31-46).

"Premillennialists believe that the Lord Jesus will at that time remove the curse from nature and restore the earth to its original pre-sin condition

---

[8]Ibid, pp. 10-11. First [ ] mine.
[9]See the quotation by Sholem Asch on the opening page of our introduction.
[10]Several of these cases were related to me by Arieh L. Bauminger, a rabbi, Holocaust survivor and former keeper of Yad VaShem (Israel's Holocaust Memorial Museum). I interviewed him in Israel regarding the number of righteous Gentiles who saved Jews, in connection with his famous work, *Hasdi Umot Ha Olam*, now translated as *The Righteous Among The Nations*.

during the one-thousand-year Messianic Kingdom (Isaiah 65:17-25; Romans 8:18-25, etc.).

"The believers who survive the seven-year Tribulation period will be taken as mortals into a global Theocratic Kingdom over which Jesus the Messiah will reign for a thousand years. He will reign on the Davidic throne from Jerusalem.

"At this time, the believing survivors from the physical descendants of Abraham, Isaac, and Jacob will receive all the things promised to them in the Abrahamic, Palestinian, Davidic, and New Covenants. (These will be defined in chapters four and five.)

"Premillennialists also believe in a distinct, sudden snatching out of believers to meet the LORD in the air. In this event, believers will be instantaneously transformed from mortality to immortality without experiencing physical death (1 Corinthians 15:50-53; 1 Thessalonians 4:13-18, etc.). This is commonly called 'the Rapture.' The Church will return to the earth with Christ at His Second Advent in immortal form to reign with him as priests during the millennium."[11]

In this particular work, Hal's arguments were directed against the Christian Reform Movement and Dominion Theology, which deny the biblical truth about the millenium. We agree!

* * *

---

[11]Hal Lindsey, *The Road to Holocaust*, pp. 30-31.

A CHECKLIST ON PREMILLENNIALISTS— THEIR HISTORY, BOOKS, AND DEEDS

The Church of Rome committed some of the most atrocious acts ever recorded in history,[12] however, this does not lessen the good and loving deeds performed by those who claim to be true followers of Jesus.

Seemingly unknown to history, in the past several hundred years there were many true believers who, in the face of Catholic persecution, stood up for the rights of the Jews, as God's people, to return to their homeland! Many of these people risked and even lost their lives protecting and saving Jews from their Roman Catholic persecutors. Thus we as ardent searchers for history's hidden truths, should list these brave born-again heroes of the faith. And in so doing, not only honor these heroes, but uncover for ourselves the other side of the coin.

Few are aware of the "underground true believers" and their deeds, books, and love. While the Roman Catholic Church was murdering innocent Protestants and Jews, there was an effort of true Bible believing Christians to teach the precious truth of Bible prophecy, in order to save Jews, and organize movements, which would allow their desire to return to Israel to become a realistic possibility. It is also our strong assertion that just as Roman Catholicism has been historically noted and condemned for its vicious persecutions of Jews, space in this historical record should be taken to

---

[12]See my book *The End of History—Messiah Conspiracy,* chapter 10, "Early Christian History Versus Catholicism" for thorough documentation on this subject.

recognize and commend the true believing Christians for saving the Jews and advocating the literal fulfillment of the prophecies which predict the Jewish return to Israel. We believe this heritage of true believers has yet to be documented and credited in popular layman's terms.

WHO WERE THE CHRISTIAN ZIONISTS?

The great theologian, Thomas Brightman (1562-1607), stated in his *Apocalypsis Apocalypseos*: "...the Jews as a nation shall return again to Palestine, as the land of their early Fathers...."[13]

Joanna and Ebenezer Cartwright, Puritans who lived in Amsterdam, wrote a petition which was sent to the government of England in 1649. In it were these words: "That this Nation of England, with the inhabitants of the Netherlands, shall be the first and the readiest to transport Israel's sons and daughters on their ships to the land promised to their forefathers, Abraham, Isaac and Jacob for an everlasting inheritance."[14]

Michael Servetus and Francis Kett of England, who wrote about the restoration of Jews as God's chosen people, to their land, Israel, were burnt alive at the stake by "Church" authorities for their unwillingness to recant their faith. they were branded as Christian Judaizers and burnt 1553 and 1589.[15]

---

[13]Regina Sharif, *Non-Jewish Zionism*, p. 18.

[14]Ibid, p. 24. Sharif's source was Don Patinkin, "Mercantilism and the Readmission of the Jews to England," *Jewish Social Studies*, Vol. 8. © July 1946, pp. 161-178.

[15]Ibid, p. 17.

Isaac de La Peyrere (1594-1676), the French Ambassador to Denmark, was the leader of a large group of Christian Millennial Zionists in France. La Peyrere wrote a book entitled, *Rappel des Juifs*, calling for the "Restoration of Israel as the Jewish nation in the Holy Land."[16] He sent this treatise to the French government. This work was only allowed into publication two centuries after he wrote it, when Napoleon requested that the Jewish Sanhedrin be reestablished in 1806.

In 1655, Paul Felgenhauer (1593-1677) of Germany, published a book entitled *Good News for Israel*. In this book he: "...maintained that the Second Coming of Christ and the arrival of the Jewish Messiah were one and the same event. The sign that was to announce the advent of this Judaeo-Christian Messiah would be, in typical millenarian fashion, 'the permanent return of the Jews to their own country eternally bestowed upon them by God through his unqualified promise to Abraham, Isaac and Jacob.' "[17]

In 1696, Denmark's Holger Paulli submitted a plan to William III of England asking the King to "re-conquer Palestine for the Jews so that they might re-establish a state of their own."[18] Paulli called on Europe's Monarchs "to liberate Palestine and Jerusalem from the infidel in order to settle the original and rightful heirs, the Jews."[19] In his plan

---

[16]Ibid, p. 27.
[17]Ibid, p. 28. Sharif's source was *Rengstorf and Kortzfleisch*, pp. 59-60.
[18]Ibid.
[19]Ibid.

to the King of England, he referred to the King as "Cyrus the Great and the Almighty's instrument."[20] Cyrus had allowed the Jews to return to Israel from their Babylonian captivity 2600 years ago (Isaiah 44).

Germany's Anders Pederson Kempe (1622-89), who became a theologian after leaving the army, was forced out of Stockholm because of his outspokenness regarding German Messianism. In 1688, near Hamburg, he published his book, *Israel's Good News*, in which he wrote: "You heathen Christians, you let yourselves be persuaded by false teachers, especially the Grandmother of all fornication, Rome, to believe that the Jews were forever disinherited and rejected by God and that you were now the rightful Christian Israel, to possess the Land of Canaan forever."[21] These were statements clearly in defense of the Jews against Catholicism and in support of their right to return to Israel!

MEN OF THE CLOTH, PHILOSOPHY AND SCIENCE WERE ALSO AVID CHRISTIAN ZIONISTS

John Locke, the great English philosopher, wrote in his New Testament commentary on Paul's epistles: "God is able to collect the Jews into one body...and set them in flourishing condition in their own Land."[22]

---

[20]Ibid.
[21]Ibid. Sharif's source was *Rengstorf and Kortzfleisch*, p. 63.
[22]Ibid, p. 36.

Sir Isaac Newton, the greatest scientist who ever lived, quoted elsewhere in this work, wrote "in his *Observations upon the Prophecies of Daniel and the Apocalypse of St. John*, first published five years after his death...that the Jews will indeed return to their homeland: 'The manner I know not. Let time be the interpreter.' He even attempted to set up a timetable for the events leading to the Restoration and expected the intervention of an earthly power on behalf of the dispersed Jews to effect their return."[23]

Joseph Priestly, the famous chemist who discovered oxygen, was a Zionist. Regina Sharif writes of him: "...Priestly remained convinced that Judaism and Christianity were complementary....His plea to the Jews to acknowledge Jesus as the Messiah was therefore coupled with his prayer that 'the God of Heaven, the God of Abraham, Isaac and Jacob whom we Christians as well as you worship, may be graciously pleased to put an end to your suffering, gathering you from all nations, resettle you in your own country, the land of Canaan and make you the most illustrious...of all nations on the earth.' "[24]

James Bicheno published his work, *The Restoration of the Jews, The Crisis of All Nations*, in 1800. In 1802, Jung-Stilling, the famous eye specialist, wrote in his book, *Das Heimweh von Heinrich Stilling*: "...'God has proclaimed through the prophets of old that the people of Israel would be scattered throughout the world. Who can deny that this has taken place? Yet the same prophets have

---

[23]Ibid.
[24]Ibid, pp. 36-37.

prophesied that in the latter days God would gather his people again from the four corners of the earth, and bring them back to the land which he promised to their fathers long ago to be an everlasting possession....The land of Palestine will again become the possession of the Jewish people.' "[25]

In 1894, William Hechler, the chaplain of the British Embassy in Vienna, an Evangelical Christian and the closest friend of Theodore Herzl (the father of modern political Jewish Zionism), wrote in his book, *The Restoration of the Jews to Palestine*, of "...'restoring the Jews to Palestine according to Old Testament prophecies'. "[26]   This book predates Herzl's great work *Der Judenstaat* by two years. Herzl spoke fondly of the chaplain in his diary, writing "The Reverend William Hechler, Chaplain of the English Embassy here, came to see me. A sympathetic, gentle fellow, with the long grey beard of a prophet. He is enthusiastic about my solution of the Jewish Question.   He also considers my movement a 'prophetic turning-point'—which he had foretold two years before.   From a prophecy...."[27] Hechler often expressed his "great love"[28] for the Jewish people.

* * *

---

[25]Kurt E. Koch, *The Coming One*.   Grand Rapids, MI: Kregal Publishing, © 1972, p. 88, used by permission. This book was first published in German under the title *Der Kommende*, © 1971.
[26]Regina Sharif, *Non-Jewish Zionism*, p. 71.
[27]Ibid.
[28]Ibid.

Prime Minister Benjamin Netanyahu.

Benjamin Netanyahu, Israeli's Prime Minister, presently in 1998, loves Christian Zionists! Grace Halsell, in her 1986 book, *Prophecy and Politics*, noted,

"In a February 6, 1985, address on Christian Zionism at the National Prayer breakfast for Israel, Israeli U.N. Ambassador Benjamin Netanyahu praised the 'historical partnership that worked so well to fulfill the Zionist dream' Journalist, he said, in recent time 'have made much of the support of evangelical Christians for Israel. Many have been puzzled and surprised by what they consider to be a new-found friendship. But for those who know the history of Christian involvement in Zionism, there is nothing either surprising or new about the steadfast support given to Israel by believing Christians all over the world...' 'For what, after all, is Zionism?...'

" 'There was an ancient yearning in our common tradition for the return of the Jews to the Land of Israel. And this dream, smoldering throughout two millennia, finally burst forth in Christian Zionism...British and American writers, clerics, journalists, artists and statesmen all became ardent proponents of facilitating the return of the Jews...'

" 'There was, for example, Lord Lindsay who wrote in the 1840s that the 'Jewish race, so wonderfully preserved, may yet have another stage of national existence open to them, may once more obtain possession of their native land.' And there was George Grawler, who in 1845 urged: Replenish the farms and fields of Palestine with the energetic people whose warmest affections are rooted in the soil.'

"Christian Zionism, Ambassador Netanyahu continued, was not only a current of idealism. Practical plans were actually drawn up for the return of the Jew. In 1848, Warder Cresson, the American Consul in Jerusalem, helped establish a Jewish settlement in the Valley of Refaim, supported by a joint Christian-Jewish society in England. And Claude Condor, an aide to Lord Kitchen, carried out an extensive survey of Palestine, concluding that 'the country could be restored by the Jews to its ancient prosperity.'

"**Christians** had **provided** a 'long **intimate** and ultimately successful support' for Zionism, Netanyahu continued, a support that expressed itself in **English literature**....Christians, Netanyahu said, helped turn 'a sheer fantasy' into a Jewish state. 'Consider, for example, Edwin Sherman Wallace, the U.S. Consul in Palestine, who in 1898 wrote, 'The Land is waiting, the people are ready to come, and will come as soon as protection to life and property is assured...This must be accepted or the numerous prophecies that asserted so positively must be thrown out as worthless...(Yet) the present movements among Jews in many parts of the world indicate their belief in the prophetic assertions. Their eyes are turning toward the Land that once was theirs and their hearts are longing for the day when they as a people can dwell securely in it.'

" 'The writings of the Christian Zionists, British and American, directly influenced the thinking of such pivotal leaders as Lloyd George, Arthur Balfour and Woodrow Wilson at the beginning of this century,' Netanyahu said. 'These were all men versed in the Bible. These were men whose imagination was ignited by the dream of the great in gathering. And these were all men who had a crucial role in laying the political foundations, internationally, for the restoration of the Jewish State. Thus it was the impact of Christian Zionism on Western statesmen that helped modern Jewish Zionism achieve the rebirth of Israel.' "29

---

29 Grace Halsell, *Prophecy And Politics*, Westport, Connecticut: Lawrence Hill & Company, © 1986, pp. 138-9, bold mine, Used by permission. Halsell's book is very critical of Israel and Zionist and in

MILTON, AUTHOR OF *PARADISE LOST*, A ZIONIST?

John Milton (a giant in English literature), in his celebrated *Paradise Regained*, wrote of Israel's restitution. However, few may recall his exact words, which were: "Yet He at length, time to himself best know Remembering Abraham, by some wondrous call May bring them back...."[30]

Sharif grudgingly documents Milton's deep fundamental prophetic faith: "Milton stated it clearly: Israel would be restored to Palestine, not by conquest but rather by some supernatural event. His *De Doctrina Christiana* (not published until 1825) testifies to Milton's own millenarian convictions and belief in Israel's revival."[31]

BROWNING'S ZIONIST POETRY

The well-known English poet, Robert Browning, was also a true believer in Jesus! As a Millennial Zionist Christian, he made his points of view known in his poetry. He was an expert[32] in Jewish literature and often read the Bible (Old Testament) in the original Hebrew. In Browning's poem "The Holy Cross Day," written in 1855, he beautifully illustrates his enthusiastic faith in the

---

my opinion is very un-Christian. We only made use of it as a source of Netanyahu's praise of Christian Zionists to illustrate facts and beliefs we in no way endorse her bias against Evangelical Christian's support of Israel.

[30]Regina Sharif, *Non-Jewish Zionism*, p. 34.
[31]Ibid.
[32]Ibid, p. 45.

return of Jews to Israel, according to Bible prophecy. A portion of this poem reads: "The Lord will have mercy on Jacob yet, And again in his border see Israel yet, When Judah beholds Jerusalem, The strangers shall be joined to them; To Jacob's House shall the Gentiles cleave, So the Prophet saith and the sons believe."[33]

OLIPHANT'S ZIONIST IDEAS RAISE HOPE IN THE GHETTOS

Laurence Oliphant of England (1829-1888), though he may be unknown to most of the world, is honored in Israel to this day. An Israeli reporter, Beth Uval, noted: "His parents were fanatically religious and raised him with...Evangelical strictness...."[34]

Oliphant was known for being "the only Christian member of the English Hovevei Zion branch [a Jewish Zionist charter]."[35] Later in his life he settled in Haifa, Israel. He lived there in 1882 with his wife, Alice.[36]

In an article which pictured a street named for him in Jerusalem, Uval, in the March 1989 *Jerusalem Post*, wrote: "Oliphant became interested in Zionism....His interest was based on...the belief, prevalent in the Evangelical circles in which Oliphant grew up, that the Jews' restoration to

---

[33]Ibid.
[34]Beth Uval, "An Oliphant Not Forgotten," *Jerusalem Post*, March 3, 1989, © used by permission.
[35]Ibid. [ ] mine.
[36]Ibid.

Jerusalem was a prerequisite for the Second Coming
of the Messiah....Oliphant's efforts to obtain a
Turkish concession for Jewish settlement in
Palestine took him to Damascus and the Sultan's
court in Constantinople (in 1879)....Oliphant's
public support for the Zionist idea raised high hopes
in the ghettos of Eastern Europe, and he was
inundated with letters calling him 'Redeemer' and
'the second Cyrus.'

"Laurence and Alice Oliphant settled in Haifa
toward the end of 1882. Their Hebrew-language
secretary was Naphtali Herz Imber, who wrote
'Hatikva' [*The Hope*—Israel's national anthem]...."[37]

The Christian Zionist Congress
held in Jerusalem in 1988.

[37]Ibid. [ ] mine.

MARCH 3, 1989 **IN JERUSALEM**

Oliphant Street looking south toward Pinsker from D'Israeli. Inset shows Laurence Oliphant in 1854 at age 25.

An Oliphant not forgotten

Street scene/Beth Uval

Talbieh's Laurence Oliphant Street, notable for its gracious homes and lush gardens, probably would have appealed to Oliphant's romantic spirit.

The son of Scottish aristocrats who became the only Christian member of the English Hovevei Zion branch, Oliphant (1829-1888) was in some ways strikingly modern. After spending most of his life in an adventurous search for action and meaning – that included travel throughout Europe and the Far East and prolonged involvement with a dubious mystic sect in the U.S.– Oliphant embraced Zionism as his final cause and spent his latter years in Haifa.

His parents were fanatically religious and raised him with a curious mixture of indulgence and Evangelical strictness, a combination that left its mark on his character, according to his biographers. One writer described him as "brilliantly intelligent, perceptive, and intuitive, with a gift of wit and fluent expression, but also impulsive, emotional, moody, and given to precious brooding about religion and morality."

These qualities found expression in a remarkably chequered career that included writing popular travel books, satire, novels, and religious tracts; a stint as London's *The Times* correspondent in the Franco-Prussian War; and international diplomatic activity as a secret agent of the British government.

The same qualities apparently also made him susceptible to the ultimately disastrous influence of Thomas Lake Harris, one of the self-styled prophets who roamed the U.S. at the time. Unfortunately for Oliphant, Harris was preaching in England at a time when Oliphant, despite the promise of a brilliant political career and the success of his writing, was suffering a bout of depression and, some speculate, syphilis as well. Oliphant fell into the clutches of the unscrupulous and manipulative Harris, who had formerly been preaching in the backwoods of Georgia.

In the summer of 1867, Oliphant left his Parliamentary seat and invitations to dine with royalty for Harris's "Brotherhood of the New Life" commune on the shores of Lake Erie in upperstate New York. According to one biographer, "[t]he rest of [Oliphant's] long journey from Mayfair was an empty shed with a few wooden crates out of which he had to construct his bed, a table and a stool to sit on. His meals were sent over to him in a basket and he was not allowed to speak to more than one or two people."

Like many 20th-century sect leaders, Harris somehow convinced people like Oliphant to hand over their money, spend their days carting manure, and maintain celibacy though married while he, Harris, lived in a 30-room mansion which he shared only with a few select women, his wife not among them.

Oliphant became interested in Zionism after a crisis precipitated by Harris's refusal to let him see his wife, Alice. His interest was based on both British strategic considerations in the Middle East and the belief, prevalent in the Evangelical circles in which Oliphant grew up, that the Jews' restoration to Jerusalem was a prerequisite for the Second Coming of the Messiah. He was probably also motivated by his taste for international intrigue and a genuine desire to be of service to humanity in a big way.

Oliphant's efforts to obtain a Turkish concession for Jewish settlement in Palestine took him to Damascus and the Sultan's court in Constantinople (in 1879). Like Herzl several years later, Oliphant left the Sultan empty-handed. According to an eyewitness account, Oliphant himself "put a stopper on it [the concession] by telling the Sultan's secretary that he was seeking to fulfil the Scripture that the end of the world was to come when the Jews were restored to their native land, and his Majesty had no desire to hurry that event."

Although his diplomatic efforts were ultimately fruitless, Oliphant's public support for the Zionist idea raised high hopes in the ghettos of Eastern Europe, and he was inundated with letters calling him "Redeemer" and "the second Cyrus."

Laurence and Alice Oliphant settled in Haifa toward the end of 1882. Their Hebrew-language secretary was Naphtali Herz Imber, who wrote "Hatikva" while working for them. In addition to befriending the local Druse and helping the Jewish settlers in the Galilee, the Oliphants (although finally free of Harris) became deeply involved in increasingly far-fetched mystic doctrines.

According to a contemporary observer, "the Turkish authorities themselves learned to reckon with the Oliphants for they were naturally credited with that measure of madness which is deemed throughout the East to derive from God."

Expressing what seem to have been the sentiments of many of his contemporaries, the same observer wrote that it was "difficult to understand Oliphant, but impossible not to love him."

A *Jerusalem Post* article by Beth Uval, featuring Laurence Oliphant, a nineteenth century Christian Zionist. The photo is of a street in Jerusalem named for Oliphant.

GEORGE ELIOT FORESEES AND ENCOURAGES THE EXISTENCE OF ISRAEL

The famous English novelist, George Eliot,[38] who may be familiar to you from your high school English literature classes, made a landmark contribution to what we are calling the "Christian Zionist Movement," as a millennial Zionist! She was a true believer who loved, supported and encouraged the Jews in their right to reestablish the State of Israel! In 1874, she began writing *Daniel Deronda*. Sharif describes the novel as follows: "Eliot's debt to...Evangelism, though unacknowledged, must be considered. The Gentile author created in *Daniel Deronda* a true Zionist hero who discovers for himself his Jewish nationality and heritage.

"The novel represents the apex of non-Jewish Zionism in the literary field, the culmination of a long tradition that began with the Protestant idea of

---

[38]George Eliot was the pen name used by Mary Ann Evans to increase her readership. In her day, the literary works of men were more widely read and respected than than those of women. *The Jewish Encyclopedia* says that George Eliot was: "...a friend of the talmudic scholar Emanuel Deutsch, and began to study Hebrew and to show an interest in Jewish matters at an early age. *Daniel Deronda* (1874-76), her celebrated 'Zionist' novel....the hero of this novel, after discovering his Jewish identity only in his 20's, eventually leaves for Palestine to help 'revive the organic center' of his people's existence. *Daniel Deronda* influenced the early Zionist thinker Eliezer Ben-Yahuda, and such Hebrew writers as I.L. Peretz and P. Smolenskin....George Eliot discussed the Jewish question again in 'The Modern Hep-Hep' a strong attack on anti-Jewish prejudice published in a collection of essays entitled *Theophrastus Such* (1878)." *The Encyclopaedia Judaica Jerusalem*, Vol. 6. Jerusalem: Keter Publishing House Ltd., © 1971, pp. 663-664, used by permission.

Restoration....George Eliot....was a deeply religious Christian...caught up in the full tide of the Evangelical movement....She regularly visited Jewish synagogue meetings and....met Moses Hess, the Jewish Zionist....[of her novel *Daniel Deronda*, Sharif comments] *Daniel Deronda* displays the possibility of having contemporary Jewish prophets and leaders as in ancient times. The heritage of the Jews is presented as most worthy of rediscovery and accepted as a way of national revival and final redemption. She strongly believed that 19th Century Jews in Europe were renouncing their own unique national heritage by striving for assimilation and amalgamation with other nations.

"*Daniel Deronda* was the 'literary introduction' to the Balfour Declaration....[part of Eliot's *Daniel Deronda* reads] 'There is store of wisdom among us to found a new Jewish polity, grand, simple, just, like the old—a republic where there is equality of protection, an equality which shone like a star on the forehead of our ancient community, and gave it more than the brightness of Western freedom amid despotisms of the East. Then our race shall have an organic centre, a heart and a brain to watch and guide and execute; the outraged Jew shall have a defence in the court of nations, as the outraged Englishman or American. And the world will gain as Israel gains'...."[39]

Eliot, in 1879, wrote in "The Modern Hep, Hep, Hep": "The hinge of possibility is simply the existence of an adequate community of feeling as well as widespread need in the Jewish race, and

---

[39]Regina Sharif, *Non-Jewish Zionism*, pp. 46-47. [ ] mine.

hope that among its finest specimens there may arise some men of instruction and ardent public spirit, some new Ezras, some modern Macabees, who will know how to use all favouring outward conditions, how to triumph by heroic example over the indifference of their fellows and foes, and will steadfastly set their faces toward making their people once more one among the nations."[40]

"ELIOT'S" (EVANS') SEVENTEENTH CENTURY FEAT—AN EXAMPLE FOR ALL EVANGELICALS TO FOLLOW IN THEIR ZIONIST SUPPORT OF ISRAEL

Quite a feat of inspirational support for a nation yet to exist, coming from this famed true believer in Jesus, isn't it? An example for today's Evangelical Millennial Zionists, found among the Baptists, Church of God,[41] Plymouth Brethren and several other denominations, who cheer Israel on in total agreement with the prophecies found in the Old and New Testaments of the Bible!

PROFESSOR POPKIN REMINDS US THAT CHRISTIAN SCHOLARS OF THAT TIME STUDIED HEBREW AND BUILT JEWISH TEMPLES

Richard Popkin tells us in his book, *Jewish Christians and Christian Jews*: "In the Netherlands,

---

[40]Ibid, p. 47.

[41]The Church of God should not be confused with the Worldwide Church of God, which is a cult. We are referring to the Church of God, such as the one in Atlanta, Georgia with Pastor Paul Walker. This church sticks to the Scriptures and is pro-Zionist. We will recommend Pastor Walker any day.

from the 1620's onward Christian scholars were learning Hebrew and were discussing religious points with Jews. Christians were also attending Jewish religious services. Two rabbis became quite involved with Christians in projects of joint concern. Rabbi Judah Leon and the leader of the Collegiants, Adam Boreel, joined forces to construct an exact accurate model of Solomon's Temple. Boreel financed the project to the point of having rabbi Judah Leon living in his house for some years. The Temple model became one of the glories of Amsterdam, was on display in rabbi Judah Leon's garden for years until he took it to England to give to Charles II, after which it has still not been traced. They also joined forces in a project, which lasted at least thirty years, on editing the *Mishna* in Hebrew with vowel points, notes, and translations of the text into Spanish and Latin.

"The other rabbi who became important, and much more important, in Christian circles, was Menasseh ben Israel, who was born in La Rochelle, France, was raised in Lisbon, and then turned up in Amsterdam in his teens, and became a teacher of Hebrew. It is not known where he received his education, but Menasseh by the 1620's exhibited a broad knowledge of Jewish and Christian literature."[42]

* * *

---

[42]*Jewish Christians and Christian Jews*. Dordrecht, Holland: Kluwer Academic Publishers, © 1994, p. 59, used by permission. Richard H. Popkin and Gordon M. Weiner, editors.

A RABBI OF THE 1620'S TEACHES CHRISTIANS HEBREW, AS HE SHARES THEIR EXPECTATION OF MESSIAH

Professor Popkin tells us: "We find in the late 1620's that Menasseh was teaching Christians Hebrew and that they were consulting him on various subjects. He became the first Hebrew printer in The Netherlands, and was an important bookseller, obtaining Hebrew books for Jewish and Christian scholars from Poland, Italy and the Levant....one finds Menasseh in contact with all sorts of learned Christians, people coming from various countries to hear him preach and to confer with him....He became friendly with John Dury, the Scottish Millenarian who was preacher for Princess Mary. He was in contact with the leading mystical Millenarians, and apparently shared their expectation....Boreel started the publication project with his work with rabbi Templo on the Hebrew text of the *Mishna*, (finally published in 1646 by Menasseh, and paid for by Dutch Millenarians). Menasseh's name was listed as editor instead of Boreel, because as Boreel explained the Jews would not buy the edition if a Christian was the editor. One of the reasons for the *Mishna* project is that the texts include the most exact descriptions of the Temple and the ceremonies held therein. This would be crucial information if Jerusalem was about to be restored....When Menasseh came to London in September 1655 he was wined and dined by leading English Millenarians. Robert Boyle's sister, Lady Ranlegh had dinner parties for him. Adam Boreel, the leader of the Dutch Collegiants, came to London and held a dinner for him with Boyle and Henry Oldenburg."[43]

A BELIEVER OF THE 1600'S FINANCIALLY BACKS A HEBREW PRESS, WHILE PUNISHING THOSE WHO ACCUSED THE JEWS

Allison Coubert reminds us of this little known fact: "...von Rosenroth spent his entire adult life in the service of Christian August of Sulzbach; for Christian August had equally wide interests and ecumenical sympathies. Not only was he intrigued by the Christian Hebraica to the point of subsidizing a Hebrew press, but his policy toward the Jews, whom he invited to settle in Sulzbah in 1666, was both liberal and protective. The charge of ritual murder was brought against the Sulzbach Jews twice during Christian August's regime, in 1682 and again in 1692. On both occasions he actively combatted the charges and ordered corporeal punishment for anyone bringing false accusations against Jews in the future....it is apparent that seventeenth-century Europe was criss-crossed by networks of millenarian Christians...."[44]

A MEMORIAL PRESENTED TO PRESIDENTS HARRISON AND WILSON— GIVE PALESTINE BACK TO THE JEW

Arthur Kac documented: "On March 5, 1891, William E. Blackstone, of Chicago, presented a

---

[43] Ibid, pp. 60-61, 63.
[44] Ibid, p. 75.

memorial to President Harrison on behalf of Israel's restoration to the Holy Land. This was signed by over five hundred of America's leading Protestant clergymen, civil leaders, editors, and publishers. In 1917 Mr. Blackstone repeated his effort, reintroduced his memorial, and that time sent it to President Wilson. Part of the memorial reads as follows: 'Why not give Palestine back to them [the Jews] again? According to God's distribution of nations it is their home—an inalienable possession from which they were expelled by force. Under their cultivation it was a remarkably fruitful land, sustaining millions of Israelites, who industriously tilled its hillsides and valleys. They were agriculturists and producers as well as a nation of great commercial importance—the centre of civilization and religion.

" 'Why shall not the powers which under the treaty of Berlin, in 1878, gave Bulgaria to Bulgarians and Servia to Servians now give Palestine back to the Jews? These provinces, as well as Rumania, Montenegro, and Greece were wrested from the Turks and given to their natural owners. Does not Palestine as rightfully belong to the Jews?' "45

GO BACK TO THE LAND OF ABRAHAM

In 1897, John Stoddard wrote: "In a place so thronged with classic and religious memories as Palestine, even a man who has no Hebrew blood in his veins may indulge in a dream regarding the future of this extraordinary people....'Take again the

---

45Arthur W. Kac, *The Messiahship of Jesus*, pp. 296-297.

land of your forefathers. We guarantee you its independence and integrity. It is the least that we can do for you after all these centuries of misery. All of you will not wish to go thither, but many will. At present Palestine supports only six hundred thousand people, but, with proper cultivation it can easily maintain two and a half millions. You are a people without a country; there is a country without a people. Be united. Fulfill the dreams of your old poets and patriarchs. Go back,—go back to the land of Abraham.' "46

PROPHECY IN MODERN HISTORY

Concerning today's evangelical love and support of Israel among the millennial Protestants, in their lineage and in relation to their counterparts of centuries past, Regina Sharif says: "One of the most definite effects of the Protestant Reformation was the emerging interest in the fulfilment of Biblical prophecies concerning the End of Time. The core of millenarianism was the belief in the Second Coming of Christ whose return would establish God's kingdom on earth, which was to last for 1,000 years (that is, a millennium). Millenarians regarded the future of the Jewish people as an important element in the events to precede the End of Time. In fact, the literal interpretation of the apocalyptic writings in

---

46John L. Stoddard, *John L. Stoddard's Lectures*, Vol. II. Boston: Balch Brothers Co., 1897, pp. 220-221. There are ten volumes of his lectures: "Illustrated and embellished with views of the world's famous places and people, being the identical discourses delivered during the past eighteen years under the title of the Stoddard lectures." This author thanks Dan Levine for pointing out these long-forgotten lectures.

the Bible led them to conclude that the Millennium was to be heralded by the physical Restoration of the Jews as a nation (Israel) to Palestine....Pre-Reformation semi-sectarian minority movements expressing millenarian yearnings had to remain underground. They were persecuted and suppressed by the Church in Rome and their teachings were branded as heresies....it [millenarianism] did maintain a certain presence and its ideas percolated down to the masses. It continued to find followers in every period of history after the Reformation and finally culminated in 20th Century American fundamentalism which insists that the state of Israel presents the literal fulfilment of prophecy in modern history."[47]

PRESIDENT HARRY S. TRUMAN
BAPTIST—ZIONIST

President Harry S. Truman was elected in 1948, the year of Israel's rebirth! Sharif said: "...Truman had shown a sympathetic understanding of Zionism. His own Southern Baptist background and training stressed the theme of the Jews' Restoration to Zion. The members of the Southern Baptist convention were the most enthusiastic pro-Zionist congregations, championing both the religious and historical claims of the Jews to the land of Palestine. Most Baptists were theologically conservative or even fundamentalist and tended to regard the creation of the Jewish state as the evident fulfilment of Biblical

---

[47]Regina Sharif, *Non-Jewish Zionism*, pp. 16-17.   Spelling of fulfillment per original. [ ] mine.

prophecies....Truman's religious background played a great part in his later life. By and large a self-taught man, like Abraham Lincoln, he had educated himself in part through the Bible itself. 'As a student of the Bible he believed in the historic justification for a Jewish homeland and it was a conviction with him that the Balfour Declaration of 1917 constituted a solemn promise that fulfilled the age-old hopes and dreams of the Jewish people.' Truman's autobiography, full of Biblical quotations and allusions, also indicates his marked tendency to dwell upon the Judaeo-Christian tradition.

"As a Baptist, Truman sensed something profound and meaningful in the idea of Jewish Restoration. It was a known fact that his favourite Biblical passage was the Psalm 137, beginning 'By the rivers of Babylon, there we sat down, yea, we wept, when we remembered Zion'. Truman once confessed that he could never read the account of the giving of the Ten Commandments at Sinai without a tingle going down his spine. 'The fundamental basis of this nation's law,' he declared, 'was given to Moses on Mount Sinai.'

"When Eddie Jacobson introduced Truman in 1953 to an audience at a Jewish theological seminary as 'the man who helped create the State of Israel', Truman's response invoked the enduring Zionist theme of exile and Restoration: 'What do you mean 'helped create'? I am Cyrus, I am Cyrus.' Who could forget that it was Cyrus who made possible the return of the Jews to Jerusalem from their exile in Babylon?"[48]

---

[48]Ibid, pp. 106-107.

There is no doubt of the President's loyalty and great contribution to Israel and the Jewish people, is there? President Truman further stated in October of 1948: "...'What we need now is to help the people in Israel, and they've proved themselves in the best traditions of pioneers. They have created out of a barren desert a modern and efficient state with the highest standard of Western civilization....' "[49]

President Truman is honored in Israel with a forest named for him. I have visited this wonderful place on several occassions.

REAGAN AND REXELLA ARE ZIONIST

President Ronald Reagan once called Israel "a young, strong, brave nation," in the face of liberal criticism while she was defending herself against terrorism in the 1980's. Reagan, who allotted annual grants of three billion dollars to Israel, often listened to the evangelical ministers Mike Evans and Pat Robertson and was thoroughly convinced of the importance of supporting this biblically prophesized nation (Genesis 12:3).

In 1993, Rexella Van Impe, of Jack Van Impe Ministries, interestingly pointed out that several Christian scholars of the past four centuries, whom we have yet to mention, had very accurately foreseen the rebirth of Israel. In the May/June 1993 edition of *Perhaps Today* magazine, Rexella Van Impe said: "In 1669 a man by the name of Increase Mather, the president of Harvard College, wrote a book entitled *The Mystery of Israel's Salvation*. In it

[49]Ibid, p. 135.

he stated: 'There is no doubt the Jews will return to the land of their fathers.'

Dr. Winchester wrote a book in 1800 explaining that the return of the Jews to their own land was certain.

In 1852 Reverend Bickersteth wrote a volume entitled *The Restoration of the Jews to Their Land*....Were these biblical scholars right? Did it happen? Let's see. In 1900 there were 50,000 Jews in Palestine. In 1922 there were 84,000. In 1931 there were 175,000. In 1948 there were 650,000, and in 1952 there were 1,421,000. Today, there are approximately three and one-half million Jews in Israel. Thus, the number of Jews has increased one hundred and twenty times in the last one hundred years. That's prophecy on the move."[50]

Jack Van Impe, Rexella's husband, an eminent Bible prophecy scholar and teacher, added: "Think of this—it had never happened in twenty-five centuries. Thus, what occurred was not just happenstance. It was the fulfillment of God's Word as predicted by these scholars. But where are these prophecies found? In Ezekiel 36:24, God says, *I will* [gather] *you from among the* [Gentiles—all nations], *and will* [put—place] *you into your own land*."[51]

After reading these pages, no self-respecting rabbi[52] or liberal Protestant can say with a straight

---

[50]Jack and Rexella Van Impe, "1999? Global March to Israel," *Perhaps Today*. Troy, MI: Jack Van Impe Ministries, May/June 1993, p. 5, used by permission.

[51]Ibid.

[52] Rabbi Pinchas Stolper wrote in an orthodox anti-missionary publication entitled *The Real Messiah* "If God is 'love', how can

face that most Christians are anti-Semitic or against the Jews. True Christians truly love the Jews. Jesus said, "for salvation is of the Jews" (John 4:22 KJV), and no one who follows His teachings, thus becoming true Christians, can love Jesus, "THE KING OF THE JEWS" (Matthew 27:37 KJV), and still hate the Jews!

THOUGH FEW "CHRISTIANS" ARE CHRISTIAN, THIS DOES NOT MAKE THOSE FEW ANY LESS TRUE

Clearly the minority, as far as world Christendom is concerned, those who are referred to as born-again believers (I Peter 4:12), are truly

---

Christians explain the silence and indifference of the Church..." with respect to the loss of life in Germany. Many Christians, as we document in chapters 12-15 of *The End of History—Messiah Conspiracy,* risked and even lost their lives in their Godly duty as they saved Jews in the Holocaust. Christine Gorman wrote in a March 16, 1992 *Time* Magazine article entitled "The Conspiracy of Goodness", "The rescuers have not escaped controversy. Their very existence has been denied by some Jews who feared the horror of the Holocaust might be whitewashed by acknowledging their presence." The well-known Jewish author and Israeli statesman Abba Eban wrote in the forward to Arieh L. Bauminger's book, *The Righteous,* "In this book, writing from the depths of our hearts, we render infinite thanks and homage to the Righteous People who risked their lives to rescue Jews during one of the most tragic periods in the history of the Jewish nation." Bauminger was keeper of Israel's Yad VaShem Holocause museum, in Jerusalem for many years. My point in addressing this issue is not to say "Let's pat those Christians on the back for saving the Jews," but rather to note they did and why they did. They did because of Jesus' commandments, and therefore Jesus' messiahship should be investigated on the basis of His true follower's willingness to risk their lives (as well as on the basis of the Messianic prophecies He fulfilled), for if He is the Messiah, who He claimed to be, we will all be the better in the end, at the resurrection, for believing in Him.

Christian and practice Jesus' words. Thus no one can truthfully say real Christians persecuted Jews in the past or present to indict Jesus or His true followers in order to cause doubt about His Messiahship. If they were true Christians in accordance with these passages, they would not have hurt anyone. In fact, they would have done the exact opposite; helped and pitied the Jewish people in troubled times.

We believe, along with others, that true Christian attitudes toward the Jewish people and Israel are represented in these words from several of today's well-known evangelical ministers, quoted from the television documentary *Israel—America's Key to Survival*. The quotes run as follows:

"The primary target of Soviet expansionism in the Middle East is Israel. World public opinion is turning against Israel. Once again, acts of anti-Semitism are on the increase throughout the world. As a supporter of law and justice, as a born-again Christian, as a God-fearing person, you have a responsibility to do something to stop these forces of destruction right now!"   Hal Lindsey,
author/film maker

"As Evangelicals, we're not ashamed to say that our God is the God of Israel. As Americans, we're not ashamed to say it...."   Mike Evans,
evangelical minister/author

"We look to Israel to be a leader among the nations of the earth. A leader of peace, a leader of technology, a leader of the improvement of mankind. We feel that all of us here in America who call ourselves Evangelical Christians are prepared to stand behind you in your struggle for peace, in your struggle for dignity, in your struggle for liberty in these critical days. You can count on us. We are with you in every respect."

Pat Robertson, evangelical broadcaster

"What a fulfillment of prophecy, what a testimony, what a future Israel has, and what a contribution Israel has made, is making and will make. All of us in the Christian faith here in America, salute you. We send you our warmest love and greetings. You're constantly in our prayers and we too say, 'Oh Jerusalem, Oh Jerusalem' and we send our love and our prayers. God richly bless you."

Oral Roberts, evangelist

"We are also praying for the peace of Jerusalem, because the word of God commands, 'Pray for the peace of Jerusalem.' We see fulfilled the prophecies of the Old Testament daily in all of the things that have taken place in your great land [Israel]."

Rex Humbard, television evangelist. [ ] mine

"Our heart is with you one hundred percent upon the biblical positions of the word with no compromises, no discussions. We are putting together 10,000 leaders and one million Evangelicals backing them up, that are going to be personally praying. More important than anything is prayers to God, but secondly after that, standing upon the biblical positions of the word of God [supporting Israel]."[53]

Mike Evans, evangelical minister and author, to Prime Minister Begin. [ ] mine

---

[53]From a meeting with Prime Minister Begin and key evangelical leaders in Jerusalem, led by Mike Evans.

"This is one of the great phenomena in our generation, the Christian friends of Israel—indeed an historic phenomenon."[54]

Israeli Prime Minister Menachem Begin's reply

"Many of you who are watching this program may be having a hard time believing that Israel's survival is actually being threatened by such ominous forces as the PLO, the Soviet Union and more recently, by world public opinion. Now, if you are one of the skeptics, I urge you to do two important things. First, if you haven't already done it, undertake a serious thorough study of what the Bible says about the fate of modern Israel. Second, start being more analytical about what you see, what you hear, what you read in the media. Don't take everything at face value. Finally, I would encourage everyone of you to pick up your phones right now and call to add your name to the petition which is going to be given to our President [Reagan] urging him and other members of our government to stick by Israel at this most crucial time. Our leaders must understand that forcing Israel into some quick easy solution can only result in international catastrophe. Please, will you call and will you do it right now?"

Pat Boone, Christian singer/entertainer. [ ] mine

"It was prophesied in the word of God and He has done it. And I thank God for it. I believe in the fact that God has raised up the nation of Israel again. Think about how fortunate we are as Christian people—we're watching God Almighty—the God of Abraham, Isaac and Jacob. We're watching Him move again just like in Bible days. Praise God."

Kenneth Copeland, television evangelist

---

[54]Ibid.

"We believe that God honors His word, God blesses His people and God honors those who honor His word and His people. For humanitarian reasons, we support the State of Israel. For historical reasons, believing that Palestine belongs to the Jewish people, we support the State of Israel. For legal reasons dating back to 1948, we believe the land of Palestine belongs to the Jewish people. And for theological reasons, first and foremost, we believe that God has given the land to the people."[55]

Reverend Jerry Falwell,
renowned television preacher

"It's not possible for a man to say, 'I'm a Christian,' and not love the Jewish people. You cannot be a Christian without being Jewish in spirit."[56]

Reverend John Hagee

---

[55]Mike Evans, *Israel, America's Key to Survival,* broadcast aired June 1983. Menachem Begin, Prime Minister of Israel, presented the prestigious Jabotinsky Award from the government of Israel to Jerry Falwell in appreciation of his Christian support for Israel and the Jewish people. After Israel bombed Iraq's nuclear reactor, Begin first called Jerry Falwell, because of his great trust in Falwell's love of Israel, and asked him to "tell America why Israel needed to protect herself." Dan O'Neill and Don Wagner, *Peace or Armageddon,* pp. 83-84.

[56]Rev. John Hagee, *Why We Honor The Jews.*

Christians celebrate the Feast of Tabernacles in Israel.

Christian Zionism continues until this day, and shall continue.

AUTHOR'S NOTES

Many of the events, circumstances, places and objects in this work are based on reality and documented history.

CHAPTER 2

♦ Adolf Eichman was a real individual who had helped murder six million Jews. He was captured by the Israeli Secret Service in 1960 and tried in Jerusalem in 1962.

♦ Joseph Mengele, alias Angel of Death, was a fellow Nazi war criminal of Eichman's rank who lived near him in Venezuela. He fled his home just 5 days prior to the Israeli Secret Service' discovery of his residence in 1960. To this day his death or whereabouts is still uncertain.

♦ Time travel according to Einstein would be possible if you could surpass the speed of light. Time does stand still at the speed of light. As you approach the speed of light, objects shrink in size, however at the speed of light objects become pure energy and therefore it is impossible for them to travel *faster* than the speed of light and go back in time.

♦ Hydric Himmler was the head of Hitler's SS.

♦ The Brudenschaft was an underground organization created to give Nazi war criminals new identities and help them to escape capture after the war.

CHAPTER 3

♦ Smirsh was a secret Russian Police loyal to Stalin.

♦ Hitlers & Eva Brown's charred remains were recovered outside his bunker and secretly buried and reburied three times. This was documented in an ABC special entitled, "What Happened to Adolf Hitler?" which aired in 1994. In this special the graves were shown to reporters by ex-Smirsch Agents, Ivan Tarashenko and Ivan Blashuke, and excavated on camera, however, they had been emptied of their contents years prior. Russia still was holding out valuable information. In 1997, in a PBS special, hosted by Henry Kissinger, signed orders were shown which proved Hitler and Eva

Brown's grave had been emptied, for the final time, in 1970 and their remains, with the exception of Hitler's teeth and skull cap were crushed and scattered over East German marshlands, Hitler's remains were hidden, so to speak, so Stalin could accuse the West of harboring the Führer in cold war propaganda. He claimed Hannah Reich, who visited the bunker the day before Hitler shot himself, could have rescued him and flown him to safety.

◆   "Nazi Gold" - Hitler's Army took vast amounts of gold from all of Europe and stock piled it in underground hide outs, caves and salt mines around the world to fuel his war effort. It is rumored that much of this gold still exists today, and is yet to be discovered.

CHAPTER 4

◆   Classified Weapons / Phaser Gun - The authentic phaser type of hand gun may be under development now. In the national news magazine, *U.S. News & World Report*, an article entitled, "Wonder Weapons- The Pentagon has a huge classified program to build sci-fi arms that won't kill the enemy. Some warriors ask, 'What's the point?' " (July 7, 1997). It was documented, "Tucked away in the corner of a drab industrial park in Huntington Beach, Calif., is a windowless, nondescript building. Inside, under extremely tight security, engineers and scientist are working on devices whose ordinary appearance masks the oddity of their function. One is cone shaped, about the size of a fire hydrant. Another is a 3-foot-long metal tube, mounted on a tripod, with some black boxes at the operator's end. These are the newest weapons of war. For hundreds of years, sci-fi writers have imagined weapons that might use energy waves or pulses to knock out, knock down, or otherwise disable enemies-without necessarily killing them. And for a good 40 years the U.S. military has quietly been pursing weapons of this sort. Much of this work is still secret...." p. 38. © used by permission.

◆   *General Hans Krebs was Hitler's last Chief of Staff who hung himself to avoid capture.

◆   *Doctor Goebbels was Hitler's propaganda Minister. He ordered the SS to shoot him in 1945. Prior to this his wishes were to be burned upon his death. He was shot and burned to avoid capture.

   *The photos of these individuals are authentic.

CHAPTER 7

♦ Doctor Morel was Hitler's private physician who administered pills which contained small doses of arsenic during the final years of his life. This may have partly accounted for this failing health and partial senility at the end.

CHAPTER 8

♦ Martin Borman was Hitler's Deputy. Elwood McQuaid has documented: "Considering the devastating attacks on the Bible and biblically orthodox Christianity brought by liberal theologians and their secular-humanist counterparts, it is little wonder that many nominally religious Germans were less than incensed at events taking place about them....the Nazis intended to destroy Christianity in Germany. Martin Bormann and Heinrich Himmler, encouraged by Hitler, promoted a return to the old paganism of the early tribal Germanic gods and a brand of neo-paganism created by Nazi fanatics. In 1941, Bormann stated publicly that 'National Socialism and Christianity are irreconcilable'" See my book, *The End of History-Messiah Conspiracy*, Chapter 13, for further details on this subject.

♦ Mufti is the title of a high ranking religious official, equivalent to today's Pope, in the Muslim religion.

♦ Hitler's hatred towards Christians - Hitler hated true Evangelical Christians. He recognized them as the offspring of Judaism, killed many of them and had planned to exterminate them as well had he been victorious. See *The End of History- Messiah Conspiracy*, Chapter 13-14 for documentation.

♦ Bible, Propaganda - Hitler considered the Bible harmful to his government. See Appendix 2 for details.

♦ Hitler's View of China - In the last will and testament of Adolf Hitler, on April 2, 1945, just twenty-seven days before he committed suicide, he wrote: "If North America does not succeed in evolving a doctrine less puerile than the one which at present serves as a kind of moral *vade mecum* and which is based on lofty but chimerical principles, it is questionable whether it will for long remain a predominantly white continent. It will soon become apparent that this giant with the feet of clay has, after its spectacular rise, just sufficient strength left to bring about its own downfall. And what a fine chance this sudden collapse will offer to the yellow races! From the point of view of both justice and history they will have exactly the same arguments (or lack or arguments) to support their invasion of the American continent as had the Europeans in the sixteenth century. Their vast and undernourished masses will confer on them the sole right that history recognizes—the right of starving people to assuage their hunger ..." While the U.S. did not interfere with the communist takeover of China (which set them back decades from being a threat to us), we now appease them with large amounts of trade, which robs our citizens of work, as they build an atomic arsenal which will one day be used against us. If China had been saved from Communism, and prevented from obtaining the bomb and set up as a democracy based on Judeo-Christian values and beliefs, things would have been different today and much safer for all. However, it is clear (from my research) that if Hitler had won the war he would have just depopulated their country using race as an excuse. From his quote above, we can definitely see his fear of the "yellow race", aside from his views of the "inferior" races and his victory would have meant their destruction.

♦ Black Race: Hitler considered the people of Africa inferior. At the Olympic Games in Germany, he was angered when American blacks won over Germans, claiming it was not fair to allow "animals" to compete with weaker human beings. He once said: "The large mass of Jews is as a race culturally unproductive. That is why they are more drawn to the negro than to the culturally higher works of the truly creative races." Thus, it is clear he would have annihilated the black race, along with the Jews and Christians, if he had obtained victory at the end of World War II. God created red, yellow, black and white, and loves all, unlike Hitler.

CHAPTER 9

♦ Professor A. S. Yehuda was a true historic individual and great collector of Newton's religious writings. They were willed to the Hebrew University in Jerusalem upon his death in 1951. They speak highly of the Jews and predict their return to Israel in the twentieth century. My books, *The End of History - Messiah Conspiracy* and *Apocalypse Prophocies of Isaac Newton* both cover this subject in detail.

♦ Volks Wagons - Ferdinand and Hitler designed the V.W. Beetle. *Volks means people* in German and Hitler intended to have most of the world driving this affordable car after his world conquest. *The Atlanta Journal-Constitution* newspaper (May 15, 1998) noted in an article entitled "Conceived in '30s, VW Beetle became all-time best seller" by Bill Vance: "Despite its origin as a brainchild of Adolf Hitler, the Volkswagen Beetle from the old original Bug to the new 1998 model—is the world's best-selling car." The article also noted that "Hitler wanted to call it the KdF-Wagon (for Kraft dorch Freude, or Strength through Joy)…"

♦ The Ark of the Covenant is truly the most ancient and holy artifact of the Hebrews. It's where abouts to the day are unknown. However, according to Bible prophecy, it will shortly be discovered. See Appendix 1 for details.

CHAPTER 10

♦ Houston Stewart Chamberlain was a real person and through his writings on Richard Wagner, his book, *Foundations Of The Nineteeth Century* and his friendship with Adolf Hitler, instigated much German Anti-Semitism. See Appendix 5 for details.

♦ Linz was to be a Hitleropolis and Hitler desired to be buried under the tallest Bell Tower in the world which he himself would have constructed there. This was documented in the film, *The Last Ten Days Of Hitler*, which was taken from eyewitnesses in the bunker, instead his final grave was in the inspection pit of a garage in Magdaburg which was covered with a large number of garbage cans in the 1990's. This was documented in the ABC special, *What Happened To Adolf Hitler?* in 1994.

CHAPTER 11

♦ Christian Protection of the Jews - Nearly one half million Jewish lives were saved by Christians. See *The End of History—Messiah Conspiracy*, *Volume 1*, Chapter 13-14 and The *Time* Magazine article, "A Conspiracy of Goodness" dated March 16, 1992.

PHOTO AND ILLUSTRATION CREDITS

P. numbers following names represent the P. numbers in this book.

International Christian Embassy, Jerusalem: Pp. 195-6, 256 (bottom), 304, 320.

State of Israel Government Press Office, Photography Department: Pp. Page facing introduction, p. 6 introduction, 14, 117, 140-43, 172-93 (except those listed on page 168), 205-206 (top), 221, 239, 256 (top), 259, 268, 315.

Frankenberger, James: Pp. Back Cover Author.

Franklin Roosevelt Library: Pp. 46.

NASA: Cover earth, Pp. 59, 148.

Cathy Taibbi: Pp. 107, 124.

Clarence Larkin Estate: Pp. 137, 228.

Jerusalem Post: Pp. 160, 198, 321.

Philip Moore: Pp. 161, 168, 169 (top), 170, 199, 201-204, 206 (bottom), 280, and photos listed on page 168.

"My hair stood on end as I read some of the things that Philip ... found."[1]   Hal Lindsey

ABOUT THE AUTHOR

Philip Nicholas Moore was born in Atlanta, Georgia in 1957. For many years, he studied Greek in Atlanta and Hebrew at Ulpan Etzion in Jerusalem. He spent eight years in Israel researching ancient Jewish beliefs and dedicated several years to researching the theological manuscripts of Isaac Newton at the Hebrew University in Jerusalem.

Moore was a volunteer at the army base, Base Machena Natan, in Beersheba, Israel. He was also a volunteer on the Temple Mount excavation with archaeologists Elat and Binyamin Mazar, which yielded the discovery of the "first Temple gateway" in 1986.

For several years, Moore assisted in research for the well known Christian author Hal Lindsey. From 1988 to 1990, Moore was instrumental in the Hebrew dubbing and release of a Genesis Project film for C.C.C. in Jerusalem.

Presently, Philip Moore, residing in Atlanta, Georgia, is completing research for his sixth book, *Israel and the Apocalypse Prophecies of Newton.*

The author and Hal Lindsey examine high-priestly garments recently woven in Jerusalem by Othodox Jews.

---

[1] Philip Moore, *The End of History: The Messiah Conspiracy* Vol. I, page xxi.

Order other titles by Philip Moore.

ORDER FORM

Please Print

Name _____

Address _____

City _____ State _____ Zip _____ Phone _____

Quantity	Code	Description	Price	Total
	Book 1	The End of History—Messiah Conspiracy, Volume I (1200 pgs.)	$29.00	
	Book 2	Israel and the Apocalypse Prophecies of Newton	$17.00	
	Book 3	Nightmare of the Apocalypse—The Rabbi Conspiracy	$15.00	
	Book 4	Eternal Security for True Believers	$ 5.00	
	Book 5	A Liberal Interpretation of the Prophecy of Israel—Disproved	$ 5.00	
	Book 6	What If Hitler Won The War?	$19.95	
	Book 7	The End of Earth as We Know It (Available 1999)	$15.00	
	Tapes	Testimony Tapes of Israeli Messianic Believers	$ 3.00	
	Video	Garden Tomb Tour Video	$17.00	
		One low shipping and handling fee (per order)	$ 4.95	$ 4.95
			Total	

Mail along with your check or money order to:

Ramshead Press International, Inc., P.O. Box 12-227, Atlanta, Georgia, USA, 30355-2227
Toll Free 1-800-RAMSHEAD (1-800-726-7432) or FAX (404) 816-9994 - Main (404) 233-8023

"In the 20th century the Jews will return to Jerusalem...." "The manner I know not. Let time be the interpreter." Sir Isaac Newton, the greatest scientist of history, three centuries before the event. Newton also predicted the 2nd coming would occur in the 21st century.

This work contains long lost material that, until now, was forbidden reading, plus insights, from a biblical perspective, into the old and infamous prophecies of Nostradamus - a first!

ISBN 0-9648623-0-1

NIGHTMARE
OF THE
APOCALYPSE
ΑΠΟΚΑΛΥΨΙΣ

THE RABBI CONSPIRACY

Excerpts from
**THE END OF HISTORY—MESSIAH CONSPIRACY
VOLUME II—ESSAYS**

Goethe-Museum

PHILIP N. MOORE
Researcher for Hal Lindsey

Hebrew prophecies regarding Jesus' (ישוע) two Messianic Comings—The Apocalypse and Israel are briefly covered and compared with rabbinic anti-missionary arguments. Germ warfare (for a 'peaceful depopulation'), petra and abortion are also discussed within a context to the End Times. A lecture by Rabbi Johnathan Cahn and a discourse on the stars by Dr. D. James Kennedy are included.

ISBN 1-57915-998-2

ISBN 1-57915-999-0

Eternal Security For True Believers
The Rabin Assassination—Predicted

An Excerpt from The End of History— Messiah Conspiracy Volume II—Essays

Included is an appendix on Hebrew Bible word codes which have foretold the future. One made nearly four thousand years ago seems to have predicted the fate and

assassination of the Israeli Prime Minister Isaac Rabin in 1995! We present new insights into the second coming of the Messiah, which may take us to the 2020s-2030s.

PHILIP N. MO
Researcher for Hal I

"Now if any man build upon this fou cious stones ... If any man's work a upon it, he shall receive a reward. I burned, he shall suffer loss; but he him by fire." (I Corinthians 3:12,

Is Israel's Rebirth Represented by Jesus (ישוע) in the New Testament Fig Tree Parable? Yes!

A LIBERAL INTERPRETATION ON THE PROPHECY OF ISRAEL—DISPROVED
NOSTRADAMUS: BIBLICAL SAGE OR SORCERER?

An exerpt from
THE END OF HISTORY—MESSIAH CONSPIRACY
VOLUME II—ESSAYS

PHILIP N. MOORE
Researcher for Hal Lindsey

Featured is an astonishing Hebrew word equidistant Bible code associating Israel with the Fig Tree and an Appendix on the false prophecies of Edgar Cayce, Jeane Dixon and Nostradamus (versus the truth of the Bible), revealing novel information on the 'inerrant prophecy' of the Kennedy assassination.

ISBN 1-57915-997-4

ISBN 1-57915-994-X

ISBN 1-57915-995-8